Praise for Eden Bradley

'*The Dark Garden* is a masterpiece'
Larissa Ione

'People are constantly looking for books similar to
Fifty . . . well look no further, I have what you need!
. . . Eden Bradley writes the most sensual books
I have ever read' *My Secret Romance*

D0492431

The Dark Garden

EDEN BRADLEY

BLACK
LACE

3 5 7 9 10 8 6 4 2

First published in the United States of America in 2007 by Bantam Dell
A Division of Random House, Inc.
Published in the UK in 2012 by Virgin Books,
an imprint of Ebury Publishing
A Random House Group Company

The Random House Group Limited Reg. No. 954009

Addresses for companies within the Random House Group can be found at:
www.randomhouse.co.uk

A CIP catalogue record for this book is available from the British Library

The Random House Group Limited supports The Forest Stewardship
Council (FSC®), the leading international forest certification
organisation. Our books carrying the FSC label are printed on FSC®
certified paper. FSC is the only forest certification scheme endorsed by
the leading environmental organisations, including Greenpeace.
Our paper procurement policy can be found at:
www.randomhouse.co.uk/environment

Printed and bound by CPI Group (UK) Ltd, Croydon, CR0 4YY

ISBN 9780753541296

To buy books by your favourite authors and register for offers visit
www.randomhouse.co.uk

To my grandmother,
who gave me her romance novels to read
and taught me that first and foremost,
in literature as in life, love is most important.

ACKNOWLEDGMENTS

I need to thank so many people for helping me to create *The Dark Garden.*

First, to B., for giving me the opportunity to write full time, and for always believing in me.

To my fabulous critique partners, Gemma Halliday and Jennifer Colgan—I couldn't have done this without you! To the dynamic duo, Jax and Amanda, the writing team of Cassidy Kent, for spending an entire weekend brainstorming this story with me. To my amazing agent, Roberta Brown, for convincing me that I could do this and for being endlessly enthusiastic about my work. To Sunny, for pushing me in the direction of New York. To Sasha White, for cheerleading me through this book and making me write more than I ever thought I could. To my Divas, for the constant support. And last but not least, to my brilliant editor, Shauna Summers, for making this the best book it could be.

The
Dark
Garden

ONE

Rowan ran her hand over the cool metal of the chain suspended from the ceiling, drawing her fingers along the sleek, steely surface, one link, then the next. She curled her fingers around the length of it, slid her hand down until she felt the soft touch of leather against her skin, moving her fingers absently over the buckles of the cuffs.

She breathed in the familiar, earthy scent of leather. Club Privé. The most exclusive BDSM club on the West Coast. Rowan's second home.

She surveyed the space where her friends and acquaintances were preparing for the play party tonight. The room was, as always, womblike, with its dark red walls and dim purple and amber lights. The mesmerizing, tantric cadence of a Gregorian chant filled the air. She crossed the expanse of wood floor to find a seat on one of the red velvet couches that edged the play area, nodding quietly to those she knew, careful not to intrude as they cleaned and prepared their equipment and set the mood with their partners.

The familiar faint buzz of sensual anticipation that was

always present at a play party was heavy in the air, a palpable shared energy that built up as the evening wore on. And as had happened all too often lately, a surge of disappointment rose up in her at the emptiness inside that this place had once filled so beautifully.

When had it all begun to mean so little, when at one time it had been everything to her?

She watched as more people filtered into the room and willed herself not to fidget. Why was she even here? She had no intention of playing tonight; she wasn't in the mood. She was far too edgy, and dominating even the most beautiful boys at the club, the most obedient, was no longer satisfying. She'd been like this for months, and nothing seemed to help. Yet at the same time, her writing, her dark secret writing, was going better than ever. Words seemed to flow out of her fingertips effortlessly in a tide of language and emotion. It should have been a release, yet she never came out of it feeling sated anymore.

The music changed to the familiar trancelike tones that signaled the official beginning of the evening. Submissive men and women were bound to the large wooden crosses, the spanking benches, the racks. They were beautiful, all of them, regardless of their shape or size. She had always thought so. There was beauty in the act of submission itself, something which never failed to amaze her.

She had talked about it at the discussion group she ran one Tuesday night each month for those new to the lifestyle. They talked a lot about the psychology of BDSM, of the rituals and symbols that were the basis of it all. She was glad she was able to help people make the transition into accepting this secret side of themselves. But in the five years she herself had been involved, there was a part of her that never quite felt whole.

Don't think about it now, don't think about why.

One of the male submissives she often played with approached her with a smile of greeting, knelt on the floor before her. He was one of her favorites. Blond, with soft, curling hair and a cherubic face, he had a sweet temperament and the stamina of a racehorse. She shook her head, letting him know she wasn't prepared to play.

"Are you sure, Mistress?"

"Not tonight, Eric. But don't worry, you're sure to catch somebody's eye." She reached out and stroked a finger over his shoulder with a sigh.

"May I serve you, Mistress? A drink, maybe?"

"Thank you, no. Go play. Enjoy your evening. I'm going to observe tonight."

"As you wish." He boldly took her hand and brushed a kiss over her skin.

Rowan smiled. "Off with you, now."

"Yes, Ma'am."

She forced her focus back to the floor. The club was crowded tonight. Almost every play station was in use. Groups lounged on the couches, as she did, or sat at the small café tables placed here and there, the submissives, or bottoms, serving food and drinks to their Masters and Mistresses, or kneeling on the floor at their feet. A small group of new submissives were huddled against one wall like a bunch of teenage girls at their first dance, waiting to be noticed. All wore the white leather protective collar of the club along with their scanty lingerie, signaling their availability and their status as bottoms. Rowan was glad that as a dominant at the club, she'd never had to go through those first excruciating experiences, that waiting to be chosen. *She* chose her partners. It would never be any other way for her. Controlling her sensuality was key. She had allowed herself to be controlled by another once and had paid far too high a price.

She shivered, pushing away the memories, down deep where they belonged, where she had kept them locked away for so long.

When she glanced up, a shining cascade of strawberry blond hair caught her eye and April, a new friend from the monthly discussion group, came to sit on the floor near her feet.

"Good evening, Mistress Rowan." The pretty young woman's voice was light, lilting. Her warm smile reached her round, cornflower blue eyes.

Rowan laughed. "Don't be silly. I'm not your Mistress, no need for such formalities." She patted the seat next to her. "Come, sit with me."

April smiled, tugged at the hem of her short baby pink leather skirt, and settled onto the cushions close to Rowan.

"How are you, April?"

Her lashes fluttered as she looked away. "Nervous. Yearning."

"Ah. Who is he?"

April gestured with her chin toward a large man with close-cut dark hair and a goatee, dressed in the standard Dom attire: black jeans, a black T-shirt, a black leather vest. He was strapping a naked woman to a St. Andrew's cross, a large wooden X on a platform with hooks to which he attached the girl's leather wrist and ankle cuffs.

Rowan nodded. "Decker. He's Irish, but he's been here in the States for a while, and he's been at the club at least as long as I have. Does something in the music industry; a sound engineer, I think. He's very experienced, has great technique. You could do worse. He plays with all the girls here, and they're all half in love with him. But he's never stuck with one woman. He won't scene with anyone for more than one night at a time. He's not the commitment type. You should know that."

April sighed softly. "I know. They never are."

"Not true. Most of the members of the club are part of a couple."

"But not you."

"No, not me," she answered quietly.

"I'm sorry, Rowan. I shouldn't have said that. It's none of my business."

"No, it's alright. I just ... don't know what to say."

"You don't seem yourself tonight. And you look tired."

"I haven't been sleeping well," Rowan admitted.

"I'm sorry. Is there anything I can do to help?" April's eyes were full of sincerity. She was a lovely girl, sweet, innocent in her desire to please. The man she ended up serving would be very lucky.

"No, nothing. Thank you, though." She squeezed April's hand.

There was nothing anyone could do to help her. She didn't know herself what this inner restlessness was about.

A cool rush of night air caught her attention as the door opened for a late arrival. An unfamiliar figure stood for a moment in the doorway, surveying the room. He was tall, well over six feet, with broad shoulders and a tapering waist. There was something elegant in his stance. As he turned to survey the room, she could see his long, pale blond hair was pulled back into a narrow leather thong. He had noble, chiseled features. And even from across the half-dark room, she could see his wide, lush mouth.

A small shiver went through her.

He is not for you.

She could see instantly that this man was a top. Dominance radiated from him like heat. Not one of her pretty boys to play with. But then, she wasn't in the mood to play, was she?

Still, she couldn't take her eyes from him, this stranger dressed all in black. And then he looked at her, locking gazes from across the room. Her stomach tightened beneath the dark blue leather corset she wore.

She forced herself to blink, to look away. Why should this man have such an effect on her?

April leaned over and whispered, "He was looking right at you, Rowan. Through you, almost. Did you see that?"

See it? She'd felt it all the way down to her bones.

"He's a Dom."

"Yes, but still . . ."

Rowan shook her head. "It's impossible."

"But you find him as beautiful as he obviously finds you."

Rowan was surprised to feel heat flare in her cheeks. She didn't bother to deny it.

April, seeming to sense her discomfort, stood. "Why don't I fetch you a drink? San Pellegrino with a squeeze of lime, yes?"

"Thank you, yes." Good girl, remembering her drink of choice.

She bent her head and rubbed her temples with her fingers as April walked away. What was wrong with her?

When she glanced up again, he was moving across the room in long strides; graceful, predatory. She had no idea why his presence here made her so uncomfortable, so hyperaware of her own skin, her own breath.

He stopped to talk to Master Hawke, the owner of the club, an enormous man with a full brown beard. They both turned to look at the group of bottoms. Yes, he would choose one of the new girls. What would it be like to watch him play?

Again her stomach quivered. What was going on with her?

She turned away once more, focusing her attention on a triad playing at a spanking bench. The bottom, a lovely young woman, was bound to it, facedown, the arch of her smooth, bare buttocks high in the air. The tops, a man and a woman, were taking turns applying tiny plastic clothespins to her flesh. The bottom remained obediently still, until the man began to use a crop to knock the pins off. The girl squealed, squirmed, then moaned as the evil little pins flew onto the floor.

Rowan smiled. She had played that game before, knew how the blood rushed painfully back into the skin after being pinched away by the pins. It always gave the bottom an exquisite rush of endorphins. She'd watched it happen, that glazing of the eyes, the Mona Lisa smiles.

She was still smiling when a light touch on her arm brought her head up. Master Hawke stood over her with the new Dom at his side. God, he was even more gorgeous up close. His face was a symphony of fine planes and angles, his mouth even darker and more sensual. But it was his eyes that started a warm knot that began in her stomach and spread outward until her limbs went weak. Eyes that were a startling shade of turquoise and jade that shifted like the ocean at twilight.

Control, Rowan.

Master Hawke leaned over her. "I'd like you to meet Master Christian Thorne, just back from Berlin. He's an old member at Privé. Thorne, this is Mistress Rowan."

Before she had a chance to respond, the stranger leaned in, took her hand, bent over it, and brushed a kiss across her knuckles. She felt his touch as though it were made of fire, those lush lips against her skin. But she forced herself not to react, her racing pulse to still. Reminded herself that he was just a man, like any other.

Why did that feel like a lie?

"It's very nice to meet you, Rowan."

She'd expected a German accent, but he appeared to be as American as she was. His voice was deep, smooth, elegant.

She nodded to him, cleared her throat. "Yes, it's nice to meet you, too. I hope you'll enjoy our club."

"I'm enjoying it immensely already."

Was that a wicked gleam in his eye? Suddenly her corset was too tight against her ribs.

Get ahold of yourself, Rowan.

"Thorne, let me introduce you to some of the others."

Master Hawke led him away and she could finally take a breath.

April arrived with her drink. She handed it to her as she took her seat once more. "I saw you talking to him. Who is he? What is he like?"

"Christian Thorne." Rowan wasn't likely to forget that name anytime soon. "He's arrogant, cool, sophisticated. And utterly self-confident." She paused to sip her drink, watching him.

She'd sensed immediately that he was the kind of man those in her group would call a true Dom, someone who was so naturally dominant that everyone—waiters, sales clerks—automatically deferred to him without being aware of it or knowing why.

And Lord help her, he was as beautiful a man as she had ever seen. His face was flawless. Strong, proud, beautifully made. He had one of those mouths that made a woman want to kiss him, to feel his lips on her flesh.

"He's gorgeous." April was smiling at her.

"He's a dominant, April. Any connection between us, other than being friends, is impossible. And I don't know that he's the kind of man I'd want to be friends with."

"But is he the kind of man you . . . want?"

The girl had a habit of asking the most revealing questions. But Rowan wasn't interested in pursuing the answer.

"I need to find a playmate for the evening."

She patted April's hand and rose from her couch. She still wasn't very much in the mood, but she obviously needed some distraction from her wandering mind, from the lust still singing in her veins from that momentary contact of his lips on the back of her hand.

Ridiculous. Ironic. But there it was.

Christian Thorne was the first man who had excited her in a long time. And she could never have him.

∞

It was well after midnight when Rowan let herself into her nineteenth-floor apartment in Century City. She paused at the wide expanse of windows overlooking the city. Los Angeles sparkled like a blanket of diamonds in the dark, illuminated by a brilliant, almost full moon. She loved this view; it had been the main reason why she'd bought this place. But tonight it did nothing to soothe her.

Neither had paddling Jeffrey, one of her usual boys. He was very pretty, with the kind of youthful, androgynous features she liked in her playmates. He was an experienced submissive. Experienced enough to know her heart wasn't in her play tonight. Finally, he'd called an end to the scene and asked her if she was alright. Of course she wasn't. She'd left him with a brief hug and an apology.

She pulled the sheer drapes closed and went to her small granite-and-brushed-steel kitchen to pour herself a glass of wine. The aromatic scent of the fine cabernet hit her nostrils as she opened the bottle.

She carried the glass into her bedroom, set it down on the dresser, and removed her corset, her black pencil skirt, her stiletto-heeled shoes. She placed the shoes into their cubbyhole in her custom-built closet, hung up her skirt, and carefully laid the leather corset in a drawer, comforted somehow by the small ritual of organization. Naked, she carried her glass into the slate-tiled bathroom, sipping as she went, and turned on the water in the tub. A hot bath would relax her, help her to free her mind from the nagging images of this annoyingly fascinating stranger.

While the tub filled she caught her reflection in the enormous bronze-framed vanity mirror. She pulled the pins from her hair and it fell in coal black waves around her shoulders. The dark smudges beneath her blue eyes were a stark contrast against her pale skin. She was bone-tired, and she looked it. Of course, it was late, but there was more to it than that. She hadn't been sleeping well lately. The edginess she'd felt at the dungeon tonight was nothing new.

She ran her hands over the red marks left on her white skin by the boning in the corset, over her ribs, her full breasts. Her nipples peaked at the touch of her own soft fingertips. Yes, it had been far too long since she had enjoyed a man.

She never had sex with the submissive men she played with. Oh, her boys would service her when she allowed them to, but it wasn't quite the same, was it? She'd dated several men out of the lifestyle, had slept with a few, but it never seemed to work for her, and none of those relationships had lasted more than a month or two. She was much more intimate with the small collection of vibrators in her nightstand drawer.

Her muscles tensed at the thought, and she turned off the now full tub, then went back into her bedroom, thinking of the new waterproof toy she'd bought recently. She needed it tonight, needed some release, some relief.

The small, textured lavender vibrator in hand, she returned to the bathroom and slid into the steaming water. It moved like silk against her skin as she sat back, leaning her head against the edge of the tub.

Oh, yes, she was sensitive tonight, every nerve in her body on alert. And all because of him.

Christian Thorne.

She turned the vibrator on high and lowered it beneath

the surface of the water. It wouldn't hurt to think of him, to imagine it was his hands on her body. When she touched the tip of the vibe to her clit a shiver of pleasure ran through her.

She was so sensitive tonight she could probably come in a minute flat. But she wanted to draw it out, to make it last. She closed her eyes, allowed herself to see his face; that beautiful, lush mouth, those mysterious ocean eyes. His hands were big, she'd noticed. What would they feel like on her skin?

She ran one hand over her breasts, caressing them as she imagined he would. But no, he would be cruel about it, wouldn't he? She pinched one of her nipples, hard, and felt the shock of painful pleasure course through her. Yes, that was more like it.

She lowered the vibe once more, let it slide over the lips of her sex. They filled with need as she teased herself. She spread her thighs apart so she could push the tip of the phallic-shaped vibrator inside.

Oh, God, it felt good. And it was his face in her mind, his fingers pushing into her. And then his beautifully masculine face lowering between her legs, that gorgeous, hot mouth on her sex. His tongue flicking over her tight, hard clit.

Her hips bucked, moving into the vibrator as she rubbed it over her cleft, over the slick lips of her sex, dipped inside, then out again, still teasing herself.

His mouth would be warm and wet. *God, yes.* She was so close. She pressed the vibe over her hard little nub, reached down and slid two fingers into her tight, aching hole, pumped them, imagining it was Christian's cock inside her.

He would be thick and heavy, filling her. She added one more finger, moved her hips against her hand, against the trilling buzz of the vibrator, saw his face.

The first wave of her orgasm rolled over her, a stinging wave of pure pleasure. And as her climax gathered in intensity, turned into a sharp, stabbing pulse beat that reverberated through her entire body, the image of Christian in her mind changed, and he was pulling her naked body over his lap, his hand coming down in a stinging slap on her ass. She came harder, moaned aloud. Her legs tensed against the onslaught of sensation, the vibe held firmly as she shook and shuddered. And in her mind's eye, Christian Thorne gave her the spanking of her life.

ର

It was after four A.M. when she finally slept that night. Her dreams were dark, veiled in a chiaroscuro cloud, as though she could never quite see what was going on. But she could feel his presence. Christian. He was strong, dynamic. She could feel him, even though she couldn't quite see his face. It was frustrating. Tantalizing.

She woke in the lonely predawn light in a sweat of need and reached into her nightstand drawer, pulling out a small hand-held bullet. She switched it on and slid it down between her trembling thighs, letting the buzzing tremors sweep through her, pressing down hard. She came fast, furiously. Her climax left her shaking and weak. And again, it was his face in her mind. He was all she could see. She fell immediately back into a deep, dreamless sleep.

In the morning she felt as though she had a hangover.

And she cursed herself for her new obsession. She really had to get it under control.

Sunday stretched interminably before her, with little to keep her occupied. A good day to write, perhaps.

Still in her favorite sapphire silk robe, she sat down at the desk in her bedroom with a fragrant cup of Earl Grey tea and flipped open her laptop. She always took a few minutes to read whatever she had written last to get her in the mood, to set the tone in her head.

Ashlyn stared at Gabriel. What had he just offered? A chance to experience the things she had only ever dreamed about, had never dared to discuss with anyone until now. All of those strange yearnings that had pulled at her for years, for as long as she could remember having sexual feelings in her body, sexual thoughts in her mind.

He had offered to give it all to her, if only she was brave enough . . .

Was she?

Images of Gabriel standing over her while she lay tied to a big, four-post bed, his dark golden eyes shining, that evil-looking goatee that she loved, a flogger in his hand. Oh, yes, she knew what it was called. She'd read her secret books, those dark stories of pain and pleasure, of dominance and submission. This was exactly what she wanted. If only it didn't frighten her so much.

Before she could allow her fears to force her to protest, to lose it all, she murmured, "Yes."

Rowan found herself getting wet just reading this simple scene. There wasn't even any sex, just that moment of submission, of giving in. It was that yielding that was the turn-on. She remembered what it had been like for her, all those years ago, that first moment. She didn't want to think now about how horribly wrong it had gone after that. No; now she wanted to feel again that excruciating, exquisite thrill.

She typed furiously for the next hour, as though she burned with fever. She was hot, and everything seemed hazy. Everything except this driving need to put words on paper. To purge some of the confusion and lust from her body.

Yes, let her character experience these things, so she wouldn't have to.

Ashlyn looked up from her kneeling position on the floor at the man who would be the first she would call Master. His dark eyes were unreadable. Was he pleased with her?

The wool rug was scratchy beneath her bare knees, but she didn't care. All she wanted now was to make him happy, to have him touch her, hurt her. It was still strange to her, that she craved the pain. But right now she didn't want to think too much about it.

How surprised she'd been when he'd first turned her over his knee and spanked her last night. His hand had been fire to her flesh, pain and pleasure coursing through her, uniting, becoming one. By the time he had finished she would have done anything for him.

She wanted him to do it again. A titillating bolt of anticipation shot through her. She knew he would. And much more. He had promised to do things to her she had never imagined. She trembled at the idea.

*Despite her inner struggle to accept this side of herself,
she was half in love with him already.*

Rowan shifted in her seat. She was wet again, soaked, in
fact, her sex pulsing. Images of her dream last night flashed
in her mind. Christian's hand coming down hard on her
bare flesh. *Yes.* But how many times in a twenty-four-hour
period could she bring herself to orgasm? She pushed back
her chair and stood. Perhaps just once more.

ೲ

Christian stalked the length of his third-floor studio in his
house on the Venice Canals, that section just off Venice
Beach that was loosely modeled on the canals of Venice,
Italy, with meandering waterways lined with houses of
every description. As he moved past the windows he could
see the small blue and white beach cottage next door, the
contemporary two-story brown shingle next to it, and beyond, the enormous stucco-and-tile structure that made
him think of an old Italian palazzo.

He was restless, couldn't seem to settle anywhere.
There was plenty to do, but he couldn't focus on any one
task. He'd hardly had time to unpack since his arrival in
L.A., except for his studio; it was the first area of the house
he'd set up. His tools were in order on his high workbench:
chisels, planes, buffers. Except he hadn't touched his tools
since he'd arrived back in the States, had he? Or for months
before he'd left Berlin. Work had grown stale for him. He
hadn't found a subject that interested him in far too long.

He was bored with it all, bored with the work. Bored with himself, perhaps. It was one reason why he'd come home to the States. Europe no longer held any inspiration for him. The women who posed for him all seemed the same after a while. Sleeping with them hadn't helped. He'd been telling himself it was about the art, but that was a lie. He hadn't met a woman in a long time who challenged him, who made him think. They were all too easy. Too easy to figure out. Too easy to get into his bed.

He sat down on an antique chaise longue covered in decaying gold velvet that was piled with pillows and several old quilts at one end of the enormous room. He'd picked up the old chaise at an antiques market in London and it had traveled with him all through Europe. He sometimes slept there after working through the night, which he did fairly often, not even bothering to cross the floor to where his big bed stood against the only solid wall on this level of the house. Pulling an all-nighter made him feel achy and edgy, but he did some of his best work in the early hours before dawn. Lately, though, even that almost hypnotic state brought on by lack of sleep had left him empty of inspiration.

Too on edge to sit, he rose and went to smooth his hand over a large piece of raw marble he'd acquired recently, nearly five feet of gorgeous white stone. Normally the stone spoke to him, and he would buy a piece knowing exactly what he intended to do with it, but this one piece remained a mystery to him. Yet he'd had to have it.

He had that same feeling about the glorious Mistress Rowan.

Mistress. He didn't think so. And he was rarely wrong about such things. But he had to admit the magnetic pull he felt for this woman may have obscured his thinking.

He'd immediately seen the strength in her delicate frame, in the dark blue fire burning in her eyes. Lord, she was beautiful. He'd never been so attracted to any woman before in his life.

He'd spent the last number of years in Europe, moving from London to Spain, Italy to France, and finally to Berlin. He'd seen some of the most beautiful women in the world. But none compared to this little beauty.

He had to sculpt her. Had to have her.

And he was pretty damn sure the feeling had been mutual.

He sipped his black coffee and looked out the long bank of windows at the view of the ocean in the distance. To the north lay Santa Monica, to the south Marina del Rey. The coast, only a few blocks away, was still fogged in, obscuring the point at which ocean met sky on the horizon. He loved the ocean, had always found it soothing. But his nerves were stretched tight as piano wire today and even the somnolent gray sea did nothing to calm him.

He'd been wound up tight ever since meeting Rowan at the club last night. Master Hawke had generously gifted him with his own pair of female submissives and Christian had played them well into the night. But he'd been distracted the entire time. He'd been able to see Rowan playing with a male sub out of the corner of one eye. Her scene hadn't lasted long and she'd left. She'd also left him with the impression of her beautiful, regal face imprinted on his mind.

Despite her claim to dominance, he was convinced there was more beneath the surface. But how to convince her? There had to be a way.

He knew he wouldn't see her again until the next play party at the club, which was next weekend. But what then? And meanwhile, he had to concentrate, had to get some work done.

He turned back to the five-foot-tall expanse of untapped marble. It reminded him of Rowan's pale skin. He ran his palm once more over the sleek surface. Lord, she would feel just like this beneath his hands. Silky, cool.

Maybe that was what he found so incredibly attractive about her. That cool control, that composed detachment. And she really was regal; elegant and lovely. She would be a perfect model for him, with her flawless skin and her long, delicate bones...

Frustrated, he grabbed a sketchbook from his workbench and flopped down on the ancient lounge, quickly drawing her face. Yes, that was it, the strong yet fragile-looking jaw, the generous mouth. The mouth of a prostitute really; lush and forbidden. Pure sex. He quickly added the high, rounded cheekbones and the slight tilt to her eyes. He sketched the long, narrow column of her neck, the slope of her shoulders, shaded in her collarbones. But when he tried to imagine her bare breasts it was too much for him and he flung the sketchpad to the wood floor and muttered, "Damn it."

He had to see her again. Had to find out if his instincts were right. Had to find out what it was about this woman that made him doubt himself, that challenged his self-control.

And meanwhile, he had better find a way to distract himself or he was going to lose his mind. He jumped up, determined to put his house in order. The physical activity of moving furniture, hanging his paintings, would work some of this energy off. And seeing the artwork he'd collected over the years always gave him pleasure; surely a good distraction. Then maybe he could manage to concentrate on his work. He had a show coming up in a few weeks and he still had to crate up several small pieces to ship to the gallery. That would keep him busy for a while. But he had a feeling that nothing would keep the mysterious Mistress Rowan out of his mind.

 တ

The discussion group at Club Privé began at eight o'clock, but Rowan always tried to arrive a few minutes early, work allowing. Her job as a freelance corporate analyst was all-consuming while she was working on a project, and incredibly detail-oriented. The perfect job for the utter perfectionist she freely admitted to being. And for the control freak she knew she was on some level, even if she didn't like to think about herself in those terms. But today, even though she had really applied herself, even working right through lunch, she'd been distracted by random thoughts of *him*.

Being here at the club wasn't helping. As she set up the circle of chairs around the main staging area, all she could think of was his face in the dim, colored lights, the hot brush of his lips on her hand when he'd kissed it.

Would she ever be able to be here again and think of anything else?

People began to filter in and Rowan greeted them as they took their seats. April ran in, flushed and breathless, her long strawberry hair flying, just as the meeting was about to begin. Rowan smiled at her.

"Welcome, everyone," she began. "Tonight we're going to talk about making the transition into the BDSM lifestyle. Few of us can do this without questioning ourselves; who we are, what we want, why we want it. And if what we're doing, what we crave, is wrong, dirty somehow."

There was a flurry of agreeable nods. Rowan continued. "In the past there have been those in the psychology community who have looked at our fetish as a kind of sickness, but more modern thinkers have come to understand that it can be a healthy expression of our desires, even a constructive way to work through painful experiences in our pasts."

It had helped her, hadn't it? But she had to concentrate on what she was saying.

"Still, there tends to be a lot of shame accompanying the pleasure and relief we find in this sort of play. I'm sure some of you have felt it."

Again, a round of nods. April raised her hand.

"Yes, April?"

"Does it ever go away?"

"For most of us, I think it does. But it's something you have to recognize and work through. And it's a bit different for the tops than it is for the bottoms. The tops, the sadists, have to stop and wonder why they enjoy being in command, why they gain pleasure from 'hurting' people. And the bottoms, the masochists, why they enjoy being ordered around, why they crave pain."

A short, dark-haired woman raised her hand.

"Patricia?"

"How do you know if you're a top or a bottom?"

Rowan shifted in her chair. "Ah . . . I think that answer may be different for everyone. Is this something you're questioning?"

The woman nodded. "I've been playing as a submissive for the last few months, but I don't think I really like being told what to do. And I don't like any of the humiliation stuff."

"These are things you can negotiate with the top you're playing with, Patricia. Not every bottom is a submissive, necessarily. Many enjoy the sensation play, but aren't truly submissive inside."

"I think that describes me. But I also have these thoughts . . ."

"Go on," Rowan encouraged her.

"Well, I've seen some of the sub boys here, and . . . I've often wondered what it would be like to administer a spanking, to have them at my beck and call . . ." She blushed a bright red.

"There's no need to be embarrassed, Patricia. You may be a switch; one of those people who enjoys playing both sides. And they do say those who have experienced bottoming make the best tops. I think if you really have that urge, you should allow yourself to explore it."

April spoke up. "Have you ever bottomed, Rowan?"

"Me? No." She laughed, trying to cover the lie that had come out of her mouth so automatically. She had conditioned herself not to think about that episode in her life. But it wasn't fair for her to be so scornful of the idea. Especially when she had just recommended it to everyone in the room. Especially when she'd been fantasizing about nothing else for two days. Her cheeks burned, and once again Christian's features flooded her mind. And then a brief, unwelcome flash from long ago. The experience she never talked about, dwelled on ... Why was this coming up lately, over and over again? She had spent a number of years trying very hard to put that year of her life behind her. And she'd been successful. Until she'd met Christian.

How was it this one man was so easily undoing all the years of work she'd put into gathering her strength? Why was she so full of questions, confusion? And the sudden yearning to experience sensation, to submit.

She had an uneasy feeling that this was only the beginning of a complicated issue she would have to face at some point, and perhaps that point was now. Her insane attraction to Christian Thorne, a thoroughly dominant man, was already something she was unable to dismiss. Could she handle it? She wanted the answer to be a quick "Yes!" but she was no longer entirely sure of herself. And she felt on some deep level that Christian's introduction into her life was going to force the issue to the surface. Could it be that somehow this one man was going to change her life forever?

T W O

Saturday night. Christian made his way through the streets of L.A. in his sleek black Cadillac. He loved this car, loved the sheer size of it, the power of the engine. It made him think of a giant panther, prowling the streets rather than driving. He knew it was extravagant, over the top. But he didn't care. He'd only had the car for a month, since he'd returned to the States from Berlin, and it was his new toy.

He didn't miss Europe. It was supposed to be *the* place for an artist, but he'd had about as much as he could take of having to remember what language he was speaking, of missing simple, familiar comforts. He'd had his adventures. He was thirty-four, and he'd already experienced more of the world than many people did in a lifetime.

He was glad to be back in L.A. for now, winding through the familiar streets. And particularly glad to be heading to Club Privé in the Valley. If he'd had to wait even another day, he might have gone out of his mind.

It was her. Rowan. He'd sketched her face countless

times during the week, from every possible angle. Was she really as beautiful as he remembered? Or had she grown in his fantasies into something larger than life? How many times this week—hell, how many times each day—had he closed his eyes, in his bed, in the shower, on the old chaise longue in his studio, and taken his throbbing cock in his hand and stroked himself to climax with her face in his mind?

He was as rutty as a teenage boy.

He pulled his car into the parking lot next to where the dungeon hid behind a high stone wall. Not the best section of North Hollywood, but this kind of facility was better off in an industrial area.

He flashed his membership card at the man guarding the gate and passed into the outdoor courtyard of Club Privé, surrounded by high concrete walls. Immediately the music from inside the dungeon hit his ears. The scent of cigarette smoke met his nostrils. For some reason, in this context, it was almost pleasant, wicked and dirty and faintly sexual.

There were two females and a male tonight in the eight-foot-tall steel cage that took up most of one corner of the patio, all of them naked except for the collars around their necks and the exotic decorations they wore. The male sported some kind of complicated chastity device. Both of the females had their nipples clamped and weighted. Beautiful, all of them, but his interest tonight lay elsewhere.

He scanned the groups and couples who sat at the little café tables, talking and laughing. The subs were serving food and drink to everyone, some on their knees, some chained together in pairs. The mood was expectant and jovial, the Doms at the tables teasing and pinching the serving girls and boys, making them squeal in delight and pain. He liked this group, liked that although they took their roles quite seriously, they could have fun as well, something he'd found lacking in the European BDSM groups he'd encountered during his years abroad.

He didn't see Rowan. Thinking perhaps she was already inside, he crossed the patio, nodding a greeting to a few people he had met the previous week, and pushed through the big double doors into the main room of the facility.

It took a few moments for his eyes to adjust to the darkness inside. As before, the lights were dim, in shades of gold, red, and purple. The colors of sex, of sensuality. And the colors that shone most alluringly on naked skin.

Several Doms had already laid claim to pieces of equipment, their bags of "toys" left to signify that they intended to play there this evening. A few were already setting up for their scenes; testing ropes, lining up their floggers, paddles, whips, and canes. At one end of the room a man was already beginning to loop lengths of red and black rope through the eye hooks on a huge square wooden frame, sliding them through and starting to build what would be an enormous web by the end of the night. His bottom, a small female with gorgeous, gleaming skin the exact shade of milk chocolate, was already in position in the middle of the frame, collared and decorated with white ropes woven in a complicated pattern over her otherwise nude body.

But still no Rowan. He commanded himself to quiet a quick surge of frustration. Temper had no place here. It was all about control. He would do well to remember that.

He found a seat on one of the couches and prepared himself to wait while the music pumped up to a higher volume. The strains of some sort of Celtic trance made him all the more uneasy. Odd, since it was exactly the sort of music he liked to scene to. It usually relaxed him, helped to get his head in the right place. But now it was nothing more than background to his impatience.

Minutes passed and he found himself tapping his foot. Try as he might, he couldn't seem to focus on the scenes beginning around him. Nothing held his interest. More people filtered in, settled into the seats to watch the activity, to wait for a preferred piece of equipment to be free. Christian glanced around the room once more, waiting, searching.

Unbearable.

He'd never waited for a woman in his life.

Disgusted with himself, he went to get a drink. No alcohol allowed at the dungeon; it blurred the senses when the point here was to use the senses to their fullest. A strong cup of black coffee would have to suffice. He made his way to the small kitchen area where food and drinks were available to the club members and ordered a shot of espresso. The submissive woman at the counter smiled and flirted with her lashes, but despite her creamy skin and full breasts, she held no attraction for him. It was only Rowan.

Where the hell was she?

He must be losing his mind. That was the only answer to this strange fixation. And he was a fool to play into it. Perhaps he'd be better off going home, trying to forget her. Yes, screw it. He'd find Master Hawke, say good night to his host, and head back to his house in Venice, to his work.

Back in the main room the play had begun in earnest. The earthy tang of leather was heavy in the air. Moans of pain and ecstasy came from the dark corners, as did the sharp crack of whips and the thuddier sounds of paddles and the big buffalo-hide floggers.

And suddenly, there she was.

Rowan.

She stood at the other end of the room, dressed tonight in a clingy, sheer, long-sleeved black top, the same long, narrow black skirt, and a pair of impossibly high red stiletto pumps with little straps around her delicate ankles. Gorgeous. Fuckable, with those whorish red shoes on.

She looked unsure of herself, distracted. A small frown creased her forehead. She didn't look up as he made his way across the room to her and came to stand at her side.

"Mistress Rowan. Good evening."

"Christian. Hello."

Was that a flush on her pale cheeks? Her eyes were dark and shining, her lips full and painted a deep red that made him think of sex. Red on that hooker's mouth of hers; it was too tempting.

"Have you just arrived?" he asked her.

"I had to work today and I was late. Are you enjoying the dungeon?"

So, she wanted to make small talk. But he could see her breasts rising and falling in short, quick breaths beneath the sheer fabric of her top. Spectacular breasts, full and high, but not too large. They would fill his hands beautifully. "Not as much as I could be if you were here to play with me."

Rowan bit her lip, anger suffusing her, even as lust

curled hot in the pit of her stomach. God, she could smell him, he was so close. Something woodsy and all male. Why should she feel this terrible attraction to him when he was being so arrogant? But damn it, something about him made her melt, the heat at the core of her body making her legs weak. She was furious.

"May I remind you that I am no submissive girl, Mr. Thorne?"

"Aren't you?" His voice was low, smoky.

"If you attended the mandatory introductory lecture, you will know that all submissives at Club Privé not owned by anyone wear a collar of protection. Do you see a collar around my neck?"

"Only metaphorically speaking."

"What is that supposed to mean?"

He smiled down at her with those ocean eyes. He looked as though he was considering his answer.

She didn't wait for him to speak. "You're just like all the others who think that because I'm a woman, you can be the one to bring me to my knees. It's not going to happen, so don't waste your time. There are plenty of unattached subs here to choose from."

"But I only want you." He moved closer until she could feel his breath warm on her hair as he spoke. "And you're wrong. About me, about yourself."

"What are you saying?" A quick shiver of heat ran down her spine.

"I'm not playing at converting you to submission, Rowan. I understand you are not to be toyed with. But I can see a side of you that perhaps others can't. You hide it well. But not well enough."

"You're very full of yourself, aren't you?"

"Perhaps. Or perhaps I'm right. Why don't we try to find out?"

"I don't think so." But her body was belying her words. Her nipples had gone taut beneath the silky fabric of her bra just from his nearness, from his solid presence so close to her, from his scent, which was making her wild with need whether she wanted to admit it or not.

"It's not that I don't believe you," he said in conciliatory tones, his gaze calm on hers. "But I do believe there can be parts of ourselves that are hidden. Hidden beneath layers of what we think we should be, or what others expect from us. Digging down and discovering what lies beneath the surface can be freeing."

"And of course you think you're the one who can free me?" Her temper was rising as quickly as her desire, making each all the more potent.

"I have a proposition for you."

"Of course you do."

"Give me thirty days to show you that I'm right about you."

"You must be joking. Why should I?"

"Because you have nothing to lose and everything to gain."

"That's a ridiculous cliché!"

"Maybe not. Everyone knows the best tops are those who have bottomed, who have experienced the other side. If I'm wrong about you, you'll have that experience and will be a better top for it. And if I'm right, you will have discovered your true self. A gift either way."

He was looking down at her; his strong, beautiful face

was perfectly serious. He wasn't playing games. But how could she? There were reasons why she was a dominant. Reasons she didn't want to discuss with him.

But he was right. It would make her better at what she did. And she would love to feel the smug satisfaction of proving him wrong. Needed to, maybe.

"Come on," he whispered right next to her ear. "What have you got to be afraid of?"

That warm, whispering breath sent a hot shiver through her. He was standing so close, he was almost touching her. Every cell in her body cried out for him to move closer, as though she wouldn't be satisfied until her flesh met his.

God, she was a fool.

"I'm not afraid of anything." She was trembling all over, and desperate that he not see it.

"Shall we find out together?" That soft breathy whisper again.

Why did she feel this intense need to prove him wrong? Perhaps it was more that she had to prove it to herself, had to test her strength.

"Alright. Thirty days."

He pulled away and looked into her eyes. "Thirty days," he repeated.

God, his eyes were intense, their watercolor depths bottomless. His pupils were utterly black, the irises outlined in dark blue. Who was the man inside there? All she knew was that he made her weak with desire.

She had to regain her balance with him, exert some control. "I can't begin until late Monday evening. I have other commitments."

"Agreed."

"And we're going to have rules. Negotiate a contract, just as we all do before playing together."

"Of course."

"And the first provision is that there will be no sex. It's only proper under these circumstances."

He smiled. "I agree. But I think we'll both live to regret it."

She regretted it already.

❧

He absolutely could not believe Rowan had agreed to his proposal. Despite his cocky grandstanding, he'd known there was a good chance she'd refuse him.

She would be his for thirty days.

Stepping on the gas, Christian steered his car onto the 405 freeway and headed for home. The lanes were still full of traffic, even at two in the morning. But this was L.A., and the freeways were busy twenty-four hours a day.

He had seen instantly that there was more beneath the surface where Rowan was concerned, but he wasn't as certain she would dare to face it. He would do everything in his power to make sure this was a memorable experience, that he fulfilled her every need. As a Dom, it was his responsibility, and his driving desire.

She was a special case and he would handle her delicately. Oh yes, he was making plans already, had all sorts of surprises in store for her. He must get his house in order before she arrived for her first visit. They had agreed they would spend the first few weeks in private, then make an appearance at the club on the last weekend only if they both felt Rowan was really functioning as a submissive. He could tell that, even as she had agreed to this particular stipulation, she didn't believe it would ever come to pass.

He had other notions.

He merged onto the 10 freeway, toward Santa Monica, passing a low-slung silver Porsche. If Rowan were a car, that's just what she'd be. All sleek, clean lines, deceptively strong and powerful for her size. And her pale skin would glow in the moonlight just as the luminous silver paint of the Porsche did in the lights of the passing cars.

He couldn't wait to get his hands on her, to touch that fine, silken skin. To bind her in ropes, in chains, which he loved. To bend her over his knee and spank that perfect, heart-shaped ass of hers.

He groaned, shifted in his seat against the tight pull of his slacks. This would be an exercise in control for him as well. Because he'd never been so turned on by any woman in his life.

What would it be like to strip her naked? To tie her up, to have that beautiful body at his mercy? Very soon, he would find out.

He reached down and stroked the raging erection that was making it difficult to concentrate on the road, pressed down hard on his pulsing cock through the fine wool of his slacks. Her scarlet-painted mouth tonight had almost been too much to bear. All he could think of was pushing his cock between those plump, red lips. He'd had to tear his eyes away from her mouth to even talk to her.

No sex.

Of course he had readily agreed to that. She was right;

these sorts of temporary contracts often implied no actual intercourse. But that didn't mean he couldn't touch her, put his hands all over her, make her come. Make her scream.

Christ.

He moved his hand away from his tight, throbbing groin, back to the steering wheel, before he crashed his car.

He had a feeling Rowan Cassidy was going to be the challenge of his life.

ൈ

What the hell had she just agreed to?

Rowan stormed into her apartment and slammed her purse down on the granite kitchen countertop. Had she lost her mind?

She yanked open a cabinet, pulled out a wineglass, and filled it from a bottle of cabernet sitting on the counter. She took a large swallow, filled the glass again, drank once more. A shame to waste a good cabernet in such a manner, but she needed it. Needed something to dull her senses.

She was furious with herself for allowing her pride to get her into such an absurd situation. And she really didn't want to think about the part of her that was afraid of what might happen.

Not that cuffs and floggers intimidated her. Nor did he. No, it was her own inner battle to keep hidden the very side of her that he wanted to bring to the surface.

Why had she felt so confident talking with him, accepting his challenge without thinking through the consequences? Perhaps she was more like her mother than she'd ever wanted to be; never backing down from a challenge had her tough-as-nails mother written all over it.

Her intense attraction to him only made it worse. She didn't like to think about the part that played in her agreeing to this insanity.

She took another long swallow. She would never get to sleep tonight, with her mind going a hundred miles an hour and her body still buzzing with the heat of him.

Christian.

His name alone sent a thrill of pure desire through her. She drained her glass, filled it again and took it into her bedroom to undress. But taking her clothes off only made her think of him all the more. Made her imagine his big hands stripping her bare. By the time she got to her panties they were soaked. She pulled them off, pausing to stroke two fingers over her heated cleft.

Yes.

But no! She had to stop this. Had to stop this mad obsession before it got out of control.

Perhaps it was already too late.

He was an experienced Dom. He would know if she was turned on. He'd be able to tell by her breathing, by the flush on her skin, by her eyes. But maybe if she took the edge off…

Standing naked in front of her tall vanity mirror, she caught her own heated gaze. Her eyes were aglow, her nipples tight and dark pink. She snaked her hand down, slid her fingers over the full lips of her sex. God, she was wet, and so aroused it hurt. She moaned.

She moved her hips into her fingers, used them to

spread her lips wide and then pinch at her clit. It was as full and hard as her nipples. She needed more.

She paused to reach into a bottom dresser drawer and pulled a pair of nipple clamps from a small velvet bag. They were tiny, wicked, with sharp little teeth. She had never used them on herself, only on the male subs she played with. But she felt a sudden craving for them.

She rolled her right nipple between fingers and thumb, pulled it out, elongating it, and carefully let the teeth close around the dusky flesh. She hissed in pain. But at the same time, a sharp beat of pleasure shot straight to her sex. Taking a few deep breaths, she tried to roll with the pain as she had instructed so many others to do.

When she had it under control she clamped the other nipple. Again that exquisite shard of stabbing pain. She breathed into it, converting the pain until it was simply sensation. She looked at her image in the mirror.

The metal clamps were shiny against her fair skin, the chain running between them swinging gently. She gave the chain a small tug, and the sensation jolted from her nipples straight to her sex.

She moved her hand between her legs again, oddly fascinated with the sight of herself, clamped, aroused. She spread her lips open so she could see the tight nub between them in the mirror, then stroked it with one fingertip. Sensation rushed through her on a wave of heat that carried Christian's face, his scent, the imaginary touch of his hands on her flesh.

There was no teasing herself after that. She rubbed her fingers over her clit, pausing to tug on it, pinch it. With the other hand she pulled gently on the chain between her breasts, torturing her nipples with the burning pain that was pleasure all at the same time.

God, it was too good, her whole sex was on fire, and the clamps only added to it. She rubbed harder; she wanted more.

Tugging hard on the chain, a sharp stab of painful pleasure shot through her system, while at the same time she pinched hard on her aching clit. Her climax broke through, needle sharp and stinging. Her hips bucked into her hand and she cried out.

"Christian!"

Still rubbing, pulling, as her sex clenched and sensations poured over her body, pounding through her like the ocean that was the same shade as his eyes.

Oh, God.

She was still shaking when she sat on the edge of her bed and removed the clamps with trembling hands. Pain lanced through her as circulation returned to the pinched flesh and the blood rose beneath her skin.

When would it ever be enough?

Maybe not until he touched her, until he made her come with his own hands.

Christian would make her come. She knew it would happen. At this moment it was her greatest desire, and her greatest fear. Because if he did, she might lose all control.

Forever.

֍

By the next morning Rowan knew she was in big trouble. She'd been a fool to think she could keep it all under control while submitting to Christian Thorne. She'd let her ego get in the way of common sense. And lust, if she were really going to be honest. It wasn't like her to be so rash. But everything had begun to change, her insides to shift, the moment she'd laid eyes on him.

She'd agreed to this ridiculous proposal of his without thinking it through. But she certainly couldn't back out now; she had too strong a sense of honor and too much pride. But how was she to get through this?

Even worse, she had told him she didn't have a job lined up for the week, so she had day after day in which she would be in Christian Thorne's house, in his hands each night.

Big, strong, undoubtedly clever hands . . . wicked hands . . .

She groaned. Always fiercely independent, for the first time in a very long time, she realized she couldn't deal with this situation alone. She picked up the phone.

"April? You're home."

"I have Sundays off work. Is everything okay?"

"Yes. Well, no. I don't know." Rowan sighed and tried again. "Can you meet me for lunch today?"

"Sure."

She could tell April was pleased to be asked. "Do you know Kabuki in Santa Monica?"

"On the Promenade? Yes. And I love sushi. Uh, you sure you're okay?"

"I'll be better when I've had a chance to talk with you, I think. Twelve o'clock?"

"That's perfect."

"See you there."

With two hours until her lunch date, Rowan decided to

distract herself with her writing. She went to her small writing desk and flipped open her laptop.

The big bed was soft beneath Ashlyn's back as she lay there, her wrists and ankles cuffed to the wooden posts. She felt vulnerable, exposed, with her legs spread wide so that her sex was open to his view. She pulled once against the cuffs, but there was no give at all. How had she ended up here? She was the good girl, and good girls simply didn't do things like this.

But how good was she, really? Because even though she'd never dared to do anything like this before, she'd been thinking about it for a very long time. Hadn't she always imagined being spanked, pinched, made to kneel on the floor?

Kissing boys in high school, her boyfriends in college, it had all been so innocent. But the entire time she'd yearned for one of them to just bite her lip.

Later, her thoughts had become less innocent by far. She wanted more than that quick little bite during a kiss. She wanted to be taken over, to give control over to another. To experience the pain her own hands could never bring her, no matter how she'd tried.

And now she was about to get everything she'd ever dreamed of, fantasized about alone in her narrow bed at night, her hand working fast and furious between her legs, her own fingers pinching her nipples until they stung. She was frightened, anxious, but as turned on as she'd ever been in her life.

Some part of her still screamed that this was all wrong, somehow. But to her body it felt absolutely right.

Gabriel stood at the foot of the bed, tall and imposing, a riding crop in one hand and a rabbit fur glove on the other. He smiled. He had a beautiful mouth, lush yet masculine, with strong white teeth. His dark hair was a little ruffled, as though he'd run his hands through it. His dark goatee was a shadow on his chiseled face. He looked absolutely wicked.

A tremor ran through her. Oh yes, this was right.

Her thighs tensed as he began his onslaught. He tapped her skin lightly at first, but soon the evil little crop was biting into her flesh, snapping against the front of her thighs, her belly, her breasts. Every painful touch sent ripples of nearly screaming pleasure coursing through her body. Her nipples were hard, her sex swollen with aching desire immediately. If only she could quiet her mind and concentrate.

But even as her body slid right into the sheer lust engulfing her, into the bite of the crop, her mind wouldn't still. She couldn't seem to convince herself that this was entirely okay.

Perhaps that was part of the allure. She knew it was.

When Gabriel paused and smoothed the rabbit fur over her tender skin, brushing across the swollen tips of her breasts, she almost came right then.

Rowan's heart was pounding so hard she had to stop and close her laptop. Her sex pulsed with need. Running a hand through her hair, she stood up and went to the kitchen to find something to drink, something to calm the heat blazing through her system.

Why the hell couldn't she write anymore without seeing herself as her character? It wasn't right. The young woman she wrote about was a submissive, innocent, yearning to be dominated. She herself was none of those things. Not anymore. That was all long behind her, hidden away beneath the dominant persona she'd invented in order to find her sense of power in the world. It had worked well for her for five years. Why wasn't it working anymore?

Perhaps because a part of her *was* Ashlyn? No matter how hard she'd struggled to bury that part of herself, it was always there, lurking somewhere beneath the surface.

She paced her small kitchen, frustration and an inexplicable anger suffusing her system.

Christian was only making things worse. She'd been a wreck ever since she'd met him: sleepless, flighty, and on fire twenty-four hours a day.

She was in very big trouble where he was concerned. And things were only about to get worse.

৩৩

Kabuki at lunchtime was always crowded. The trendy sushi restaurant was one of the most popular in the Santa Monica area. Rowan loved the décor: sleek, spare, everything in black lacquer with spots of color made by the spectacular arrangements of tall sprigs of rare orchids and bamboo placed here and there. Vaulted, raw-beamed ceilings and enormous windows gave the place an open feel, and the food was spectacular. But she wasn't particularly hungry. She was far too anxious.

April was already waiting for her at a table. Rowan crossed the crowded room to join her, sat down, and immediately ordered a saki, which was quickly delivered to the table.

"Thank you for coming on such short notice."

"Of course. Are you going to tell me what's going on with you?"

Rowan took a sip of her saki and turned it all over in her mind. Where to start?

"I'm...having some trouble..." Rowan fiddled with her cup. "I've done something very foolish and I can't get out of it. And I don't know how I'm going to deal with it."

April reached over and placed her soft hand on Rowan's arm. "Tell me."

"I've agreed to bottom for Christian Thorne."

Shock glazed April's round blue eyes. "You did what? God, I'm sorry, I didn't mean to say that, I'm just...so surprised."

"No more surprised than I am."

"I don't understand. I thought you were a top, a Domme."

"I am."

"Then how...?"

Rowan shook her head helplessly, then related the details of her conversation with Christian.

"And now I have to do this thing that feels totally unnatural to me. I can't stand the idea of it, of submitting to anyone. What was I thinking? I don't see how I can do this. Yet I can't back out of it, either. And I've been up all night thinking about it, which only makes it worse."

"Rowan, if you have to do this, then just do it. The

whole point is to discover whether or not you have a submissive side, right? If not, then nothing he tries will work.
And if that happens, I imagine he'll grow bored of the game
before the thirty days are up. And if he's right—"

"He's not!"

April was quiet for a moment. "Well, if he were right
about you, then this could be the best thing ever to happen
to you. I know that finding my submissive side, learning to
accept this part of myself, has been such a release, and em-
powering in a way I can't explain."

"You don't understand. This will be a disaster."

"You're right. I don't understand."

Rowan bit her lip. How much to tell? How much did
she want to face herself right now? She was wide open
again already, and she hadn't even begun. How much more
raw might she be under Christian's hands?

"April, there are experiences in my past that have...
that have led to my becoming a dominant. Ugly things.
Things I don't think about much anymore. I don't want to
go into detail now—"

"You don't have to."

"Being a dominant has been my way of finding myself
again, of finding my strength. And I have to tell you, I grew
up with this very domineering mother. She's a brilliant trial
attorney. She can argue her way out of anything. She's very
good at manipulating people. She did it with me my whole
life and I...I buckled under to her control."

It was frightening and freeing at the same time, talking
to April about these things, things she hadn't told anyone
for a very long time. But some of her history would be left
unsaid.

"I didn't even know who I was apart from what she wanted me to be, what she demanded of me. Until I left for college and, well..." She paused, deliberately skipping over the important part. "After college I swore no one would ever manipulate me again. Do you understand? Being a dominant has been good for me, it's been exactly what I've needed. I can't give that up."

"Why do you think submitting to a man you're obviously incredibly attracted to means giving anything up? Haven't you told us at the discussion group that submission is a gift? That the bottoms hold the ultimate power within the dynamics of a D/S relationship? Why would it have to mean something different for you?"

"Because *I'm* different. I didn't come into this lifestyle seeking a submissive role. That's not what I want."

"Forgive me for suggesting this, but are you sure? Because it seems that people sometimes come into the lifestyle with ideas about what they need, and those ideas turn out to be wrong. Or sometimes they discover they want more. Like that woman at the meeting last week, Patricia. You suggested she try the other side, since she's been thinking about it. So, are you sure it holds absolutely no appeal for you, deep down somewhere? Can you be absolutely certain of that?"

Rowan shook her head and murmured, "That's exactly what I'm afraid of."

THREE

"YES, SIR."

"Louder, April. I can't hear you." Decker's voice was deep, dark smoke in her ear, laced with a hint of an Irish accent that made her knees weak.

"Yes, Sir," she repeated. His voice alone could make her tremble, even over the phone. The receiver was hot against her ear.

"I've read through the e-mail I asked you for with your list of desires and limits. Now we'll talk about mine. When I play, it is always sexual. And I demand absolute obedience. If you're one of those subs who thinks it's attractive to have a smart mouth or who only wants some sensation play, then you're not the girl for me."

"That's . . . that's not a problem, Sir."

"Excellent. I use the standard safe words: yellow for slow down, red for stop the scene. Is that understood?"

"Yes, Sir." Why did simply saying these words to him give her a small thrill?

"I will respect your hard limits, will push you hard on

your maybes. Don't expect me to be gentle with you, to show you moments of sweetness. That's not the kind of Dom I am. But I will play you well, will play you hard. Is that what you want, April?"

"Yes, Sir!" She was trembling all over already just imagining it, in response to his thoroughly commanding tone.

"Be here at nine o'clock. I'll e-mail you my address and directions. I want you to wear a simple, dark skirt and a white blouse. You've read *Story of O*?"

"Of course, Sir." She didn't know a submissive woman involved in the lifestyle who hadn't.

"Then you know what I mean. Nothing underneath, no pants, no stockings. I want to see your bare flesh. Is that understood?"

"Yes, Sir." She was damp already. The mere idea of going to him naked beneath her skirt, of driving to his house that way in her car. It was sexy, but more than that, it made her whole body quiver with yielding. To *him*.

It felt dangerous. Reckless. Yet she was comforted by the fact that she was doing this at his instruction, that he was in control.

"And, April . . ."

"Yes?"

"Be prepared for anything."

She was glad he wasn't able to see her small triumphant smile. "Of course, Sir."

Her heart fluttered as she hung up the phone. It had been pounding since the moment she'd answered and heard his voice. She still couldn't believe he'd actually called her.

She went to her closet to find the appropriate outfit.

She undressed, then slipped on a short black skirt that flared a bit at the hem. She wished her legs were longer, but at a little over five feet, she was used to wearing the highest heels. She found exactly what she was looking for on the top shelf of her closet: a pair of black patent-leather pumps, with a little point to the toes and tall, spiky stiletto heels. She slid them on, stood back to look at the effect in the full-length mirror on the back of her closet door.

The skirt and the shoes were perfect. She moved her long, straight hair aside and cupped her full, bare breasts in her hands. Tonight it would be *his* hands touching her. Her pale pink nipples peaked at the idea, and she brushed her fingers over them, quickly, teasing.

She hoped she would be what he wanted, that she would please him. Her stomach clenched. She wasn't terribly experienced. She'd only been in the lifestyle for a few months, played with a few people at the club. She didn't have any real formal training yet, and couldn't take as much pain play as some of the other submissives did.

Decker had a reputation as one of the top players at the club. He'd been a Dom for years. She'd seen him there, watched him scene with other girls. He was a master with the flogger, the snake whip, with his large, punishing hands. Would he be happy with her?

She breathed out on a soft sigh. All she could offer him was her self, her submission. It would have to be enough.

It's just one night of play.

Even though she knew better, she couldn't help but hope for more.

⊗

April sat in her car in front of Decker's house in the Hollywood Hills. In the dim glow of the streetlamps and the amber light coming through the shaded windows of the house, she could see it was a large redwood structure, all sharp, modern lines and tall windows. She felt a quick rush of intimidation at the austere beauty of the house, at the idea of the man who lived there. What would a man like him, a man who could have any woman he desired, want with a simple girl from Oregon?

A night of play with nearly virgin flesh.

She was a novelty, nothing more. And that sense of newness would wear off as soon as he'd spent a night with his hands on her. But if it was all she could have of this man with whom she'd become so oddly fascinated, then she would take it.

She checked her watch. One minute before nine. She got out of her car, locked it, and began her ascent up the steep stairs set into the hillside that led to his house. The night air was thick with the scent of the eucalyptus trees that grew all over the hills in Los Angeles. Her heart hammered in a sharp, staccato beat that had nothing to do with the climb from the street. She took a deep lungful of air before she knocked on the door.

He answered immediately, as though he'd been waiting on the other side. Perhaps he had been.

"April." He smiled, a dimple flashing in one cheek, bringing her eyes immediately to his mouth. "You look lovely. Come in."

He held the door, inviting her to move past his big frame and into the house. A small tiled foyer led into a large living room with vaulted ceilings. Floor-to-ceiling bookshelves lined two walls, overflowing with books and small pieces of ethnic art: African baskets, modern bronze sculpture, South American pottery. The furnishings were contemporary, masculine, in rich neutral shades of chocolate brown, ivory, amber, everything made on a large scale to fit both the house and the owner.

Decker gestured for her to sit on the enormous L-shaped sofa. She perched on the edge, her back straight, trying desperately to hold her hands still in her lap.

"This outfit is perfect for you. The way the blouse strains against your breasts. You're excited already, aren't you?" His mouth quirked up in a grin. "No need to answer that."

God, that accent again. That alone would have her on her knees.

He settled on the sofa next to her, close enough that she could smell the faint citrus of his cologne. She felt overwhelmed by the sheer size of him. He was tall, broad, built like a pro football player. His size intimidated her, and that was a part of the attraction. He was so powerful, in his size, his bearing, his attitude. She started to tremble all over, a soft shivering inside.

"We already discussed your safe words and limits on the phone. As I told you earlier, I intend to push your limits. Have you had any change of heart?"

"No, Sir."

"Good, then. I think you'll be very obedient. I can see that in you, your willingness to please. A very much admired trait in a submissive."

"Yes, Sir."

She tried to look him in the eye as she spoke, but his

dark gaze was too intense and she had to look away. She was quivering all over, just beneath her skin.

"Come. We're going upstairs to my...playroom."

Her pulse raced at the thought, and when he took her elbow to guide her through the house and up the stairs, her mind went blank, just emptied of all thought, except one.

This is really happening.

The staircase seemed to go on forever. At the top, he led her down a short hallway to a room at the back of the house, against the hillside. It had only one tall, narrow window, and that was shuttered.

The room was set up as a small dungeon. In the middle of the room was a large bed covered in black satin, with cuffs dangling from each corner and a black nylon suspension harness hanging over it like some twisted chandelier. She quickly took in a padded spanking bench, a high wooden chair with steel wrist and ankle cuffs set into the arms and legs, a tall T-shaped wooden cross in one corner with lengths of chain suspended from the ends of the crossbar.

A large armoire was open to reveal a variety of toys and implements hanging from hooks inside: floggers, whips, crops, paddles, leashes, coiled lengths of rope in various colors. Music was already playing, the soothing, familiar trancelike tones of Enigma.

For some reason this small, private dungeon was more daunting than the club, and more intriguing. Her sex grew damp just looking at it all.

"A nice room, yes?" Decker asked her.

"It's beautiful, Sir."

He came up behind her and stroked the back of her

hand, making her shiver with pleasure. "I love the way you say 'Sir.' I can hear your submission in your voice." He drew around to the front of her, tipped her chin in his hand. "Are you ready, April?"

She'd never felt more ready in her life. Yet she could barely get the words out.

"Yes, I'm ready, Sir."

He leaned in, still holding her chin, until she could feel his breath warm against her cheek. His dark eyes glittered. He whispered, "Strip."

∽

Venice Beach at night was always a party. The narrow streets were lined with bars, cafés, art galleries, all of which were packed with the bohemian Venice regulars. Even though it was winter, tourists still roamed the sidewalks, adding to the crowds. Rowan was glad Christian had his own parking area behind his house on the canal, a rarity in this neighborhood. She pulled her small silver BMW up next to his black Cadillac and got out of the car.

Instantly the scent of the ocean hit her nostrils, a strong jolt of salt and cool air. She took a deep lungful, trying to calm her hammering heart.

Why was she so afraid? If she was right, if he couldn't manage to make her yield to him in any true fashion, then this would simply be an uncomfortable situation, a waste of time for them both. If he was right...

She pushed the thought away.

A group of teenagers on skateboards passed her, whistling and calling to her. She'd better get going, get to the house. The possibility of young thugs wandering the dark alley wasn't any more frightening to her at that moment than the thought of what she might face in Christian's house.

Checking to make sure she'd locked her car, she stood up straight, blew out a breath, pulled her shoulders back, and followed the wood-slat walkway around the side of the garage as Christian had directed her, until she found the back door of the house.

It was a large, three-story structure, all wood, silvered from the sea air. She could see that the top story was made mostly of glass, like a greenhouse. Light shone through, and she could see the silhouette of a large easel, as well as what looked to be several objects draped in sheets.

She shifted from one foot to the other, took one more deep breath before knocking, held it for endless moments before the door swung wide.

Christian. It struck her like a blow how handsome he was, how noble looking, with his chiseled features and that lush mouth. She had to steel herself against the warm rush of desire between her thighs.

"Rowan. You're here."

"Yes. Did you think I wouldn't come?"

"It was a distinct possibility. I'm glad to see you're as courageous as I thought you were." He smiled at her, a flash of beautiful white teeth. "Please, come inside."

He was challenging her already. She lifted her chin, stepped into the large, well-lit kitchen. It was all warm wooden cabinetry, smooth wood floors. Copper bowls piled with fruit lined the tiled counters. The overall effect was warm, homey. Surprising.

She paused to take it in. Christian came up behind her, stood so close she could feel the heat of his body against her back.

"Let me show you the rest of the house."

If she leaned back a mere inch or two, she would feel the hard planes of his chest against her body . . .

He moved around her to show the way.

The kitchen led to what appeared to be a small dining area. It was empty.

"I haven't had time to buy all my furniture yet," Christian called over his shoulder.

They came into the living room. A stone fireplace with a heavy wood mantel occupied one end of the room. Two overstuffed sofas and a chair with an ottoman done in moss green velvet filled the large space. Everything was plush, made for comfort. Funny, she'd imagined him in a house filled with black leather. Of course, she hadn't seen the upstairs yet.

"Sit down."

Christian gestured to the sofas, but she chose the chair instead. He sat on the arm of one of the sofas, close to her. His long legs stretched out before him, crossed at the ankles.

"Let's talk a bit first."

She nodded, swallowing hard. "We need to discuss terms. Specifics."

"Yes. Why don't you tell me your hard limits."

She nodded. She was trembling inside, a knotted mass of nerves and barely contained lust. What the hell had she been thinking, coming here like this? But it was too late for that, wasn't it?

Get yourself under control!

She swallowed once more. "No sex, we already agreed to that." She saw him nod, tried not to notice the way his long, ponytailed hair was draped over one shoulder, how the pale blond strands shone in the lamplight.

Come on, Rowan, you can do this.

"No anal contact of any kind. None. No insertion of objects. No electrical play, no body fluids, no cutting, no age regression, no cowgirl, nurse, Catholic schoolgirl role-playing stuff."

He nodded. "Agreed. Is that it?"

"No." She paused, caught his sea-colored gaze. "No fucking with my head."

"But isn't that what it's all about?"

She had to stop and think about that. He was right, to some degree. BDSM was all about psychology. But that wasn't quite what she'd meant. Or was it?

"I just don't want any of that meaningless sweet-talk crap that some Doms use to flatter their bottoms into sub-mission. I hate that sort of insincerity."

"Not that that's my style, but I doubt very much it would work with you, anyway."

"You're right. It won't."

"But nothing will work unless you can manage to drop the attitude, the defenses," he said softly.

His eyes were focused on her, sincere, intense. She had to look away. He remained quiet for a moment, as though letting her absorb that.

"And what about your maybes?"

"I . . . I don't know," she admitted.

"Well, you know your safe words, how to let me know

to stop, or slow down. And you know I'll push you. When I push beyond your unspoken boundaries, you'll let me know. I trust you to do that, to use the safe words, rather than making a show of braving your way through an uncomfortable situation."

"Of course."

"Now I'm going to ask you something that I don't think many people ask. But it's important as far as I'm concerned. What brought you into the BDSM lifestyle? What do you want from it?"

She was so surprised that for a moment she couldn't speak. It was a loaded question, for her, anyway. Her answers were not so simple. And she certainly wasn't going to tell him everything, about Danny, about that year with him that had begun as a longed-for experiment in sensuality and had ended so horribly.

A small shiver ran through her and she had to take in a deep breath. This wasn't Danny here with her now. And she was so much stronger. That was the whole point, wasn't it? She would prove that.

"I spent too much of my life being controlled and manipulated by people. Mostly my mother. I was passive, weak. Being a Domme is my way of finding myself, taking my power back."

He leaned forward in his seat, his hands clasped. "Yes, but what about it attracts you, turns you on?"

"The same as everyone else who does these things. The exchange of energy, what goes on in our heads, is fascinating. Titillating. And the symbols are all so taboo: the ropes, the handcuffs, the whips. The forbidden is always attractive to people like us."

She smiled, tried to look as though that were the whole truth.

He was studying her face. She shifted in her seat, her body going hot under his concentrated stare.

"That'll do for now, I suppose."

He stood, offered his hand to her. She took it and let him help her to her feet. Unexpectedly, he pulled her close, leaned in so that his face was only inches from hers. He searched her eyes. "Rowan. Don't let your pride prevent you from telling me what you want. And what you don't."

What did she want? She was here, wasn't she?

She licked her lips. Her throat was so dry she couldn't have spoken if her life depended on it. Her blood was absolutely pounding in her ears.

Christian turned and led her silently upstairs.

It was about to begin.

They went up two flights, bypassing the second floor altogether. The atrium she'd seen from the street level turned out to be his studio, as well as his bedroom.

The room was enormous, covering the entire length and width of the house. The floors were a pale expanse of wood. Three walls appeared to be made entirely of glass that curved at the ceiling to create a partial dome effect. A black wrought-iron four-post bed stood against the only solid wall; gold velvet curtains covering a section of windows on each side gave privacy. An intricately patterned Persian rug in dark shades of red, black, and gold marked off the bedroom area.

An art studio took up most of the room. She spotted the easel she'd seen through the windows, but the room was devoid of paintings. Instead, stone sculptures were every-where, in every size. Small busts stood on pedestals; one figure, draped in a sheet, was six feet tall. All were portray-als of the human form. All were brilliantly done.

"They're beautiful," she breathed.

"I'm glad you think so. Come, look at the view."

She joined him at one bank of windows overlooking the town of Venice.

"During the day you can see the ocean from here. If you listen you can hear the crash of the waves. Here, close your eyes."

He slid a hand over her face, covering her eyes. She tried to listen for the waves, as he'd said, but she couldn't stop thinking about the fact that he was touching her. That he was about to do much more. And so close, she could smell him, his skin. There was a faint scent of something sweet, like honey.

She was losing control of the situation, and she knew it. But there was nothing she could do to stop it. And he hadn't even really started yet.

With one hand still over her eyes, she felt him gather her hair in the other and move it aside. Then he placed a palm on the back of her neck. She stiffened.

"Shh, Rowan. Be still," he whispered, as though sooth-ing a frightened animal. But maybe that's what she was right now.

She was totally out of her element already.

She tried to relax her muscles, but they remained rigid. She was hot all over.

When he moved his hand and placed his lips on the

back of her neck her legs almost went out from under her. The gesture was so unexpected, so soft and warm. Her sex went damp immediately.

"That's better," he whispered. "We'll begin now."

He drew his mouth away, then his hand, and she stood blinking, confused.

He turned and began to move across the room, turning lights out as he went until only a few small lamps shone in the vast, dark space. When he reached the bedroom area he turned to her. "Come, Rowan."

He waited. Her feet were rooted to the floor. She was standing in the dark now. She was vaguely aware of the stars shining beyond the windows, of the half moon hanging in the sky. She could not get herself to move.

"Stop fighting it, Rowan. There's no point in your being here if you don't."

She bit her lip. Why did she feel like crying?

"Rowan." His voice had gone very soft. Yet there was still a tinge of command there. "Come." And then more sharply, "Now."

Something in her loosened. Perhaps it was the tone of his voice. Perhaps it was that she knew she had to do this, had to give herself over to the experience. Either way, her feet moved, and she crossed the room until she stood before him on the Persian rug.

"Good." He smiled again, that devastating smile. But it did nothing to reassure her.

He began to move in a slow circle around her, his fingertips lightly brushing her shoulders, her arms, the back of her hands. She stood there, unsure of what to do with herself, trembling already beneath his touch. She hadn't felt so confused and weak in a very long time. Perhaps never. She didn't like it.

But she didn't want him to stop touching her.

Finally he drew away.

"Remove your clothes, Rowan. Everything but your bra and your underwear."

"What?"

"Just do it."

"I can't!"

"You can. And you will. For me."

She was suddenly furious. "I will not."

Christian took a step back and stood there, arms crossed, looking at her. "Are we doing this or not, Rowan? Because if not, then I imagine we both have better things to do. But if we are, then you're going to have to find it in yourself to yield to my command, because it won't work any other way, and you know it."

"I told you I'm not a submissive," she said quietly, still steaming.

"Yes, you did." He stroked a hand over his jaw, exhaled a long breath, dropped his hands to his sides. "If you've decided we're finished, then go now."

There was still strength in his voice. He wasn't defeated. Her mind was spinning. She wanted more than anything to bolt, to run downstairs and out into the night, into the safety of her car.

But she was too proud to back down. And her body was still humming with need. And something more . . .

She still felt like crying.

She shook her head. "No. I'll . . . I'll stay."

"Then take your clothes off."

He sat down on the edge of the big bed, his hands braced on his knees, and waited.

With defiant but shaking hands, she unbuttoned her blouse, took it off. Her narrow black skirt followed, leaving her in the sweet white lace bra and panties she'd chosen earlier tonight with some perverse sense of irony, and her black stiletto heels.

She'd never been one to be self-conscious about her body. On the contrary, she worked hard for her sleek, fit figure and was proud of it. But she'd never felt more naked in her life.

She raised her chin as Christian looked her over.

"Beautiful."

He ran a finger along her abdomen and she went warm all over.

Again he circled her, this time feathering a light touch over her bare skin; her shoulders, her collarbone, her rib cage, the small of her back. He continued to move around her, touching her lightly, his fingertips mesmerizing in their gentleness.

Her sex filled, grew damp, and her nipples peaked beneath the lacy cups of her bra. When he brushed the swell of one breast she gasped.

"Relax, Rowan. Enjoy my touch. There's much more to come."

Oh, God.

He went down on one knee before her. "Off with these shoes now."

He helped her step out of her high heels, his big hands wrapping around one thigh as she stumbled, setting her flesh on fire.

Control, Rowan. Control.

But that was impossible already. He had her. And no doubt he knew it.

He traced the line of muscle in her calves before he stood up to face her. Without her heels on he seemed taller than ever, looming over her. He tilted her chin with one hand and his ocean eyes held hers.

"There will be no pain tonight, Rowan. Only pleasure. Don't be afraid."

"I'm not."

He searched her face, his brows drawing together. He was so intent, so thoughtful. "What is it, then? You're still struggling."

"Yes." She wanted to look away, but she couldn't.

"Don't think about it. Just do it. Just give it all over to me. Let me handle everything. Let me take care of you." He was still looking deeply into her eyes. "Do you trust me?"

"I . . . yes." It was herself she didn't trust.

"Then come with me. Sit here."

He took her to an antique carved wood chair, upholstered in dark red velvet. She sat. The old velvet was scratchy against the back of her thighs. Christian bent down and pulled a large basket from behind the chair.

"Tonight is about learning to give yourself over to me, to this experience. This will be a mental exercise, an exercise in yielding. Do you understand?"

Rowan nodded. She was barely able to think straight.

He pulled something out of the basket.

"Flowers?" she asked, startled.

"I'm an artist. For me, everything must have a certain aesthetic."

He didn't bother to explain further, just pulled the garland of flowers from the basket, bit by bit. And then he wrapped it around one of her wrists, binding it to the arm of the chair.

She could hardly believe this was happening, that this was how he intended to begin. That it was her sitting in this chair, being bound in flowering vines. It was too pretty to be real. Where was the leather, the whips, the chains?

But this was part of his genius in all of this. He knew she'd never come to it willingly, in any normal way. He'd known she'd need something different. Something to take her totally by surprise.

Very clever.

It was working.

The perfume of the flowers rose as her body heated, as he wrapped her in the fragrant vines. First one wrist, then the other, then around her waist, drawing her firmly into the chair. He went to work on her ankles next.

By the time he was done she'd never felt so helpless, so vulnerable. She had to struggle not to tear the vines off her, which she knew she could easily do. But it seemed important to her that she fight the urge to run away from this.

"Submission is all about symbols, Rowan," he said quietly.

Yes, she knew that. Knew it down to her very soul as she fought not to tear herself from the chair. A series of emotions rushed through her, one after the other: frustration, rage, desire, and finally, sadness. She didn't know why. But it soon engulfed her. Tears threatened, but she would not give in.

She would not give in.

She took a deep breath, let it out slowly. And began to cry.

She couldn't control it. The tears welled up, spilled down over her cheeks, and she couldn't do a thing to stop them. With her wrists bound to the chair she couldn't even wipe them away.

"Rowan?"

Dimly, she was aware of the concern in Christian's voice. God, she couldn't stand it. Couldn't stand to feel like this; the fear, the absolute panic. Couldn't stand for him to see her like this. For him to pity her.

Anger suffused her, and she yanked hard on her fragile bonds, pulling free. She stood, tearing the twining flowers from her body.

"I have to get out of here. I have to go." She found her clothes and pulled her skirt on, then her blouse.

"Rowan, wait. Let's talk."

"No. I'm leaving." She bent over to retrieve her shoes from the floor.

"Rowan, stop. Look at me."

She turned to look over her shoulder. The damn tears still hadn't stopped. "Don't let this make you think you've won," she hissed. She heard her own voice like a snake's.

As she ran down the stairs she heard him mutter, "It was never about winning."

Downstairs, she paused long enough to slip into her shoes, then ran out into the damp night, her pulse speeding, her heart thundering in her chest. She fumbled with her car keys, finally fit the key into the ignition, and pulled out of the driveway.

Why was she crying? Still? What the hell had happened

to her in there? She tried to go over it in her mind, but she couldn't think straight. She was too barraged by emotions.

All she knew was that she had to get far away from this place, from him. Christian.

It was too much, he was too much. She couldn't go through with this mad plan. She couldn't face the old fear and defeat it brought to the surface, already, without him having really even touched her.

God, she was a mess.

She'd gone on believing she was strong, that she'd found her strength after the pain of her past, grown beyond it. What a fallacy that had turned out to be!

As she sped through the night, all she could think of was that Christian Thorne had turned out to be her downfall. She would never forgive him. She would never forgive herself.

ლე

The idea of taking her clothes off had been simple enough, but April hesitated, her fingers paused on the buttons of her blouse. Would he like her naked body? Would she be pretty enough for him?

"It's all going to come off, April." With one dark brow lifted, Decker looked faintly amused. "But leave the shoes on. I like them."

She nodded, undid the buttons, one at a time, stepped out of her skirt. He eyed her full breasts admiringly, making her feel all the more naked, for some reason. Her mind was emptying already, and the sinking sensation that marked the descent into subspace, that dreamy place of endorphin-induced pleasure, made her light-headed.

His big hand engulfed hers as he led her to the wooden cross in the corner of the room. With his hands on her waist, he turned her to face him.

"Have you ever been bound to a cross?"

"Yes, Sir. At the club."

"Very good. Raise your arms over your head."

She did as asked, immediately, without any thought of struggle. She loved his deep voice, the way it rumbled in his wide chest. Commanding, with no room for doubt or discussion. Not that she had any intention of arguing with him. She was here because she wanted to be, because she wanted to please him. And now, naked before him, with her wrists being buckled into the padded leather cuffs suspended from the tall wooden cross by primeval lengths of chain, she wanted that even more. Her skin shivered with need, as though she had been brushed all over with something spiky and hot.

Finished, he pulled on the chain from which the cuffs hung, testing it. Then he checked her hands for circulation. He left her ankles unbound. Satisfied, he took a step back.

"Beautiful girl."

She'd never felt more beautiful. Bound and waiting for him to take his pleasure with her, she felt vulnerable and safe at the same time. It was an odd feeling, one she'd experienced while playing with other tops in her brief months at the club, but never to this extent. Her whole body quivered in anticipation.

She could hardly wait for him to touch her.

"A little warm-up first," he said.

He ran his hands over her body, his big, flat palms making wide sweeps across her skin. His touch left a heated tingle as he went, making her nipples harden and her sex plump between her thighs. It took every ounce of self-control to hold still, to keep her eyes cast down as a good submissive should.

She wanted to see him, to watch this enormous man who touched her so gently. But she knew that wouldn't last. And as soon as the idea crossed her mind, his hands grew a little rougher, pinching the skin at her waist, on her thighs, the undersides of her breasts, and finally, excruciatingly, her nipples.

His wicked hands seemed to race over her skin, pinching everywhere at once, and she couldn't help but squirm. The pain was giving her sharp little jolts, followed by a quick buildup of endorphins. She was flying already and he'd hardly even started.

Her sex was practically dripping.

When the pinching stopped she was panting. Her own breath was ragged in her ears, and her skin was hot, burning.

"You take it well," Decker remarked, his accent stronger, rougher, than ever.

A surge of pride ran warm through her system at the obvious pleasure in his voice.

"Let's see what else you can take, shall we?"

She didn't dare look as he moved away from her. She closed her eyes, listened to the quiet rustles and whispers as he gathered the toys he would use on her. In a moment, he was next to her again; she could feel the heat from his body without opening her eyes.

"Yes, I like that, keep your eyes closed. I don't want to use a blindfold on you. You're prettier without it."

She stood, waiting, leaning her body weight into the cuffs a bit. And then she felt the first stroke of leather against her flesh.

A flogger, she thought, a small one with a lovely little sting to it. Although she was certain he could make it really hurt if he wanted to. She knew at some point he would. A shiver of desire ran through her at the thought.

The thongs of the flogger swept over the front of her body; her stomach, her breasts, the front of her thighs. The leather was cool against her skin, with just a small bite. She concentrated on the rhythm, let her body sink into it.

The flogger moved faster, harder, the bite turning the slightest bit vicious. And she gloried in the sensation, in the pain that was pleasure moving through her body in warm waves.

A sharp smack of his hand on her ass had her jumping.

She heard a low chuckle from him. The endorphins already coursing through her body made her smile.

"Amusing, am I?" he asked. She knew better than to answer. "Let's see if you find this entertaining."

He spun her around, the chains from which she was suspended twisting, and started to work her bottom with the flogger, a slow build in speed and intensity. Pleasure flowed through her veins, a tingle of heat and excitement that warmed her all over. She breathed in the acrid scent of the leather, the male scent of his heated body.

Please touch me.

Suddenly, the rhythm changed, and he was hitting her with a hard, slow volley of smacks that forced her body to bend and flow beneath the impact. The sensation went right to her head, blanking her mind. And to her hot sex, which was slick and throbbing with need.

Touch me!

The flogger came down harder across her ass. Her skin was absolutely on fire, her body arching into the rhythm of the flogging. But she needed more.

Decker worked her expertly, staying in one rhythm long enough for her to sink into it, then switching it, surprising her, beginning a new surge of sensation. It was all wonderful, but she wanted desperately to feel his hands on her.

When he stopped she could hear the ragged panting of his breath coming in short gasps, as was her own. Then he moved up behind her, pressed close to her, so tightly she could feel every ridge of hard-packed muscle on his body. And his huge erection pressed into her back, making her groan.

His breath hot on her hair, his hand snaked around the front of her and cupped one breast. She exhaled on a long, slow breath, moved into his hand with a mixture of sharp desire and profound relief. He pinched her nipple hard.

Yes! Just what she needed, craved.

It was even better when his hand moved down between her legs and he slipped a few fingers into her drenched cleft.

"Spread for me, April," he whispered.

He hardly needed to ask. Her thighs moved apart as if of their own accord, allowing him better access. Immediately he began to pinch and pull at her clit, hard, painfully, yet it was exactly what she needed. She surged back into him, wanting to feel his body hard against hers. Her sex was burning, with pain, with pleasure. And when she was right on the verge of coming, he used his other hand to squeeze her nipple between his big fingers.

She went off like a rocket, her orgasm screaming through her at a thousand miles an hour. Fire flashed behind her closed lids. Her body surged in ecstasy, spasmed, went limp.

She sagged against him. Her legs were shaking so hard, only the cuffs and his huge body held her up.

He stood there with her like that, letting her catch her breath. Her head was spinning. She'd never come so hard in her life.

Finally, he moved away from her, leaving her suspended from the cuffs. She swayed in her heels, her body tingling, her heart thumping. She looked up and found his eyes on her.

He lifted her chin in his hand, his dark gaze bearing into her, seeming to look into her soul. "A nice beginning, yes? But I'm hardly done with you, my April."

FOUR

WHAT THE HELL HAD JUST HAPPENED? CHRISTIAN still held the shreds of flowered vines in his hands. He swore he could still smell her scent in the room, something soft and feminine and fresh, and utterly different from the scent of the flowers.

He'd never handled a bottom so carefully, yet it had all backfired. But why? He needed to think this through, to figure it out. No, he had to talk to Rowan. She was the only one who could tell him what the tears, her sudden departure, were all about.

He had some theories. Obviously, the act of submission had brought up something painful for her. He'd seen it happen before, with other people. But he'd never seen anyone react so strongly. And it convinced him that he was right about her, right about her submissive side hiding beneath the tough veneer of domination. The woman put on quite a façade, and he had no doubt that she was a good top, but he'd seen there was something else hiding behind it.

And it had all crumbled tonight, fallen apart at the merest touch, at the first act of yielding.

Christ, her skin had been like pale silk under his hands.

He threw the flowers to the floor and moved to the windows. The night was dark, the moon barely visible now behind a blanket of coastal fog. He could see the lights of the bars down on Venice Boulevard. She was out there somewhere. Hurting, raw. And it was his fault.

He had to talk to her.

He knew if he called she wouldn't be home yet. Hell, he couldn't even follow her because he didn't know where she lived. He'd have to wait, give her time to make her way home. He'd call then, in a little while, and hope she'd answer the phone.

He couldn't get the image of her tear-streaked face from his mind. So tragic. So beautiful it almost hurt to look at her.

He grabbed a sketchpad from a side table and began to draw, but as soon as he got to the eyes, it felt like a betrayal of sorts to put the emotions there on paper. The first time since before he'd left Europe he'd felt like working and he couldn't bring himself to do it. He tossed the pad down in frustration

He checked his watch. It had been only fifteen minutes. Too soon. She'd mentioned at one point that she lived in Century City; it would be a little longer before she reached home.

He was too worked up to sit still. He went downstairs to his study on the second floor, and sat down behind the big, carved hardwood desk he'd had shipped from France, and picked up the phone.

Two rings, then a deep, male voice with a British accent. Sterling Price, owner of the prestigious Price Galleries, was a world-renowned art expert. And even though the man was old enough to be his father, he was also one of Christian's oldest and dearest friends.

"Price here."

"Sterling, it's Christian."

"Christian. How are you, my boy?"

"I need to talk to you."

"Well, you have me."

Where to start? He ran his hand back over his smooth ponytail. He'd have to start at the beginning.

"I have to talk to you about a woman."

Sterling chuckled. "Not my specialty, Christian."

"Oh, come on. I know you prefer your beautiful boys, but you know people better than anyone."

"Now you flatter me. I like it. So, what seems to be the problem?"

"This woman, Rowan. I met her at the club I go to. And she agreed to bottom for me, even though she thinks she's a top."

"Interesting."

"You have no idea." Neither had he, until he'd had Rowan in his hands. *Christ.*

"The thing is, she's really fighting this. Something happened and she left in tears. She won't talk about it. I don't know how to fix it."

"Why do you have to fix it?"

"Because it was my fault!"

"Was it?"

"Her well-being was my responsibility. And I blew it.

I had her in my hands, and I mishandled the situation horribly, misread what she needed." He paused, frustrated. "This wasn't what I'd intended. I wanted to open her up, yes, but not like this. I may be a sadist, but I never want to cause anyone real pain. Not the kind that cuts soul-deep. Maybe there was nothing I could have done to prevent it, but she was in my hands, she was my responsibility. I screwed this one up royally, Sterling. It's unforgivable."

"I think sometimes you take on too much, Christian. You cannot fix everything. This woman, Rowan, she is not your mother, your sister."

"Damn it, Sterling, I'm aware of that."

"Are you?"

He blew out a long breath, tried to calm down. "Taking care of my family after my father left is hardly the same situation."

"You were twelve years old," his friend said quietly.

"I did what I had to do."

"What do you think you have to do now? Now that your mother is gone, your sister safely married . . . is this woman some sort of replacement responsibility?"

"What? No, of course not." But was there some truth there after all? "I need to think about this."

"Yes, you do. I'm confident you'll find the best way to handle things. Let me know what happens."

"I will."

He put the phone down, not sure if he felt any better. Still antsy, he went back up to his studio and took out his frustration in cleaning the mess of flowers, gathering the ropy vines in his arms and stuffing them into a trash bag.

He couldn't stand the idea of throwing them all away. They'd looked so incredible on her body, against that smooth, fair skin. She was all mock innocence in her white lingerie and bound in flowers. He'd wanted to take his camera out, to photograph her so he could draw her later, maybe paint her.

Her eyes had gone blank the moment he'd bound her wrist, and he'd thought she was giving in. He swore he'd felt at least a momentary loosening of her muscles. But then she'd snapped. Something had changed while he'd been bent over fastening her ankles to the chair, and he hadn't seen it happen.

He checked his watch again. Another ten minutes had passed. He went downstairs once more, sat down, quickly dialed her number.

The phone rang, over and over. Finally, the ringing stopped.

"Hello?" Her voice was husky, but she sounded better. Calmer.

"Rowan, it's me, Christian. Don't hang up."

Silence.

"We need to talk about what happened."

"No."

"Look, I want to understand what happened with you. I want to help."

"Please just leave me alone."

"Rowan, if you had been topping someone and the same sort of thing happened, wouldn't you feel some sense of responsibility? Would you just let it go?"

Silence again. Then a whispered, "No. I suppose not."

Her quietness was giving him a sense of desperation. "It

doesn't have to be now. Why don't you try to get some sleep, then we can talk tomorrow."

All he heard was a soft sigh.

"Will you be okay alone tonight?"

"Yes. Of course."

She didn't sound okay. In fact, she sounded defeated; the burning anger he'd seen earlier appeared to be gone. But he had no other choice. He knew she'd never let him come to her.

"Come back to the house tomorrow. We'll talk."

"No, not your house."

He rubbed a hand over his jaw, the stubble scraping against his fingertips. "We can't very well have this conversation in public."

Get it back under control. It's your job.

She sighed. "You're right." A resigned pause. "Okay. I'll be there in the afternoon. I need some time to...I need some time."

"Yes, of course. I'll see you tomorrow afternoon. But look, if you wake up later, or if you can't sleep, whatever, and you need to talk—"

"I won't."

He smoothed a hand over his hair. Of course she wouldn't. "I'll see you tomorrow, then."

He heard a click.

Christ, that was one of the most stilted, difficult conversations he'd ever had. He hadn't meant to mess with her head to that degree. He hadn't known it would, having her submit to him. If he had, he would never have done it.

No, that was a lie. He would have tried this no matter the cost. What did that say about him?

What the hell was happening to him? He was always in control, yet with this woman he was behaving completely irresponsibly.

Don't be an idiot.

But he already was. He had been since the moment he'd met her.

Taking a deep breath, he exhaled as he stood up and went back upstairs to his studio. Sleep would be impossible, but he could work. Work was his salvation.

He'd have to work until his hands bled to get Rowan out of his mind.

ख़

Decker had played her for hours. April's entire body ached exquisitely. He'd brought her to climax twice already. And now he'd taken her down from the chains, pulled off her high heels, and laid her on his big bed. Through the haze of pleasure- and pain-induced opiates surging through her brain, she watched as he stripped his shirt over his head. His shoulders were broad and muscled, his chest defined. His tawny skin was unmarked by hair, other than one narrow line dipping into the waistband of his jeans. Ah, but those were coming off, too, and now she could see his enormous erection jutting from a nest of dark curls.

God, he was gorgeous all over. Her mouth watered, wanting just to touch him, to touch his beautiful cock, covered in the same tawny skin as the rest of his big body.

"Sit up, April."

She did, perching on the edge of the bed as he approached her. Without saying a word, he grabbed the back of her head and pulled her mouth to his cock, pushing between her lips.

Yes, she wanted this, wanted to please him. She opened her throat, took him in, sucked. His hands were buried in her hair. She could hear his ragged breath, felt his cock pulsing against her tongue. When he moaned a rush of pleasure swept over her.

Anything to make him happy. Anything.

But he pulled out of her mouth with a groan. "Not yet."

Then he pushed her down on the bed again, pulled a condom from somewhere, sheathed himself. He rose over her, and she spread her legs, her sex aching, swollen, wanting him inside her, finally.

His hand snaked down between her spread thighs, his fingers brushed against her, and she let out a sigh of need.

"You're so damn wet, girl. I know you can take me."

"Yes . . ."

He used his fingers to spread her lips apart and without another word, pushed inside her, all the way to the hilt.

She gasped as he stretched her, filled her. Then her muscles relaxed, accommodating his girth, his length. He was rock hard inside her. She was going to come again, and quickly.

He slid out, in again, each motion bringing a stab of pleasure so intense, she could barely stand it.

"Please, Sir. Please . . ."

His breath was hot in her ear. "What is it, girl? What do you want? Do you want me to fuck you? Because I will." He punctuated his words with a sharp thrust. "I am going to fuck you until you come. I want to see the pleasure wash over your face."

He thrust his hips again, and she moved hers to meet him, his pelvis grinding into her mound. She was on the edge already.

Then he really started to move, his hips pistoning, his heavy cock driving into her, hard and fast. She couldn't hold back, her sex clenching. Pleasure invaded every pore of her body, making her moan, making her want to scream. She bit her lip as the tremors shook her to the core.

Before it was over she felt him tense, shudder. And then he was driving into her harder than ever, groaning over and over, before collapsing on top of her.

They were both panting, covered in sweat, musky with sex. She inhaled deeply, loving the scent. She had to hold herself back from wrapping her arms around his neck, from holding him close, keeping him there with her.

He rolled off her with a deep groan, onto his back.

They lay there for a long time. April tried to catch her breath, to still her heart. She had to keep reminding herself that mind-blowing sex was just that, nothing more. But how could this kind of sex mean nothing?

Don't be a fool, April.

It took every bit of strength she had not to roll over, snuggle into his side, beg him to kiss her.

She knew what she should do; she should get up, get dressed, thank him, and go home. Decker never kept a woman overnight; the rumors had been clear enough, and so had he. But she couldn't bear to leave the warmth of his bed, not after what they'd done tonight.

Was it only that half-in-love feeling most bottoms felt for any top who played them well? Or was it something more?

No, she'd be an idiot to think there was more to it for him.

She sat up, and felt his hand on her arm.

"Where are you going?"

"I...I thought you were done with me, Sir."

He was quiet for a long moment, then he looked at her, his dark gaze meeting hers. He said in a near-whisper, "Stay."

Her heart hammered in her chest as she lay back down on the bed. He reached out and pulled her close to his side. She didn't know what to think of it, but she wasn't going anywhere, not as long as he wanted her with him. He would ask her to leave soon enough.

This is dangerous.

Yes, it was. But despite everything she knew about him, she couldn't help but allow her heart to soar a little. Even if eventually he would break it.

∞

Rowan rolled down the windows on her small, racy BMW, letting the cold air into the car. The wind whipped her hair around her face, stung her tender skin. But she needed it. She took a deep breath, held the cool air in her lungs, trying to calm down.

She'd hardly slept all night. When she'd woken from a nightmare at three in the morning, she got up to take a bath. It hadn't helped. She was exhausted and half numb. But numb was better, maybe.

She found her exit from the 10 freeway and pulled off, following the same route she'd taken the night before. God knew she didn't want to have this conversation today, but she owed it to him. Owed him some sort of explanation, about last night, about why she intended to back out of their little experiment.

She'd known the moment she'd left his house last night that she didn't want to go back, didn't want to deal with this. As much as she hated to admit defeat, she hated the idea of being so weak and out of control even more. She could not allow it to happen.

She had been weak once and it had almost destroyed her.

Never again.

She found the little alley that led to Christian's parking space behind his house, pulled in, and parked. The scene was different in the light of day. She could see clearly the weathered wood siding on his house. Gulls cried overhead, and the scent of the sea was strong, carried to her on the moisture-laden wind. As she walked across the deck to the back door she had the distinct sensation of being watched. He opened the door before she reached it.

She wanted to cry again the moment she saw his face.

This would never do.

God, she hated this.

"Rowan. I'm glad you came." He held the door open for her. "Come in. Do you want something to drink? Tea? It's cold today."

"No, thank you. I don't need anything." The anger was still simmering in her veins.

She couldn't bear to look at him, so she sat down at the plain wooden table by the window at one end of the kitchen. He sat across from her while she played with her car keys.

"Rowan, look at me." His voice was quiet but held an air of command.

"Why? So you can gloat?"

"Of course not."

She shook her head. "I'm sorry. That was unnecessary."

"It's alright. I just want to know what happened up there."

She shrugged. "I don't really want to talk about it."

"Obviously. And I don't blame you. But if you won't talk to me, you should talk to someone. That was some pretty heavy stuff."

She looked away, out the window. A gull had landed on the railing around the deck and was preening itself against a backdrop of heavy gray sky.

She felt just as dark and heavy inside.

"Rowan, I've been thinking about this since last night. All night, if you want to know the truth . . ."

She looked at him then, saw the dark circles beneath his blue-green eyes. He was beautiful even then. And as strong as ever.

"I think what happened to you last night was a shock of some sort. I'm not asking you to go into the details of your past with me, whatever caused you to feel like that. What I'm suggesting is that you try to work past it. With me."

"I won't be humiliated again."

"You know that's not what I intended."

"Yes." She knew it was true. She also knew he was right that she should work through her old issues. She just didn't know if this was the time to do it, or the way.

"Rowan."

He reached out and took her hand in his. Her skin was

instantly suffused with warmth. His touch conveyed his concern, his sincerity, and the heat began to build between them at once. She wanted to pull away, but she couldn't let go of that heat.

"I'm asking you to trust me."

"It's not about you."

"I know that. But I want to work through this with you. I'm still convinced, I feel more than ever, that this will work for you. That this will be revealing for you."

"I'm not so sure I want anything to be revealed. Why are you pushing so hard for me to do this? We don't even know each other."

He was silent a moment, then he shrugged, a ripple of solid muscle moving across his broad shoulders beneath the gray sweater he wore. "Because I feel I must."

"You're going to leave it as vague as that?"

"I'm inviting you to do the same. Does that help?"

"Maybe."

He curled his fingers around her hand, a tight grasp, holding her so she couldn't move away. If she allowed herself to relax even a little, it would feel good. Safe.

"Come upstairs with me now," he said quietly.

"I came back here to talk to you, to apologize. I didn't intend to stay."

"Yet, here you are."

She started to shake her head.

"Shh. Just do it. Stop questioning everything, and just do it. If some small part of you didn't want to, you wouldn't have come back."

She knew there was a grain of truth in there somewhere.

"Rowan, you strike me as the kind of woman who doesn't back away from a challenge. Think of this as one of the biggest challenges of your life."

"I don't know that I'm up to it," she answered honestly.

He paused, looking at her, into her eyes. She could feel the searching in his expression as though it were a physical sensation. She squirmed in her seat, but she forced herself not to look away.

"I think you're strong enough. I know you are."

"Flattery will get you nowhere." She was suddenly angry again.

"I have no need for empty flattery. I don't use that kind of bullshit. It's simply the truth as I see it. And I also see that you're using your anger to avoid dealing with the situation."

She didn't like that he could read her so easily. Hated it, really. But having the truth laid out in front of her deflated the anger somewhat.

"I don't even know how to go about beginning again."

"Leave that to me."

She put her head in her hands, her hair falling over her face in a soft tumble. Was she actually going to do this?

"Don't think about it. Just do it." His voice was low, steady. "Put yourself in my hands. Trust me. I'll take care of everything."

When was the last time she'd had an offer like that? Maybe never.

When he stood and laid a hand on her shoulder she could feel the solid warmth of his palm through her sweater. His touch was reassuring. And at the same time, that sensual buzz she always seemed to feel whenever she was near him thrummed through her body. An irresistible combination.

She forced her mind to go blank, to stop thinking, analyzing it all. To give in. She could do this. Needed to do this.

She looked up at him. "Let's go upstairs."

He raised an eyebrow and a faint smile crossed his features. Taking her hand in his, he took her up the stairs, back to his top-floor studio.

He led her to the bed once more, and this time he undressed her with his own hands, carefully, tenderly. He helped her step out of her shoes, then her wool slacks, slipped her cream-colored cashmere sweater over her head, left her in her ivory silk camisole and matching thong.

"We're going to take things slowly." He spoke softly, soothingly. "One step at a time. I just want you to get used to my touch first. To being under my hands. You know you can always stop the scene if anything gets to be too much for you. But I want you to try to stretch your boundaries a little."

"Just being here is a stretch for me."

"I know that. That's why I haven't thrown you over my knee and given you a good, hard spanking."

His wicked grin was infectious and she couldn't help but smile.

"Ah, that's better. Come now, sit here on the end of the bed."

He pressed down a bit on her shoulder, guiding her. The bed was soft beneath her, as though it had a layer of down ticking under the rich brown and gold bedspread.

The room was warm enough, but she shivered anyway. It was impossible to hold still.

He moved to the head of the bed and she couldn't see what he was doing, only heard the slide of a drawer. She felt the mattress sink a little beneath his weight as he sat down behind her. When he touched a fingertip to her bare shoulder she jumped.

"It's alright, Rowan. It's just me." He slid that fingertip down her arm, raising a trail of goose bumps. Down her arm to her wrist, over the back of her hand, then back up. His fingers continued their stroking exploration, over her neck, the line of her jaw. She could feel the heat from his hand on her skin. Incredible, how much heat came off that one finger. What would his whole body feel like pressed against hers?

Before she could banish that thought, her sex gave a squeeze, went liquid. She couldn't fight it with him still touching her. He continued to stroke her skin, moving down to her collarbone, and her nipples peaked hard as he swept across the swell of one breast, then the other. She closed her eyes and let herself enjoy the sensation.

His hand slid over the outer edge of her camisole, down over the curve of her breast, and she wanted to arch into that hand, to make him cup her breast, but she didn't move. She was trembling inside with desire.

His hand made its way over her rib cage, the lines of her abdomen, lower, until he brushed the very top of her thong. Her sex ached. She was sure he could sense the pacing of her breath, the heated flush of her skin. But right now she couldn't find it within herself to care. She only knew she didn't want him to stop touching her.

He took his hand away, leaving her skin cold. Then his mouth was next to her ear, whispering, "I'm going to blindfold you now."

Panic hit her full force. "No!"

"Yes." It was a tone few would argue with.

"I . . . I can't do that."

"You don't have to, Rowan. That's the beauty of this arrangement. I'll do everything."

He tucked her hair behind her ears while she sat, shaking and silent. She didn't know how to fight him.

The blindfold came down over her eyes, shutting the world out. She raised her hands to her face but he quickly pulled them away.

"Still, Rowan."

How many times had she given that very command to the bottoms she'd played with?

"You know how this is done. I want you to focus. To be aware of only the sensations in your body, your own breathing. Shut out the rest of the world. It's just the two of us now. Let the rest fall away."

His voice was soothing, hypnotic, yet her pulse was racing. She understood the purpose of the blindfold: to allow her to draw inward, to concentrate only on what was happening to her in this moment. But she couldn't shut her mind off. She couldn't stop telling herself why this whole scenario was all wrong, even as her body responded to his nearness, his hands on her. Even though her sex was soaking wet, her nipples hard and needing to be touched.

Pure agony.

He was touching her again. He lifted her hair from her neck, stroked the skin there, making her shiver.

"You're very responsive, Rowan. I like that. You're like a deer; hyperaware, hypersensitive."

He let her hair fall back into place and continued stroking her skin. His fingertips moved over her face; her cheekbones, her lips, where he lingered just long enough that she knew if she darted her tongue out she could taste him.

Where had that idea come from?

His hands, both of them now, moved down and he lightly cupped her breasts. She trembled, tried to hold still, but a soft sigh escaped her lips, her body's response betraying her.

"Yes, that's it." His voice was soft, low, the tone of it intensified because she couldn't see him.

But she could smell him. She drew in his masculine, honeyed scent with every breath. She swore she could actually smell the heat of his body.

She felt pressure on her shoulders and realized he was pushing her down on the bed. Panic seized her again and she struggled against him.

"Stop fighting, Rowan."

"I can't." She almost sobbed.

He eased back, allowing her to sit upright again. "Tell me what it is. What are you thinking, feeling?"

She shook her head, mute. She wasn't ready for all this. She didn't want to think about the "whys" just yet.

"Then let's try it again. Just fall into my hands. *My* hands, Rowan. Mine. Not anyone else's. Do you understand?"

She did. And having him say it made it a little easier. When he put his hands on her shoulders again she let him ease her back onto the velvet bedspread. It was soft under her back. With his big hands still on her she felt safe, somehow.

"Very good."

Was that a small tremble of pleasure surging through her at the approval in his voice?

His hands were on her again, caressing everywhere; her arms, her stomach, her thighs, then down over her calves, her ankles, even her toes. He moved back up, gently moved her thighs apart, just a few inches. That one small motion sent a thrill of erotic pleasure through her and she eased her legs apart for him, hardly believing she was doing it.

Don't think about it.

"That's it, let it all go. Open to me. Open your body, open your mind."

His stroking hands were moving higher until they were almost at the juncture of her thighs. Teasing, his fingertips drew over the aching flesh of her inner thighs in lazy circles. She wanted to raise her hips, to ask him to touch her where she needed him most, but she refused to do it. She needed to hang on to some shred of control; it was slipping away quickly enough.

"Tell me what you want."

Damn it. He could read her even now.

She kept quiet.

"Your body tells me even if you won't, Rowan. But you won't get what you want until you ask for it."

She clamped her jaw tight.

He continued his stroking, his hands sliding over her skin while her nipples hardened unbearably beneath her silk camisole, her sex ached with need, and her breathing came in short, sharp pants. But she refused to ask for anything. She could fight that much.

He bunched the hem of her cami up beneath her breasts and she thought he'd move it away to expose her, but he stopped there, swept one flat palm over her bare stomach. When he moved his hand up over the silk fabric and brushed across her hardened nipples, it took every bit of willpower she had not to arch into his touch.

Her own stubbornness was torturing her more than he was.

Her sex was absolutely throbbing. She needed desperately to come.

Unexpectedly, he pulled away from her. She could feel the absence of his body like a palpable thing.

"What . . . where are you going?"

"Shh. No questions. You know better."

Yes, she did. But it was *her* laid out here now, not some subbie boy she played with. She couldn't stand it. But she didn't move.

She could hear him moving around the room, the slide of a drawer. She couldn't tell what he was doing. The panic started to rise in her again, but she fought it down.

She jumped when something soft brushed the back of her hand.

"Easy . . ."

She forced herself to hold still and focus on whatever he was touching her with. It was so soft, maybe a feather of some sort. And once she allowed herself to relax, she enjoyed the sensation as it moved up her arm, over her shoulder, her neck.

He touched it briefly to her lips, whispered, "Beautiful." She could swear his voice was thick with desire.

No less than hers would be right now if she spoke.

The feather continued its tickling and teasing over her flesh. She could feel the slightest trace of its touch through the thin silk of her camisole as he brushed it over her breasts. She was sure he could clearly see the stiff peaks of her nipples, but at this moment it was hard to care.

The blindfold was doing its work, helping her to shut out the world, to close off her awareness of her surroundings. It made things a little less scary. Funny, but she'd thought it would make things worse, harder. She guessed Christian knew what he was doing after all.

But she could hear him moving again, and then the sharp scent of leather hit her nostrils and she melted a little inside. She'd always loved leather, really had a thing for it. And then she felt it on her skin.

Thin straps of leather cruising over her flesh in long, slow strokes; a flogger perhaps. But he'd said no pain the first time, so she knew he wasn't going to flog her with it. Just the lazy flow of leather, the aroma of it that was pure sex to her, and the knowledge that it was him doing these things to her.

It was too perfect.

Her thighs spread a little wider of their own accord, and he moved the leather thongs between them, stroked her through the damp fabric of her thong. She had to fight not to moan aloud.

But why was she fighting? She wasn't quite sure anymore. The stroke of the leather became more steady, moved to a faster beat. Her breathing came hard. And Christian whispered in that low, sexy voice, "Tell me what you need, Rowan."

She couldn't do it. Couldn't say a word. But he kept on brushing the leather over her sex, her clit coming up in a hard little nub to meet the lovely, easy pressure of leather against the silk.

One hand came down on her inner thigh, a feather-light touch, and the heat shot through her like an electric jolt. Her hips came up off the bed.

"Say it, Rowan. Say you want to come."

"No," she panted.

"Wrong answer. I know you want it, need it. And I want to give that to you."

He moved the flogger so that it came down more heavily between her legs, no pain, just a steady beat. Her whole sex was throbbing with an incredible need. His hand gripped her thigh, his grasp burning into her flesh. He moved one thumb down and hooked it under the edge of her thong, brushing over her mound.

"Oh, God," she moaned. She couldn't help it.

"Tell me. Tell me you need to come."

This time the flogger came down in a small, thudding slap over her sex and she almost came right then. She struggled to hold it back.

"Ah, you liked that."

He did it again. Her sex pulsed, right at the edge of climax. Still, she held it off, her thighs tensing.

"Give yourself permission, Rowan. Give this to yourself. There's no point in struggling anymore. You're so close. I can feel it. I can feel it in the heat coming off your skin. And you're soaked, so damn wet. I want you to come for me. Just do it. Let it go. Tell me, Rowan."

He was stroking her sex with the leather, over and over as he spoke. With his thumb, he brushed teasingly over her slick lips. Yes, she should just let it all go. Had to, now.

"Do you want to come for me, Rowan?" he paused, stroked again with his thumb. "Do you?" He pressed his thumb once onto her clit.

"Yes!"

"Then come for me. Do it now."

He moved his thumb over her clit in a tight, hard circle, and her body seized in an agony of pleasure. Sharp, stinging, her climax shot through her, shaking her inside and out. He didn't stop pressing his hand into her mound, didn't stop stroking her with the leather flogger, driving her on, layering sensation on top of sensation while her orgasm rocked her body in a shattering embrace.

FIVE

When the last clenching waves of pleasure finally died away Rowan was left shaking. Christian pulled her into his arms. She was still blindfolded, blind to the world, to everything but the pulsing beat of pleasure still shimmering deep inside her, and Christian's strong arms holding her against his chest.

It was a long while before she caught her breath. It was then she became aware that he was still holding her, that she could hear the unsteady rhythm of his heartbeat beneath her ear. He was as breathless as she was.

"Christian..."

"Shh, not yet. Don't speak. Just feel."

She wanted to. She wanted to lie in the comfort of his arms and sink into the lambent buzzing of her climax. But suddenly she realized what had just happened to her. She struggled in his embrace.

"Rowan, stop fighting. It's over. There's nothing to fight right now. Relax."

But she couldn't. She was all too aware that she had just

given her body to this man to do with as he wished. That she had followed his commands. That she had allowed herself to be weak with him, helpless.

It scared the hell out of her.

She tried to pull the blindfold off, fumbled with it.

"I need to—"

"Stop. I'll do it."

The command in his voice froze her. She let him untie the blindfold and pull it from her eyes.

She blinked in the dim light of the foggy afternoon coming in through the windows. She tried to stand up, but he held her firmly.

"I have to go," she said quietly. She didn't want to look at him.

"Rowan, I know this may have seemed like a lot, but it was a good first step."

She shook her head. The damn tears were threatening again. "You don't understand."

"I think I understand more than you give me credit for," he said quietly, but he let her go.

She gathered her clothes and put them on. He sat in silence while she got dressed.

"A little safer now, with your clothes on? A little less vulnerable?"

"Yes." Why was she angry again?

"Then let's talk for a moment before you go."

"I can't, Christian."

"Then I'll talk."

He came to her and held her shoulders in his big hands. His eyes were intense, the colors of the ocean, but darker now than she'd seen them before; the sea at twilight. She saw the muscle in his jaw working for a moment before he spoke.

"I can see you struggle, Rowan. I know there's something going on inside of you that you don't want to face. And it makes me feel more than ever that we have to press on. I owe it to you at this point, although that's entirely selfish of me, in a way. But more than that, more than the reasons I tell myself in my head why I want to do this, there's something here, between us. I know damn well you feel it, so don't bother to argue the point."

He paused, searching her face, but she wasn't going to argue. She didn't want to talk about anything at all right now. She just wanted to give in to the fierce need to flee, to get away so she could think. She couldn't think with him standing so close to her.

His voice softened. "I want to see this through with you. I'm the one who opened this door, I owe it to you. This is my responsibility."

"My . . . issues . . . are no one's responsibility but my own."

"I'm part of it now, whether you want to accept that or not. And I want to be." He blew out a breath. "You'll come back tomorrow." It was a statement, not a question.

She paused, then nodded. "Yes."

"Eight o'clock, tomorrow night."

"Yes." She looked away. She couldn't stand to see his face, to see the strength there, the conviction. The staggering male beauty of his features.

He released his hold on her, then reached up and tucked a strand of hair behind her ear. "Tomorrow, then."

She nodded once more, then turned and left.

Breathing a long sigh of relief, she closed her car door

behind her. Why had she agreed to come back? But she couldn't have refused, could she?

This was all a tangled mess and she didn't know how to begin sorting it out. She was beginning to feel helpless against the whole process, and she hated it.

Even more, she was beginning to feel helpless against Christian Thorne. But she couldn't hate him for it. Because she had loved every minute with him, no matter how emotionally difficult it had been.

She knew why she hadn't argued about coming back. She couldn't find it in herself to stay away.

∾

Wrapped in a thick terry robe, Rowan stared out the window of her apartment, a cup of herbal tea in her hand. Lights twinkled below her, the lights of other apartments, the headlights of the cars moving on the streets. The world still went on, just as it had every day, just as it would continue to do. But she was different. Today had changed her.

She wasn't sure yet if it was a good change. All she knew was that she felt different, open and raw, yet light all over. She was scared to death.

She'd spent years building her strength, and now, after one afternoon with Christian, she felt as frightened and weak as she ever had. She didn't like it one bit.

Was this the price she was to pay in order to be honest with herself about what she wanted, craved? If being submissive even *was* what she wanted. Yes, it had been a part of her at one time, but that was long past. She'd taken great care to bury it. And now Christian wanted to bring it to the surface, had already begun to do so. And here she was, having to cope with the fallout.

Focusing again on the streets below, her eyes followed the line of Olympic Boulevard toward the sea, toward his house. The coast was fogged in, the stars obscured by clouds. But the moon was partially visible, glowing with a hazy blue light.

She would be back there tomorrow night. Sipping her tea, she thought about what might happen. Was she ready for it? Her body gave a long, convulsive shiver of need as she imagined his hands on her again, and her mind went immediately to that dark, solo fantasy she'd had of him the other night, of herself naked across Christian's lap. Of him spanking her bare flesh.

Yes.

Her sex filled, swelled, pulsed with hungry desire. If nothing else, her body was ready. If only she could stop worrying, stop fighting it. But she felt as though her struggle against giving in completely was all she had left to hang on to.

She glanced at the clock. April had called earlier and asked to come by. After standing at the window and brooding for too long, she had only a few minutes left to get ready. Hanging her robe up in the big walk-in closet, she dressed in a pair of army green cargo pants and a white long-sleeved T-shirt. Barefoot, she padded into the kitchen to prepare a snack for her guest.

It had been a long time since anyone had been in her apartment. She had always been a private person, and she hadn't brought any of her submissive boys home for months. It had been even longer since she'd had a friend visit. Since she'd had a close friend, really.

Why was that? She remembered in high school, in college, having a group of female friends always around her. They did everything together: studied, went to the movies, the mall, confided in each other. When had that stopped for her? When had she become such a recluse?

It had all happened at the same time, hadn't it? After the nightmare that changed her life at the age of twenty. After her lovely fantasies had been turned into something dark and twisted. What little sense of self she'd managed to build up after leaving her mother's house had crumbled beneath the strain. Hell, *she* had crumbled.

Never again.

She shook the edge of memory away and turned to the refrigerator, pulled out a small wedge of Brie to soften and a bunch of plump red grapes. Putting them both on a square plate of glazed green Japanese pottery, she found some nice imported crackers in the pantry and carried it all into the airy living room, then opened the sheer curtains to the view.

It was another foggy day; the sky was gray and she could almost feel the thick dampness in the air, even with the windows closed.

It would be cool and dark at Christian's house by the beach.

Why did her body surge with desire just thinking about the weather there?

She shook her head. This was ridiculous.

The ringing of her doorbell brought her out of her reverie, and she opened the door.

April was wrapped in a big ivory sweater and a pair of jeans. "Hi," she said shyly.

"Come on in."

Rowan took the girl's hand and brought her into the living room. "Have a seat. What would you like to drink? I have mineral water, some juice, or I can make tea, or some coffee."

"Mineral water is fine. Wow! This place is gorgeous. And look at this view! All I can see from my apartment is the building next door." April moved across the living room to the window. "You can see almost to the beach from here."

Rowan knew that all too well.

"I'll get our drinks. Make yourself at home."

By the time she came back to the living room with two tall glasses of San Pellegrino, April was settled on the long white modular sofa, leaning against a small sea of embroidered turquoise and jade throw pillows. Rowan set their drinks down on the aluminum-framed glass coffee table, then sat down on the sofa.

"So, you want to tell me what happened with Decker?"

April bit her lip. "I'm not even sure where to start. It was... he's the best player I've ever been with."

"Not surprising. He's been doing this for a long time. He has an excellent reputation. One of the best at Club Privé, actually."

April nodded. "But it was more than that. I mean, I think it was." She paused, blew out a breath. "I've been with some tops at the club who did a very good job, but things were really different with him. He's much more... commanding. I could feel it down to my bones. And it made me want that much more to please him. Does that make sense?"

"Absolutely." Rowan understood on a newer, deeper level she didn't want to think too much about right now.

April leaned over, plucked a red grape from the plate and popped it into her mouth, chewed thoughtfully for a moment. "For me, subspace, that place my mind goes to once the endorphins really kick in, has always been easy to attain. I've heard other subs say they have a hard time getting there, depending on who they're playing with, distractions, whatever. But it's been easy for me right from the start. All a top has to do is put a collar around my neck and I start going down. Even getting ready for a play party starts to put me there. Just showering, rubbing lotion into my skin, dressing in pretty lingerie. The whole ritual of preparation. It can all begin right then. But with Decker, I reached a whole new level. From the first moment I arrived at his house."

"Don't take that to mean too much, April," Rowan said quietly, not wanting to insult the girl, but feeling a strong desire to protect her from hurt.

"I know. I really do. But then, once we got started, it was all so perfect, as though he could read my mind, knew immediately exactly what I needed. Even the way he spoke to me... I know he's probably spoken to a dozen other girls the same way. Maybe even a dozen others just this year. But there's an intensity about him, a focus. He made me feel so special, so cared for. Treasured."

"That's how a good Dom should make you feel."

"But, Rowan, I've never felt quite like this with anyone else. It was more than that he was doing his job. It felt personal. And maybe that just means he's really good at what he does, but I don't think so."

"Honey, you know his reputation with women. Everyone in the group understands he's not the kind of man to stay with one girl. He's not built like that."

"I know, I know. I can't explain exactly what happened, but it felt different. It really did. And, Rowan, he asked me to stay the night. He kept me there all day today. I just got home earlier this evening."

"That is different, from what I know of him. Still, I don't want to see you get hurt."

"I know that, too. Thank you." April smiled and put a hand on Rowan's arm. "I can't tell you how much I appreciate your friendship, that you want to look out for me."

She smiled back, patted April's hand. "Just be careful."

April nodded. "And what about you? How did it go? Or would you rather not talk about it?"

Rowan's stomach clenched. It had been easy enough to put her own concerns aside when the focus was on April. Now it all came rushing back and she could feel herself blanch.

"That good or that bad?"

Rowan shook her head. "Maybe both."

"You don't have to tell me if you don't want to."

"I just . . . it's hard for me. This whole thing is crazy."

"Rowan, you've helped me so much, from the first day I joined the discussion group. Let me help you."

She looked into April's cornflower blue eyes, wide with

sincerity. It had been far too long since she'd had a confi-
dante, a friend. Still, it was a struggle to organize her
thoughts.

"It was..." She turned her head away. "He made me
yield to him. I still can't believe I did it. There were so
many things going through my head. There still are. It's in
my nature to analyze, I guess. And being with him like that
brought up some old memories I'd rather keep buried."
She shook her head, turned back to April. "No, that's not
true. These thoughts were beginning to rise to the surface
before I even knew he existed. Strange that I've met him
now. The timing is almost too perfect."

April remained silent, allowing her to wade through the
confusion in her mind.

"I was thinking of what you just said about Decker.
That's exactly how Christian makes me feel. That incredible combination of total dominance and utter kindness that
allows me to do things with him I never would with anyone
else. Still, there are limits I don't think I can get past. Old
fears I can't get past."

"You've hinted that you went through something terrible at some point in your life. I know it's none of my business and I'm not pushing, but maybe if you talked about it,
you'd feel better."

She really did not want to talk about it. But it was ridiculous to keep dropping hints and not tell April what had happened to her. She trusted her; who better to talk to? But her
throat hurt just thinking about saying these things out loud.
She pulled a throw pillow to her body and held it tight.

"Danny was my boyfriend in college. It all started out
just fine. More than fine, really. He was interested in the

fantasies I confided to him in bed one night shortly after we began dating. To tie me up, dominate me. That was what I asked for, and he gave me exactly what I wanted. But over time things began to change. He became more aggressive. And angry. I couldn't understand it. I thought it was my fault. Maybe I felt it was punishment for having these deviant thoughts.

"He was getting rougher with me, which might have been alright, except that his attitude had changed. It wasn't about fun for him anymore. And it certainly wasn't fun for me. But I didn't know how to make it stop. And I just kind of fell apart after a while."

"Jesus, Rowan. How long did this go on?"

She shrugged. "Almost a year."

"How did you finally get out of it?"

"I got out because I had to. One night was really bad. He was drunk." The memories flooded her mind, threatened to overwhelm her. Tears stung her eyes. But she was done shedding tears over Danny. She would not cry.

"I'm sorry, honey." April laid a warm hand on her arm. "You don't have to tell me any more."

"Do you see why I can't be a submissive, April?"

"I see why you don't want to be," she said quietly. "But we are what we are. I don't think we can hide from that; not for very long, anyway. Maybe that's why all of this is happening to you now. Christian, these memories. Maybe you need to stop hiding."

"I know you're right. I just don't know if I can do it."

Could she? Could she just ignore her fears, her struggle, and enjoy what she was doing with Christian, what he was doing to her?

What would he do to her tomorrow night? A wave of pure lust surged through her, and she felt her entire body heat.

"You okay, Rowan?"

"What? Yes, of course. I'm fine."

But was she? And would she be when she had to return to Christian's house? As much as she feared it, she could hardly wait to find out.

ↄ‌ﻼ

Christian drove along the Pacific Coast Highway as fast as he dared without risking a ticket. The scenery flashed past him—beaches, sweeping vistas of ocean crashing on the shore, million-dollar homes on the Malibu cliffs across the highway—but he hardly even noticed.

He'd gotten in the car, needing to clear his head, and this was his favorite drive, but it wasn't helping. He could not get Rowan out of his mind.

Christ, her skin had been like heated satin under his hands. And once she'd allowed herself to relax, she was as responsive as any woman he'd ever touched. He wanted to touch her again, knew he would tonight, and the thought drove him crazy.

He wanted to fuck her. There was no getting around that. Wanted to sink between those perfect thighs, have her wrap her long legs around him, and plunge his cock into her tight little pussy all the way to the hilt. And it had been hell exercising enough control to do what he was supposed to do with her. For her.

Yes, *for* her.

And that would be his mantra, to keep himself together around her. Even though he'd had the hard-on of his life with his hands on her. Torture.

But he was a man of his word. No sex. Even if it killed him. It just might.

He took a right turn and began the climb into Topanga Canyon. The scenery shifted, and he drove past rocky fields studded with small, gnarled trees, the road twisting and turning just as his thoughts were. The road was a hell of a lot easier to handle.

This was something entirely new for him. He'd never wanted more from a woman than a few nights of pleasure, or to train her to submissive perfection, only to hand her over to someone else. The need for perfection had always been a driving force for him. Pure ego, now that he thought about it. But for the first time, he didn't care about exhibiting his prowess as a Dom to anyone but Rowan.

Right now, she was the only thing that mattered. What the hell did that mean, anyway?

Frustrated, he stepped on the gas and the low-slung Cadillac swung around a turn, tires squealing. He was fighting just as hard as she was, but he wasn't sure he wanted to know exactly what his struggle was about. But deep down, he knew damn well it was her. Rowan.

For the first time in his life, he was falling. Hard. And when he crashed, it was going to be a fucking mess.

ℰ⅋

April arrived at Club Privé, showed her membership card to the collared, lingerie-clad woman at the front desk, and moved through the heavy leather curtain onto the private, walled-in patio. Music poured through the open doors of the main building, a hard-driving rock song she couldn't identify. But she felt the dynamic energy of it, understood why the club DJ played this sort of music. He had a lot of control over the energy in the room, could really manipulate the mood of the people playing there. April hadn't thought about music in this way before coming to the club, but she did now. She saw the power in it.

But this wasn't the particular brand of power she'd come for tonight.

Her stomach gave a small shiver as she scanned the crowd on the patio, looking for Decker. Not spotting him, she went inside, into the main playroom of the club. The lights were low, as always, lighting bare skin in sensual tones of red and purple. April had arrived late; the evening had begun in earnest, the members already deeply into their scenes. She wished she could have come earlier, but her boss had kept her late at work, doing inventory.

She knew Decker would be here tonight. He rarely missed a play party. She'd hoped to find him mingling, talking still with the other players. But of course, he was right where anyone would have expected him to be.

He stood in one corner of the room where a spanking bench was set up. A woman with long brown hair that hung in spiral curls around her face was strapped onto the bench, straddling the center piece, her elbows and knees resting on the padded bars made for that purpose. Her bare bottom was brown and smooth, except where it was covered in wide red welts.

Decker stood beside Master Hawke; they must be tag-teaming her. Lucky girl, April thought, trying to suppress the sharp surge of jealousy. She really shouldn't have come tonight, if she couldn't come early enough to find Decker before he started a scene with someone else. Not that he was guaranteed to play with her just because she was there. Of course not.

She watched miserably as Decker paddled the woman's buttocks and thighs while Master Hawke joined in with a long crop between the blows Decker delivered.

God, she really should just turn around and leave. But she couldn't stop watching him, the grace and strength of his arms, his shoulders, beneath his black T-shirt. She moved a little closer.

Decker stopped, wiped his brow with a small towel he kept in his back pocket. He stepped back, gestured for Master Hawke to take over. When he turned around he looked right at her.

His dark brows shot up in surprise, then a corner of his mouth quirked in a half-smile. He gave a small nod with his chin. An order to come to him, she knew. Her stomach knotted as she moved across the room.

His dark eyes were fixed on her, his gaze as intense as always. "April. Are you meeting anyone tonight?"

"No, Sir."

"Ah."

He stood quietly, inspecting her. At least, that's what it felt like. She hoped he was pleased with her appearance. Why didn't he say something?

Finally, "April, I'm going to ask something of you."

"Anything, Sir." God, she sounded eager as a puppy!

"I'd rather you don't play with anyone else here.

Tonight. While you and I are together. I don't mean this as an order. I have no rights to you. This is a request."

What did this mean? Her eyes flicked back to the girl on the spanking bench he had been paddling only moments earlier. He followed her gaze.

"Yes, I know. Look, she's from out of town, a friend of Hawke's. This was arranged weeks ago."

"I don't understand, Sir." Why was he making excuses to her?

He paused, ran a hand over his stubbled jaw. "Fuck it, neither do I. Just tell me you won't let anyone else touch you."

His eyes were absolutely burning, molten heat blazing in the black-brown depths. Her legs went weak, that heat seeping into her skin, flooding her muscles.

"Come to see me tomorrow night."

Did she hear a hint of doubt beneath the usual command in his low tone?

"I'll be there, Sir."

"Now I want you to go home. To rest. You'll need to be rested for what I have in mind for you."

He slid a hand over her bare shoulder, paused to take a strand of her long hair between his fingers. He rubbed it almost absentmindedly for a moment, then gave a small tug. April stood frozen, heat rushing through her, making her damp with need. He slipped an arm around her waist and walked with her to the door, led her outside and through the gate, onto the street.

"Where are you parked?"

He'd never walked her to her car before. The evening was getting stranger and stranger.

"Right in front, Sir." She pointed to her small blue Saturn.

"Give me your keys."

She did as he asked, amazed at this show of chivalry. He stood holding the door open for her. She went to get in, but he stopped her with a hand on her arm. He watched her silently. She could not tell what was going on behind his eyes. Then he curled a hand behind her head, burying his fingers in her hair. He leaned in and laid a soft kiss on her forehead, then on her lips. She shivered, her body flooding with desire.

"Go, April. I'll see you tomorrow night. Be ready."

Her heart fluttered, her pulse racing. He wanted her! For now, at least. And for now, it would have to be enough.

∞

She arrived at exactly eight o'clock. Christian opened the door and there she was, looking fragile and pale in the dusky light of the moon. Her pretty mouth was drawn into a tight line, and her shoulders were ramrod straight. But at least she was there.

"Rowan, come in."

She paused for a moment, and he curved a hand around her slender waist and pulled her gently inside. Hard as iron beneath her soft clothing, her body language spoke of her tension louder than words ever could, but he was sure he could handle her.

"Tonight is going to be different, Rowan. Tonight you are under my command, starting now. Do you understand?"

He looked into her dark blue eyes. Her brows shot up and she opened her mouth, to protest, he was sure, but she closed it just as quickly.

"Very good. Undress."

"What? Here? In the kitchen?"

"Yes."

He waited while a series of emotions crossed her features. Finally her dark, elegant brows settled into a frown, but she pulled her black trench coat off and handed it to him as though it were a sacred offering. He took it, and watched in silence while she stepped out of her black slacks and her soft, gray wraparound sweater. She handed him each piece of clothing as she removed it, a look of stubborn concentration on her lovely face. Her eyes were dark and shuttered, her cheeks flushed. If he didn't understand how much was at stake for her, he would have been amused.

Finally, she was left in a black mesh bra and matching thong, along with the black stiletto-heeled pumps she'd worn before. Her dark nipples showed through the sheer fabric of the bra, and he had to suck in a breath at the sight.

He turned away to lay her clothing over the back of a kitchen chair, using the time to get the lust raging through his system under control, then offered her his hand. "Come, upstairs."

She ignored his hand but moved through the kitchen and into the living room without looking back at him, her hips swaying as she walked. So, she was going to be stubborn tonight. Her attitude didn't worry him. She was here, she was following orders, and for once she wasn't arguing every point. Let her think she still remained in control of some aspect of the evening. He would shatter that illusion quickly enough.

He followed the swing of her gorgeous ass up the stairs, loving the way the thin strip at the back of her mesh thong separated the firm, rounded globes. Oh, yes, he planned to give those cheeks a little workout tonight.

Once on the top floor she moved toward the bed, but he had other things in mind for her.

"Stop there, Rowan."

She paused, and he could see the rise of her shoulders as she drew in a breath. She turned slowly.

He went to one wall and uncoiled a length of chain he'd anchored there. A metallic clink echoed through the space as he unwound a long, heavy chain from a pulley suspended high overhead. A pair of padded leather suspension cuffs dangled from the end.

He stopped the chain at the appropriate height and secured it on the hook in the wall, then went to her. She was trembling faintly all over. He put his hands on her shoulders. Her skin was warm, fragrant, that feminine scent that sifted through his veins and made him tighten up inside.

"This is the next step. I'll blindfold you if you think it will help you."

She swallowed hard, shook her head.

"Alright, then. Let's go."

With an arm around her delectably slender waist, he guided her across the room. She was surprisingly quiet as he took her hands, raised them over her head, and buckled her into the cuffs. He couldn't tell yet if she was surrendering or simply enduring it out of sheer stubbornness. Her hot little body was still taut as piano wire and shaking a bit, as though an electric current was buzzing just beneath her skin. He realized she was really and truly scared. But this was the only way he knew of to work past that.

When he was done he stepped back and just looked at her. He had never seen a more beautiful sight. With her arms stretched over her head, her body was elongated, elegant, open. Pure art. Fantastic. Her breasts rose and fell with her short, sharp breaths. Her hair cascaded over her shoulders in midnight waves, brushing tenderly against her skin. And her skin...perfect, like milky porcelain. He flexed his hands. He could hardly wait to touch her. His thickening cock echoed the sentiment.

He moved in closer, tilted her chin in his hand, looked into her eyes. The pupils were huge. He couldn't believe how long her lashes were.

"We're going to start now. I don't want you to be afraid. You need to know that I don't see this as a game. I understand the seriousness of what we're doing here. Do you trust me, Rowan?"

She swallowed, paused, then nodded.

She looked so afraid, and so determined. He couldn't help but lean in and brush his lips across hers.

It was almost his undoing.

That brief, chaste kiss went through him like a shock, heating his system almost to boiling point. He had to drop her chin, walk away, take in a deep lungful of air.

Christ, her lips were velvet, sweet and yielding, no matter how tightly strung the rest of her was.

He stood for a few moments trying to collect himself, trying to convince his swollen cock to go down. He had to pull himself together; he'd left Rowan literally hanging there.

He moved around behind her and began.

He brought his body close to hers, not quite touching, but he wanted to be able to hear every small change in her breathing as he worked. That would be the catalyst, what he would use to bring her down into subspace; her own breath and the vampire glove he had in his back pocket. It was a leather glove, the palm and inner fingers of which were decorated with tiny, pointed metal studs, like rows of wicked teeth. He quickly slipped it onto his right hand and curled it over her tight buttocks, just brushing her skin with it.

She pulled in a sharp breath, then relaxed a little when she realized it didn't hurt. He moved in closer, until the front of his body was a hairsbreadth from her back. He slid the other hand around her waist and up, until it came to rest between her breasts. Beneath his palm, he could feel the erratic fluttering of her heart.

"Just follow me now, Rowan. Listen to my voice. Concentrate on my instructions. I want you to take a deep breath, in through your nose and out through your mouth. Good...now another."

He lowered his voice, moved his face closer to her ear, breathed in the enticing scent of her hair. "That's it, breathe in, now out slowly."

She did as he asked without struggle; a good sign. Her body heated, her heartbeat began to slow. He went on for a while, just taking her through the breathing, keeping her there. When he felt she was ready, he wrapped his hand a little tighter around her bottom and squeezed.

She jumped.

"Breathe, Rowan."

She took in another breath, and as she blew it out he squeezed again, not hard enough to really hurt, just a small bite. Again she inhaled deeply, and again he squeezed as she exhaled, allowing the teeth of the vampire glove to dig into her tender flesh.

Long minutes passed, and he created a rhythm of breath and bite, a pattern she could sink into. Listening to her breath, gauging her heartbeat, he sensed it when she started to let go. Her breathing shifted, came more easily, her muscles loosened, and he knew she was going down into subspace.

He kept up the rhythm, careful to keep it steady, while she came apart under his hands.

Twenty or thirty minutes had passed when she went slack and leaned into him. He knew he had her.

Moving his bare hand up to her breasts, he caressed them through the thin mesh of her black bra. Her nipples were hard nubs of flesh beneath his searching fingers.

His cock was rock hard beneath his slacks.

Slowly, he smoothed his hand over her flat stomach, while at the same time he slid the teeth of the vampire glove over her ass. She surged first against his bare hand, then back against the glove. Moving lower, he slipped his hand to the triangle of mesh between her thighs. She was so damn hot and wet, he thought he'd lose his mind, or at least his self-control. He quickly moved his hand away and stepped back an inch or two.

Her ass was tinged with pink from the vampire glove,

criss-crossed with tiny scratches, and her body seemed weightless, suspended from the cuffs in an attitude of total submission. He loved seeing her like this. A surge of heat moved through him, lighting his nerves with sensual fire. He knew she was ready for more. And the adrenaline, that enticing rush of power, was running hot through his system.

He slipped the spiked glove from his hand; then, taking a small, flat leather slapper from his back pocket, he smoothed it over the skin of her back and buttocks. Again that surging movement as she arched into the leather. He slid it around to the front of her body, caressed her stomach with it, her breasts. She let out a small moan.

Yes, she was ready.

He gave her right buttock a small slap. She gasped, but held perfectly still, letting him know she was down, had let it all go, had yielded to this experience. He smacked her again, a little harder this time, and still she didn't move. Her breath came in a regular cadence.

He was about to change that.

He began a volley of stinging smacks with the leather slapper, moving in a pattern over her tender buttocks, watching with pleasure as her skin pinked. She began to writhe, gorgeous undulations of her slim body. And the pace of her breath quickened with each slap.

Beautiful.

His own breath was coming faster as well, as he slapped her harder, the little leather tool biting into her flesh and leaving satisfying welts on her pale skin.

He moved in closer to her body once more, continued

to smack her in short, sharp slaps while he slipped his other hand around the front of her body, under the seam of her thong, and into her hot, wet cleft.

God, she was soaked. He moved his fingers over her swollen lips and then between them, and inside her.

Her sex clenched around his fingers and she gave a small cry. It was almost too much to take. He moved his hand away, kept up the steady cadence of the leather slapper on her ass, took a moment to catch his breath.

Hers was ragged now, and her body moved back toward his, as though asking for more. He had to remind himself that he wasn't ready to let her come yet. That wasn't in his plan. He had to discipline himself just as firmly as he did her.

He could see how pink her skin was, loved the sight of the darker red welts rising there. Loved the way she moved into each blow. He knew she was ready for more, knew she could take it.

He wrapped his fist in her glorious cascade of dark hair, pulled her head back firmly, and spoke softly into her ear.

"You're doing beautifully, Rowan. But I have more in store for you. Are you ready?"

She gasped.

"Are you?" He tugged a little harder on her hair. "Tell me."

"Yes!" she hissed.

It was all he needed to hear. All he needed to know before he began to do all of the things to her lush little body he'd been dying to do since the moment he'd set eyes on her. All but fuck her, which he couldn't stop thinking about. He could do anything to her but that, all of the exquisite, pleasurable, nasty, wicked things he wanted. Everything but that one thing he wanted most of all.

Torture.

But which of them was tortured the most here, he didn't know. Didn't matter. They suffered together.

SIX

ROWAN KNEW NOTHING BUT THE SENSATIONS POUR-ing through her, the sound of her own ragged breath, and the warmth of his big body so close to hers. Except for one new thing: the aching desire to please.

She couldn't think about it now, all she could do was feel. But it was there, hovering at the edge of her consciousness.

Don't think, don't think.

Right now, she just needed him to touch her, to smack her with that nasty little leather strap. And the vampire glove—lovely! She'd seen them before, used them herself, knew exactly what it was. But now she was absolutely in love with it.

If only he would use it on her again, let it bite into her flesh. If only he would make her come.

But he had moved away from her again, leaving her skin too cool. She shivered, with cold, with lust, with pure chemical reaction to the things he'd been doing to her body.

More.

And then he was back; she could feel him behind her again. His arm came around her neck and she saw the long deerskin flogger he held. He swept it across her stomach, her breasts, which suddenly ached to be free of her bra, to be bare to the leather, to the touch of his hands.

"I'm going to flog you now, Rowan. And you're going to love it."

Yes, he was right. She would love it, wanted it now, craved it.

She felt the rush of air as he pulled his arm back and swung. The leather straps came down on her back in a soft caress that made her shiver with need. No pain, just that sweet, gentle slide of leather over her skin, again and again. She sank into the tempo of it, like a physical sensation of music on her flesh to which she could match her breathing.

When the slap of the leather came down harder, she was ready for it, needy for it. Her breath shifted its tempo, matched the rhythm of his strokes as the leather began to sting and heat her skin. The sting became sharper as her skin sensitized, became more tender, and he hit a little harder each time.

And then with one swift, sharp blow the pain shot through her in a stinging current. She yelped. But immediately she wanted him to do it again.

"Good girl," she heard Christian whisper, and pleasure suffused her at his words.

His hand came down on her heated flesh, smoothed over the soreness. God, his hand felt good. She let out a soft moan, wishing his hand was between her legs, or touching her full, aching breasts. But she understood that she had no control here. Even with her mind flying, high on endorphins, she really understood for the first time.

Something deep inside her broke, crumbled. But there was nothing frightening about it. She knew, with him, she could let it happen.

His hand slid down to her buttocks, the flesh there hot and tender. He brushed over her skin, down over the bottom curve, and briefly slipped between her thighs. She immediately parted her legs for him, her sex throbbing, but he moved his hand away.

A low chuckle from him. "Eager, are we?" Then he moved in closer until she could feel the warmth of his breath in her ear. "So am I, my love."

She was absolutely panting now, the sound of his voice, the masculine scent of him making her dizzy.

Please touch me.

And as though he'd heard her fervent wish, his hand slipped around her waist, dove down to the juncture of her thighs, and he slid his fingers beneath her thong and began a slow, steady stroke.

Her hips bucked into his hand as he rubbed his fingers over her tight, hard nub. At the same time, he was pinching the raw, sensitized skin of her buttocks with his other hand. And she was excruciatingly aware of his enormous erection pressed against her back.

Inside me, please . . .

His fingers moved over her cleft, slippery with her juices, then slid inside, back out again. And all the time the sharp, evil pinching on her sore flesh. When he pinched her clit between his fingers she came, hard, shattering into a million pieces as her mind spun into darkness. Her body shook, shuddering against the solid wall of him behind her, pain and pleasure merging, fusing, in a sharp, spinning kaleidoscope of sensation. She was whirling, falling, her legs weak, liquid.

The next thing she knew, he had unbuckled her wrist cuffs and picked her up in his strong arms, carried her to the big bed, and laid her down.

She was shivering, with the last of her climax, with cold, maybe a little shock at it all. But she'd never felt better in her life.

He laid a soft blanket on her body and bent over her, placing small, warm kisses on her palms, on the inside of her wrists. When she looked into his eyes, they appeared to be as glazed as she knew her own must be.

What was this?

But it was all too good to question it any further. She felt gloriously sluggish, dreamy. And his kisses were so sweet and hot. She didn't think she could move.

"God damn it, Rowan," he muttered.

She blinked. Was he angry with her? Hadn't she pleased him?

Then, "You'll be the death of me, girl."

She smiled. April was right. She still had some power here.

Christian's expression was tender, a little confused. Beautiful. His brows were furrowed over those sea-colored eyes, and a lock of his blond hair had come undone, falling into his face. She wanted to touch it, but she wasn't sure she could lift her hand.

"Do you need anything? Something to drink?"

She shook her head. She didn't need anything, except

perhaps another of those mind-numbing orgasms, for him to work her again, to touch her. She wanted him inside her. Now. But that was the one thing she couldn't have.

It was her own doing, not being able to have him inside her, and even now, in this altered state, she knew it was wise. Yet it was all she wanted.

Just as Christian said she would, she regretted it, this part of their little contract. But perhaps no more than he did, from what she could tell by his gasping breath and the raging hard-on pressed now into her hip as he sat on the bed beside her and pulled her into his lap.

Yes, a little power on the bottom side after all.

That would make it easier to bear, her yielding, handing over her power to this man.

Don't think about it now.

The time to think would come soon enough. For now, she just wanted to feel, to relax into Christian's arms. To pretend things could be different. Because even now, at this moment, despite everything that had just happened between them, she still knew the truth about herself.

જી

He held her for almost an hour. She lay there in a dream state, basking in the endorphins he knew had flooded her system. He'd had no such release. His cock had remained hard and aching the entire time. But at least he had a chance to explore her face, to really look at her.

Her lips were a deep cherry pink, even without lipstick. And they were so damn lush and kissable he could barely restrain himself. It would be easy enough, just bend down and kiss her. Just kiss her softly, brush his lips over hers while she was still warm and lambent in his arms. But no, it wouldn't be like that. If he touched her lips now, he'd crush her mouth, open it with his tongue, thrust in and taste the sweetness he knew would be there.

Christ. Get ahold of yourself, man.

He forced himself to move his gaze to the rest of her face.

She had those high, curving cheekbones that made her face look as though it had been sculpted by a master hand. And her skin really was flawless, even this close. With her eyes half closed, a deep glow of blue glistened beneath her barely parted lids, lids that were fragile and translucent. They begged to be kissed almost as much as her mouth did.

His eyes roved lower, over her long throat, which was slender and swanlike. She had the body of a dancer, and the grace to go with it. The blanket he'd laid over her had slipped off one breast, and he could see the dark halo of her nipple through her bra. It was still hard, pushing against the delicate fabric. His groin tightened and pulsed in response. He was pretty damn sure if he touched her now he could make her come again. The idea seemed self-indulgent in some way, even though she would be the one to climax.

Too lovely to resist.

His hand moved as though of its own accord, pushing the blanket down, smoothing over the silken flesh of her stomach. He was dying to get the bra off, to pull her nipples into his mouth and suck. But instead he moved his hand downward, slipping beneath the thong she still wore and right into her still-damp cleft.

She let out a small moan as he brushed the tips of his fingers over her mound, over the silky hair. He'd love to bury his face there, to breathe in the musky scent of her desire, but he had to maintain some control, and he knew damn well that would be the end of him, to taste her honeyed sex on his tongue.

He used his fingers to part her swollen lips, all slick and hot beneath his touch. But she was even hotter when he slid his fingers inside her.

She writhed, bucked her hips, let out a soft gasping breath.

"Shh," he told her. "Just lie still."

He moved his hand so that he could press on the hard little nub hiding in her wet cleft with his thumb, his fingers still inside her. God, she was fucking drenched, and so damn tight he couldn't help but imagine how that velvet sheath would feel clenched around his cock.

He worked her with his fingers, sliding them in and out of her, all the while circling her clit with his thumb, concentrating on her pleasure, on the rasping pant of her breath. When he looked at her beautiful face, her eyes were squeezed shut. He continued to watch her as he pushed his fingers into her. He pressed harder, faster, until he felt her tighten around his fingers, all wet heat and the glorious scent of her arousal hitting his nostrils. She cried out, trembling, and her inner walls clenched at his fingers.

He almost came when she did.

His cock throbbed with need, hard and hurting. But he was too fascinated with her writhing body, her ragged breathing, her slick sex pulsing under his touch.

Finally, she calmed and he withdrew his hand. He was

panting as hard as she was. Her features relaxed, went slack, and still he watched her. At that moment, he felt as though he could never get enough of her. He wanted to make this woman come in his hands over and over. He never wanted to stop touching her, never wanted to stop pleasuring her.

He hadn't even come himself, yet this was one of the most intense sexual experiences he'd ever had. How was that possible?

She lay there quietly for a long while, giving him time to think, to search her face again. But he couldn't find an answer to the questions that burned through his brain, that had made him restless and sleepless and half crazy with need since he'd first met her. He wanted to enjoy this moment with her, but his mind wouldn't stop.

What the hell was going on here? Was he obsessed? What made her so different from any other woman he'd known? What did it all mean?

He wasn't someone who was used to questioning himself. He found it confusing, exhausting. At some point he lay down beside her and drifted off to sleep.

❧

When Rowan awoke it was dark, except for the faint fog-hazed glow of moon and stars through the big windows. Christian was warm against her side. Her head was pillowed on his shoulder; one arm was thrown over her body in a protective gesture. She was surprised to see he'd fallen asleep. It seemed tender to her somehow.

Was that what caused the gentle ache in her throat?

As she blinked into the dark, the events of the evening came back to her, bit by bit. She had submitted to a man, to *this* man. And he had made her feel nothing but pleasure. He hadn't hurt her, not in any way that hadn't felt good at the same time.

Why was her heart beating so damn hard?

Panic filled her, a slow tide, thick and heavy, weighing her down. She had to get out of there, away from him. She had to think. Or not think, she wasn't sure which. All she really knew was the pressing need to run.

Carefully, she lifted his limp arm, and tried to shift away from him without waking him. She noticed the hard ridge of his arousal pressing into her hip before she rolled away. Scrambling from the bed, she stood for a moment beside it.

Christian's brows were slightly drawn together, his features strong, even as he slept. Strong and beautiful. It scared her how much she wanted to keep staring at him; even more how much she wanted to kiss him, his face, his hands.

With her pulse racing, she made her way quietly down the stairs. The harsh light of the kitchen made her blink hard as she got dressed. She slipped out into the night.

The air was cool and damp around her, and she paused to take a deep breath before she got into her car. She knew she was running again, but damn it, she had to. She couldn't stay in there with him. It was too hard. It forced her to feel too much. She wasn't ready.

She gunned the engine of her quick little BMW as she pulled onto Venice Boulevard and headed east, toward home. Her body ached; her skin was tender all over, her arms and legs felt stretched and used. It would have felt good if she'd been in a better frame of mind. But there was so much racing through her brain she could hardly breathe.

She sped through the early morning, dawn beginning to light the horizon in front of her in a deep blue glow. The sky was tinged in pink by the time she reached her apartment.

Once there, she stripped down, crawled naked under the covers and shut her eyes against the gathering light of day. But she couldn't shut out images of Christian's face, drawn in concentration as he made her come. And she couldn't forget the surge of her heart as she allowed herself to yield to his touch.

By the time the sun rose to fully light the sky outside her windows, she was so tired she couldn't keep her burning eyes open. Finally, she slept.

She dreamed of him. Christian stood before her, gloriously naked, gloriously erect. She itched to reach out and touch him, but she was bound, her hands tied and stretched high over her head. Her body burned with need, yearned for his touch. Slowly, he lowered himself over her prone figure. She could feel the heat of him, could smell his clean, masculine scent. She closed her eyes, waited...and was shocked to feel a sharp slap across her face. She tried to open her eyes, was sure they were open, but all she could see was black. Hands pulled at her bound wrists, dragging her. She struggled, tried to scream, but a hand came down over her mouth, hard and bruising.

Punished. He was punishing her, but why? What had she done?

Tears gathered at the corners of her eyes, and still she struggled against the hands that were rough now on her flesh, dragging her legs apart. She could feel body heat over hers again, but this time it was too hot, a rank, unwanted heat. Fear gripped her. She screamed.

"*No!*"

Bolting upright, she sat in her bed, alone and shivering in the beams of sunlight streaming through the windows. She buried her face in her hands, her hair falling in loose waves, shutting out the light.

It had been a long time since she'd had one of her nightmares, those ugly flashes of buried memory. But this time Christian had been there. What did it mean? She wasn't even sure if it had been him hurting her, or Danny...

No, don't think about it, can't think about it. Shut it away.

It had all been a long time ago. It was too ugly and too long past. She was over it. Wasn't she?

Then why was she still shaking?

The phone jangling on her nightstand made her jump. She reached for it, still half in the dream haze.

"Hello?"

"You left without telling me, Rowan."

"I...yes, I'm sorry, but I had to—"

"It won't happen again."

His tone hit her like a soft, thudding blow to her chest. She heard command there, and hurt. Was it possible she had hurt him?

"Rowan, did you hear me?"

Some anger, as well.

"Yes. I heard you. And it won't happen again." Why did she feel comfort in acquiescing to him? But the fact was, she did.

"I'll give you until noon to come back. This time, don't plan to leave until I tell you that you can go."

She swallowed. She wasn't sure what this was making her feel. Anxiety? Relief?

"Christian, I had to leave—"

"You don't have to tell me why. Not now. But you should spend the time until you get here trying to figure it out for yourself."

She glanced at the clock on her nightstand. Nine A.M. "I think it'll take a lot longer than three hours to figure out," she said quietly.

"Then I suggest you get started." He paused. "Twelve o'clock."

He hung up.

Oh, yes, he was angry. But wouldn't she be, if she were in his position? She'd be furious.

Meanwhile, she was quivering with nervous anticipation and a deep pulsing need that even her nightmare hadn't managed to drive from her body. The sound of his voice on the phone had brought it all rushing back.

But that dream . . .

She really didn't want to think about why it had come back to her now. She knew damn well that what she was doing with Christian was responsible for it. Yet she didn't want to stop.

When had that happened?

They had to talk before things went any further. As much as she didn't want to talk about anything, to lay it out on the table all raw and open, she knew they would have to. She didn't have to tell him everything, but she at least had to apologize for running off.

She got up, stepped into the shower, and took a long time washing her hair, standing beneath the warm, soothing water. She let it flow over her, relaxing her muscles, the comforting heat driving away the last shreds of the dream that tried to cling to her mind.

She felt much better by the time she was done. She took care in smoothing lotion into her skin, drying her hair, applying a little subtle makeup. And she sank a little into the ritual of preparation. There was something about getting herself ready to present to him that made her feel unexpectedly and exquisitely objectified.

In her walk-in closet she pulled on a pair of tall black boots with dangerously high heels, a long, narrow knit skirt, a fitted black sweater. She slipped a pair of small, dangling bloodred garnets through the holes in her ears and purposely left off her undergarments. She would go to him properly today.

Before she had a chance to second-guess herself, she left the house.

In Venice the sun struggled to cut through the coastal fog in dim shafts, warming her skin as she waited at Christian's door once more. Her stomach lay in a tight knot. She purposely kept her mind blank. But she couldn't help giving a little start when he pulled the door open.

There was a scowl on his handsome face and he looked tired, his eyes hollow and stormy; the sea in winter. He didn't say anything, just held the door open for her. She walked past him and into the kitchen, then stood there, waiting. He'd shut the door, but kept his back to her, and she could see the tension that set a hard line along his broad shoulders. She was nervous, but willing to be compliant. What else could she do? Arguing wasn't going to help.

Finally, he turned around. His eyes locked on hers, his now burning with a fine green fire.

Banked emotion as he spoke in a tight voice. "I'm glad you saw fit to come back."

His gaze was so intense on hers, she had to look away. "I'm not here to fight with you, Christian. I'm going to try very hard not to fight anymore. I understand it defeats the purpose."

When she looked back at him his features had relaxed a little, his eyes were softer. But his tone was as firm as ever. "I won't continue if this sort of thing happens again. There's no point."

"I understand. And I'm sorry."

He raised one hand to smooth back his already perfectly smooth hair. "I'm not in the habit of being abandoned without notice by one of my girls."

Her stomach and her fists clenched in unison and she went hot all over. "I am not one of your girls. I'm not some innocent neophyte."

"No. You're not. But the same rules apply."

She nodded. He was right. She let her fists uncurl. This whole thing wouldn't work if she didn't show him respect.

He was watching her very closely, and she suddenly wished he would take her in his arms, kiss her. She took a deep breath, exhaled. "What now?"

"Now we spend some time together. I think it's time we got to know each other, don't you?"

"Wh-what do you mean?"

"We're going to take a drive up the coast today. Talk. Eat."

"That's it?"

"Until later, yes."

She wasn't quite sure what to make of that, or of the calm, cool, matter-of-fact way he spoke. Why couldn't he just take her upstairs, strip her down, tie her up? That, she knew how to deal with now.

He walked over to her then, put his big hands on both shoulders, leaned down, and brushed a quick kiss over her lips, leaving her burning, needy. She didn't have time to respond. Before she had a chance to think about it, to react, he'd moved away again, but he was holding on to her hand.

"We'll go now."

ஒ

The view from the Pacific Coast Highway was beautiful, miles of shoreline with the blue and green surf crashing on beaches and against the craggy rocks. The coast was dotted with houses, some of them million-dollar homes, some no more than beach shacks, pale and battered with wind and sun.

It had been a long time since Rowan had taken this drive. Christian's big black Cadillac headed north, skimming over the highway so smoothly she barely had any sense of motion apart from the passing scenery. It added to the dreamlike quality of the day, driving along with the sparkling winter sea out the window, and Christian at her side. The car seemed to fit him perfectly: big, sleek, elegant.

They'd hardly spoken a word on the drive. The silence between them felt heavy, almost sacred somehow, as though it would be a sin to break it now. And there was something strange about being out in the world with him, away from the confines of his house. She wasn't quite sure what the dynamic was supposed to be between them, away from the private, intimate environment of Christian's house.

She was trying very hard to stop the million and one questions hammering away at the edges of her mind.

When they reached the small town of Ventura, Christian pulled off the highway and onto a frontage road. Sand dunes ran along the edge of the road to their left, and beyond them, the sea. She sat quietly as he made a sharp left turn into a parking lot, drove through it toward a long pier with a row of wood-sided structures perched on it. He found parking close by the wooden stairs leading up from the parking lot.

"I hope you like oysters," he said, getting out of the car to come around and open her door.

He kept his hand on the small of her back as they went up the stairs. The gesture was protective, territorial. She loved it.

They were seated at a table next to a long bank of windows looking out onto the beach. The water here was more gray than blue, with bits of green and reddish-brown seaweed twisting among the waves. The ocean looked cold and lonely, and she found herself glad to be inside, to be there with Christian.

"Incredible view, isn't it?" His voice sounded lighter, more relaxed.

"It is, even now, at the end of winter. I love the drift-wood that's washed up on the shore. The shapes and the textures are so sinuous, so beautiful. It's like a still life. Like a garden of dead wood, with the sand the dry earth. Yet it's not really dead, is it? It's strangely alive, just...stilled. Serene."

"You have an artistic eye, Rowan."

"Me? I've never thought so. I'm more...analytical."

"That, too."

He smiled, and her insides warmed, went a little soft and loose.

"Tell me about your work. Master Hawke mentioned you're a corporate analyst."

When had he asked Hawke about her? "You want to hear about my job?"

"Yes."

He waited expectantly while she tried to shift gears in her head.

"It's boring, really, for most people. But I love it. I love to take all the tiny bits of information, find the patterns, see what doesn't fit."

"And when those pieces don't fit, you dispose of them."

"Well, yes, but don't make it sound so dispassionate."

"Isn't it?"

She gave a little laugh. He was right, maybe. She shrugged. "That's my job. And there's certainly nothing artistic about it."

"Maybe not. But I see it in the way you dress, in the way you look at things. You see the beauty in the world. And that, my Rowan, is art."

He slid his hand over hers, his palm curling possessively

around her fingers. A warm shiver went through her, from his touch, from his words.

My Rowan.

Lovely.

The waiter brought wine, a delicate French Pinot Noir. Christian took his hand away from hers to lift his glass.

Rowan sipped the wine. It was like silk gliding down her throat, some of the best she'd ever tasted.

"So, it's your turn. Tell me about your work."

"Ah, well, that's a long story. But to make it bearable, I began to draw as a child, to paint by the age of sixteen, and then at eighteen I discovered sculpture."

"What do your parents think of your being an artist?"

He was silent a moment while a cloud passed over his features. He stroked his wineglass with his fingers. "My mother and my sister have always been very supportive. They came to all of my shows until my mother passed away a little over six years ago. Then my sister got married and moved to Boston. That's when I left for Europe."

She could sense a great deal of tension in him; his face was absolutely stormy, yet she wanted to know more.

"And your father?"

"I haven't seen him since I was a kid. I don't know where he is, if he's even still alive. Doesn't matter." He threw back a gulp of the wine.

She shook her head. "Of course it matters."

He caught her gaze. His eyes were dark, shuttered. "Change of subject, Rowan."

There was no arguing with him. And she understood that he was hiding some kind of hurt. It certainly wasn't her job to bring that to the surface.

"Alright, then. Tell me why you never paint anymore. I saw the easel in your studio, but no paintings."

The tightness around his mouth relaxed, his face softened. "I sometimes use paint to make preliminary sketches. And I often draw in pencil or charcoal. But I haven't painted for some time. Sculpting comes easier for me. It's more tactile. I don't have to feel my subject as much to sculpt as I do to paint." He shrugged. "Nothing has inspired me to paint in a long time."

He looked at her then and smiled a slow, mysterious smile. She couldn't figure out what it meant. Then, "I want to draw you, Rowan. To paint you. Maybe to sculpt you."

"Me?"

"Yes."

"Why?"

He spun the stem of his wineglass in his fingers as he spoke, his pose relaxed as he leaned back in his chair. But his eyes never left her face. "Because you're beautiful to me. Because I love the lines of your body, the shape of your face, even your hands. Your bone structure is perfect. And maybe because I never want to forget you."

Her heart stirred, fluttered. Her throat was tight; she could hardly breathe.

But what was she, some insecure teenager whose head could be turned by a few pretty words? Yet she felt he was perfectly serious.

"Maybe..."

He leaned in a little, across the table, and said quietly, intimately, "If I tie you up, bind you in chains, you'll have no choice, will you?"

He let that sink in a minute while she felt her mouth

open in a small o. There was a wicked twinkle in his eyes. Why should she find that so irresistible?

Even more irresistible was the image he'd created, of her bound in chains, helpless against him.

Yes.

He lowered his voice to a whisper that nevertheless went right through her, deep into her body, heating her core. "It could happen at any time. Something for you to think about."

He lifted his hand, stroked a strand of hair from her face, sending a shiver of desire racing through her, then he sat back in his chair as the waiter brought their oysters to the table.

Yes, his eyes held a wicked gleam, dark and burning with desire. No more, she was sure, than did her own.

Ah, the thought of him doing exactly what he'd said: binding her in chains, helpless, while he drew her.

She really was losing her mind. But as time went by, that little fact seemed less and less important to her. All she had to do was gaze into those eyes of his, blue and green as the ocean, and she was lost, adrift in the sea.

SEVEN

THEY WERE ON THE WAY BACK DOWN THE 405 FREE-
way when Christian asked her, "Where do you live,
Rowan?"

"Century City."

"Give me an address."

"What?"

"We're going there now."

He expected her to balk, but she didn't.

"It's three-three-oh-five-three Olympic Boulevard."

He'd also expected her to ask why they were going to
her place, but after giving him her address, she sat quietly.
He pulled off the freeway at Olympic and headed east.

Her building was one of those gargantuan, shiny affairs,
probably a good thirty stories, towering over the city like
some sleek, black-mirrored monolith. He'd bet anything
her apartment was done all in black leather, aesthetically
spare and Zen-like. And no doubt perfectly organized. He
had a feeling Rowan kept every aspect of her life in a neat

little pocket. He knew he'd disturbed her perfectly ordered life. Was it the sadist in him that made him want to smile at the idea?

She directed him to an underground parking lot, gave him a pass code at the gate. The garage was dark and womblike as they walked to the elevators. They stepped in and heavy doors slid closed behind them. When he looked over at Rowan, her face was pale, but a deep pink blush stained her high cheekbones. She caught his gaze. Her dark blue eyes glittered and he could feel the tension emanating in waves from her small body, could see the rise and fall of her firm breasts beneath her sweater. And he could just as easily make out the hard tips of her nipples. She was turned on by it all, maybe by the mystery of it, by silently following his commands.

He had a quick flash of taking her in the elevator; it was one of his long-standing fantasies, one of many. What would she say if he grabbed her, backed her up against the sleek wood paneling, lifted her skirt and pushed into her? The back wall of the elevator car was mirrored; he could watch himself fuck her, holding her ass in his hands.

Christ.

When he glanced at her face she was watching him, biting her lip, which made it even worse, made his cock swell and pulse beneath his slacks. What he wouldn't give to kiss that hot little mouth. But it seemed too intimate, somehow, more intimate than making her come with his hands.

Her gaze was tracking him, shifting from his eyes to his mouth, as though she knew what he was thinking. When she licked her lips, her pink tongue darting out, then back in, he couldn't resist. He moved right in, bent down, and pressed his lips to hers. She made a small sound, as though to protest, and he pressed his lips more firmly.

Her mouth was soft and pliant, and he knew if he wanted her to, she would open to him, let his tongue inside to taste, explore. He pulled back, just to prove to himself that he still held some semblance of control. But his cock was harder than ever, and he couldn't stop thinking again about taking her in the elevator.

He was in big, fucking trouble with this woman.

He took a step away from her, looked at her face. She was still flushed, her lips more lush than ever. She was blinking rapidly, as though she were confused by his actions. Still, she didn't say a word.

The doors opened with a soft *ping* and they stepped out into a plush, carpeted hall. Sconces lined the walls, casting a soft golden light as they walked down the long hallway to the end. Her keys were already in her hand and she opened the door and let him in.

The place was open, airy, and decorated in smooth, spare lines. No black furniture, as he'd expected. Instead, everything was white, with small splashes of color here and there: in the pile of embroidered pillows in shades of water and sky on the long, modular sofa, in the matching hand-woven throw blankets, in some of the astounding framed photographs on the walls.

He moved closer to the wall nearest him.

Jesus.

"Rowan, this is a signed Mapplethorpe, for God's sake."

"Yes. I have a small collection."

"You have more?" But he wasn't ready to tear his eyes

from the piece in front of him, a color print of an orchid in graduated shades of white and green against a stark black background, classic Robert Mapplethorpe. It looked more clear and vivid than if he'd been staring at a live flower. More real. Amazing.

"I have two of his black-and-white nudes in the bedroom."

"Show me."

She led him down a hall and into her bedroom. The room was modern, lush despite the simplicity of the furnishings. The high platform bed was covered in a raw silk duvet the color of garnets. Pillows covered in Indian printed silk in reds, purples, and golds were piled against the wall at the head of the bed. There was an armoire, a pair of nightstands, and a long, low dresser made of imported wood: heavy pieces with clean, simple lines. Two chairs done in deep eggplant stood on each side of a wide window. It all spoke of a great sense of spare balance and form, yet the fabrics were incredibly lush and sensual. Just like her. Beautiful.

"Tell me you didn't have a decorator."

"No, of course not."

He turned to smile at her. "Of course not. Where are the prints?"

She gestured with a graceful arm toward one wall. A pair of framed nudes in black and white graced the wall, a man and a woman. He moved to inspect them more closely. The woman, with arms stretched overhead, her body a long arc, reminded him of Rowan in the suspension cuffs, with the same pale skin, the same sense of tension in the pose, the same look of being elongated. Gorgeous.

The man had beautiful ebony skin. He was curled up, his knees hugged to his chest. He loved that Rowan had thought to display these two pieces side by side, marking the opposition of every detail, the color, the fluidity of the woman's body in stark contrast to the tight knot of the man's. Incredible.

"How can you say you have no artistic sensibility?"

"I just always thought I knew what I liked. And I love photography. These pieces seemed worth the money."

"I'm sure they're worth a lot more by now, in addition to being spectacular photographs." He turned to her. "You are a most fascinating woman, Rowan."

She didn't say anything, just held his gaze, steady and unblinking. It was then he realized that she was already part of the way down into subspace. What had done it, exactly? Taking her unexpectedly to her house? Dominating her in her own space?

Didn't matter, really. He could analyze it later. It would do him good to know what caused that sublime shift in her head. But right now he had her in her bedroom. A delectable thought. He was sure she had some equipment here somewhere.

"Show me your toy chest."

"Wh-what?" She blinked.

"Don't think that because we're in your home, because they're your toys, they can't be used on you." He walked over to where she stood at the foot of her bed. He stroked her cheek with one finger. So smooth. "You are still mine, Rowan. Don't forget that."

"As if I could," she murmured.

He slid his hand around the back of her neck, beneath

the dark, silken strands of her hair, gave a little squeeze. Watching her, he saw her eyes widen, the pupils dilating. But she said nothing.

He had her now, he felt sure. Even if she wanted to fight it, she wouldn't. Curling his fist into the back of her hair, at the nape of her neck, she let out a small gasp when he pulled tight. He felt the tension drain from her body, that sense of sensual anticipation as endorphins were released in her system, and adrenaline in his.

He said to her quietly, "Show me your toys." He let go of her hair.

She turned and went to one side of the bed, opening the nightstand drawers. He followed her and found a rather nice selection of floggers, paddles, crops, whips, all divided into felt-lined compartments. Just like her to keep everything so neat and organized. So under control.

He ran a hand over the various leather implements. *Her* toys, the same ones she'd used on her submissive boys. He didn't like to think about it.

Finding what he wanted, he grabbed her by the waist and moved her ahead of him to the dresser.

"Lift your skirt and bend over."

She hesitated only a moment, then pulled her skirt up until it was gathered around her waist. When she leaned over, resting her elbows on the dresser, a shock went through him at the sight of her bare, smooth ass. He went to her, used a hand to press down on her back, pushing her down further, and he could see her plump pink lips peeking through.

"No underwear. Nice touch, Rowan. I appreciate your thoughtfulness."

He tried to keep some wry humor in his voice, but all he could think of was how easy it would be to pull his cock out and slide right into her.

She was bent over directly in front of the vanity mirror. He could see her reflection, her parted lips, the gorgeous crush of her breasts against the top of the dresser, the fevered flush to her skin as she waited for him. He had to take a few deep breaths to get himself back under control.

Control was everything. He'd do well to remember that. Why was it this woman threatened the carefully held control he'd built so painstakingly over the years? Why her, when no one else had even come close to making him lose it?

And why the hell was he even thinking these things now, with this perfect, porcelain ass in front of him, just waiting to be touched, to be tortured?

He mentally switched gears, focused on the waiting flesh before him. Focused on Rowan. And as soon as he did, he was right back there with her, in the moment, every other thought gone from his mind. His gaze slid over her flawless skin. Yes, he would touch her, torture her. Make her come for him.

He spun the paddle in his hand, feeling the heft of it. Pulling back, he let go with a good, solid blow, not even warming her up first, just to see how she would take it.

A small sigh out of her, that was it. He smacked her again. She stayed quiet. What would it take for her to really make some noise?

Her ass was so damn perfect: round, high, the skin silky and milk-pale. A blank slate, tempting as hell. He dropped the paddle on the bed and instead used his hand to smooth over her skin, stopping to pinch her buttocks, the back of her thighs, to give a small slap. Her skin began to pink almost immediately. He loved that. He spanked harder, beginning a rhythm of sharp, quick smacks, concentrating. It was only a few minutes before she was struggling not to writhe. She was taking long, deep breaths, converting the pain, he knew. He moved in with both hands, a volley of hard, punishing slaps, all the while listening for any shift in her breathing.

When she finally let out a gasp he knew her skin was nice and tender, sensitized. Small welts were coming up all over her flesh. Beautiful.

He raised his eyes to glance into the mirror, and saw her looking back. Her eyes were dark and glazed, glowing like fiery sapphires. He loved that she responded so beautifully, that she went so fast into subspace, got her endorphin rush with such little effort. If he'd ever had any doubts about her ability to bottom, they were long gone. The woman was made for this. Made to be his.

He couldn't get that idea out of his mind.

His.

He waited a moment, letting her catch her breath, catching his own. He moved his hand down over her lovely pink ass cheeks, slid right down in between them, over her slick, hot little cleft. She pushed back against his touch. He pushed his thumb inside her and felt the velvet clutch of her inner walls encase him. Angling his thumb, he found her g-spot, and pressed, rubbed, then began to spank her once more. He went right to a fast, controlled rhythm, moving his thumb in time with his hand on her ass. In moments she was gasping, sobbing, coming into his hands, pulsing and shuddering all over. He didn't stop until he was sure she was done, until her tight pussy ceased to throb around his fingers and she dropped her head onto the lacquered surface of the dresser.

Pulling his hands away, he gazed for a moment at her sex. He could swear it vibrated, pulsed, but it was nothing more than her ragged breathing. Still, too enticing, her hot little slit, almost begging to be fucked. But he wouldn't do it.

He would *not* do it.

How many times would he have to tell himself that before he really believed it?

ॐ

"Are you with me, April?"

Decker's voice pierced the thick fog in her head. God, she loved his accent. She let her head fall back, leaned her weight into the soft black ropes, fluttered her lashes open.

He was so big. She loved that, too. Loved his big hands, the way he touched her. The man was a devil with the flogger.

A new surge of those lovely brain chemicals welled up in her, and she wanted to laugh, had to fight to hold it in. She felt wonderful. He'd been playing her for what felt like hours, days.

He bent over her now, peering into her face with those dark eyes of his, so intense. But they were always intense. Smiling, she leaned forward and kissed his mouth. He pulled back.

"Smart-ass sub," he muttered, but he was smiling at her.

She giggled.

"Okay, I think you're done, my girl."

"Noooo..."

He laughed. "Ah yes, you are. You're just too full of endorphins to know it. We call it the Forever Place."

"The Forever Place," she repeated. "I like that."

And she did. She'd never felt so good in her life, her body worshipped and thoroughly used.

When he untied the ropes lashed around her wrists she was surprised to find she couldn't hold herself up. Decker caught her in his strong arms, sweeping her off her feet. She snuggled right into his chest, loving the feel of the solid-packed muscle there.

He deposited her on his big bed, covered her with a soft blanket, then held a glass of water to her lips, held her head with his other hand while she drank.

She'd never felt so utterly treasured. She couldn't stand the idea of ever being apart from him. Unexpected tears filled her eyes.

Decker set the water glass down and held her in his arms.

"You'll be alright in a few minutes," he whispered to her. "You're just crashing, is all. It happens."

She sniffled. Maybe he was right. Maybe not. She knew that after playing so hard she was raw and open. But she'd played hard with other people and never felt what she was feeling now; a sense of loss at the knowledge that after tonight, she'd never know when—or even if—Decker would call her again, invite her to play, allow her to sleep next to his big, warm body. She hated not knowing.

She turned her face into his chest, burrowing deeper.

Inhaling the scent of him, she tried to take in as much as she could, so that when the time came and she was alone, she would remember him.

"Hey." His voice was soft, almost tender. "What's this?" He reached down and cupped her chin in his hand, forcing her to look at him. His dark eyes were earnest, a frown creased his forehead. "Dry your tears now. You're fine. Everything is fine. You pleased me very much, April. You did well."

What did that mean? That he would let her come back to him again? She hated the sense of desperation coursing through her. But she wouldn't leave him until he said she had to. And meanwhile, she could dream of what it would be like to belong to him.

He smoothed his palm along the side of her face and spoke soothingly to her. "That's it. Nice and calm. Are you warm enough?"

"Yes."

She was, with his large frame pressed up against her. She wished he'd make love to her. They always did after the play; he would undress and take her in his enormous bed. His cock was huge, thick and long and beautiful. And he could make her come over and over again, with his hands, his clever mouth. He wouldn't call it making love, of course. But she didn't mind when he told her how much he liked to fuck her. She loved when he talked to her like that, his breath hot in her ear as he slid into her, filling her up, moving inside her in long, slow strokes. Pure ecstasy.

"Please, Decker..."

Lord, had she said that aloud?

"What is it? What do you need?"

His hand slid down and cupped one naked breast. The nipple came up fast and hard under his touch. She moaned.

"Do you need some attention still, my girl?"

My girl. Torture, that he called her such things. But she kept quiet, arching into his hand.

"Yes, I think you do," he murmured, giving her nipple a sharp pinch, making her take in a gasping breath.

Decker stood and quickly stripped off his clothes. God, his body was beautiful, so hugely muscled and strong. And his cock jutted out proudly from the nest of dark curls at his groin. It was so thick and red, the head darker, almost purple. Her sex went wet at once.

Then he was on the bed next to her, pulling the blanket from her, leaving her naked and open to him. He began to caress her immediately, his hands running over her skin in long, smooth strokes, bringing her nerves to life, his fingers lighting a small explosion of sensation everywhere they touched.

She was on fire immediately, his hands on her sending sharp lances of need straight to her sex, making her nipples harden and swell almost unbearably. She let out a long sigh of relief when he bent to take one into his mouth and sucked hard. He used his hot, soft tongue and his teeth, licking and grazing her sensitized flesh. She could almost come just from this.

Finally he pulled his head up and took a condom from somewhere beside the bed, sheathed himself, and moved his body over hers, crushing her with his weight. She loved it.

"God, I need to fuck you, April. I need to slam my cock hard into you, girl, and fuck you until you scream. Spread your lovely legs for me. Yes, that's it."

The tip of his swollen cock nudged her opening. She spread her thighs wider, as wide as she could, ready to take the full length and girth of him. He moved in, inch by inch. Her hot little sheath pulsed around his flesh.

"Oh, God."

"Yes, it's big, but I know you can take it. I'll go slow, but when I'm in, I'm going to fuck you hard, my girl."

Another inch, and then another. So slowly, it was excruciating and exquisite all at once, each small motion sending ripples of pleasure coursing through her body.

When he was finally in all the way, his balls pressed up against her ass, he began to move in long, even strokes. Her hips surged up to meet every thrust, her whole aching mound meeting his pubic bone, making her shiver with the need to come. He moved faster, and when she peered up into his face, she saw a look of concentrated lust there; his brows furrowed, his strong white teeth catching his full lower lip. He glanced down and caught her gaze with his dark, bottomless eyes.

"Jesus, April," he ground out.

He pumped into her, his eyes locked on hers, making every sensation more intense. And as he plunged into her, his face changed, softened, and he said quietly, "You really are beautiful."

And then he was thrusting into her in sharp, hard strokes, making her body scream with pleasure as she trembled on the edge of climax.

He bent his head and drew her nipple into his mouth once more, sending her right over the edge. She shattered, yelling out his name as fireworks went off behind her eyes, a blinding flash of heat and color. Her sex convulsed around his thick shaft plunging in and out of her, each thrust of his hips pounding against her, driving her orgasm on and on.

In a moment she felt his body stiffen and tremble all over, and he drove into her as his own climax took him over the edge.

He rolled onto his side, pulling her with him. She loved the heat of his body, loved that when she rested her head on his broad chest she could hear the steady cadence of his heart. But even sated as she was, her mind whirled and her own heart yearned for something more.

You can never have it, so you may as well get over it.

But she knew with a deep and clear certainty that she would never get over this sharp, stabbing yearning for Decker to be her man, her Master. She wanted to be with him, to serve him, every day. To please him, to pleasure him.

She smoothed her hand over his chest, the taut muscles of his stomach, enjoying being able to touch him, now that the scene was over and the roles of dominant and submissive were not so strictly in play. He stroked her hair, and she gloried in his gentle touch. She loved when he was like this, all soft and tender with her. She loved the contrast of it, after the intense S/M play they both enjoyed so much.

To her surprise, he began to talk, as though they were simply two normal people in bed together, under normal circumstances.

"Talk to me, April. Tell me where you come from. You're not from L.A. any more than I am, are you?"

"Is it that obvious?"

He laughed. "Yes. But that's not a bad thing, believe me."

April sighed. "I am a small-town girl. I guess you can never really change that, can you?"

"I hope not." He gave her waist a small squeeze. "So, tell me."

It was phrased as a request, not as a command; the first time he'd ever spoken to her like this. His voice was soft, husky, intimate.

"I grew up in Ashland, Oregon. Have you heard of it?"

"Aye, the Ashland Shakespeare Festival is there. You can't live in a town like L.A., surrounded by actors, and not have heard of it. Are your family actors, then?"

"Mine? No." She had to laugh. "My folks are the most normal people in the world. My dad's an engineer for the local department of water and power. My mother works as a seamstress for the theater. She does the most beautiful work. I spent my childhood surrounded by costumes; these luxurious fabrics, Elizabethan dresses that weighed thirty pounds. Of course, I had to try everything on. I've always been such a girl. I still am."

"Yes, you are," he growled, his hand caressing her breast.

She surged into the heat of his palm, lust flooding her body. But there was more to it than that. Lying there, talking quietly with him in the darkened room, she felt warm, safe. She still couldn't believe they were talking together like this.

"What about you, Decker? Tell me about your family."

"Ah, they're all in Ireland, a small town outside of Dublin; my parents, my sisters, lots of aunts and uncles and cousins. They're simple people. They enjoy a simple life, simple pleasures. But it was never enough for me."

"Do you ever talk to them, see them?"

"Hah! Mum'd have my head if I didn't phone her every Sunday."

She couldn't imagine anyone having Decker's head, but she loved the idea that he called his mother every week. It gave her a glimpse of vulnerability, made him more human.

"I had Mum and my Aunt Claire out here to visit last year," he went on, surprising her by going into detail about his family life. His voice had dropped even lower, almost as though he were talking aloud to himself. "Made the tourist rounds; Hollywood, the beach, all that. When I took them shopping at the Grove in Beverly Hills, they were like two kids in a candy store, going mad over all the pretty clothes, the handbags. But I couldn't get them to choose anything. Mum said she didn't know what she'd do with all those fancy things at home. They finally let me buy them the biggest box of Godiva chocolates I could find. And I found a gorgeous diamond pendant for Mum that she couldn't refuse, and a pair of earrings for my Aunt Claire. You'd have thought I'd bought them the crown jewels."

He was quiet for a few moments while April absorbed this new information about him. He was still Decker, still radiated dominance with every fiber of his being, yet she loved seeing this softer side of him, this sentimental side. Even if he never again let her in like this, she had this moment, knew a little more of what went on in his head. Of who he was. It felt like a gift. It felt personal.

She knew it was foolish, unrealistic. But every moment they spent together only made him more real to her, and this moment more than any other.

Don't be a fool, April.

But she already knew it was too late. Far too late for any

warnings, for the voice of reason to permeate her mind and, more important, her heart.

She was in love with him already.

ॐ

Ashlyn sat on the edge of Gabriel's big bed, waiting for him. Still naked, her hands now bound behind her back, she wanted to cry. But not because of her naked and well-used state; no, these were the things she loved. She wanted to cry because she loved this, loved it all: the flogging, the bondage, the pain, the sex, the exquisite pleasure it all brought.

How was this possible?

How could she love these things? Did it mean she was crazy, twisted somehow? And yet, she couldn't find it within herself to leave, to turn her back on everything Gabriel had shown her, taught her. She couldn't turn her back on him.

This had been meant to be a sexual experiment, an exploration of her fantasies. She wasn't meant to fall for him. But there it was. She wasn't sure exactly when, or how, it had happened. And she wasn't certain yet that she could call it love. But it was something, something big and intense and frightening.

There was so much to be afraid of. Her own dark yearnings, her feelings for Gabriel—a man who could have any woman he wanted, and probably had. She was foolish to think that anything more than their play would come out of this. But what if . . . ?

She shook her head. Things had spiraled out of control

so quickly, she'd hardly had a chance to think about it. Suddenly her mind was working at a hundred miles an hour, searching for answers to too many questions.

Who was she, really, now that she had done these wicked things? Wasn't this proof of her intrinsic weakness, that she could give over her body and her well-being to another person? That she loved it, needed it? What did it mean? About her, about who she was in the world? Had she really changed so much that she would have to rethink her entire life?

And then there was him. He was far too enigmatic for her to ever figure out. She would never presume to even guess at what was on his mind, in his heart. He was too good at what he did, too experienced, his true self shuttered behind his expertise. She'd be a fool ever to presume otherwise.

She'd be a fool to fall for him.

She wouldn't admit that she had, not even to herself, even though the idea of it nagged at the corners of her mind. She would fight against it. She couldn't allow that to happen. This beautiful, clever, wonderful man who made her feel more alive than she ever had before. But it was this same man who had brought on all of this self-doubt, this sense of spinning out of control.

She had to make very sure that, no matter what happened, no matter what they did together, she stayed true to herself, kept who she was intact.

If only she were sure of exactly who that was.

Rowan hit the save button and closed her laptop, sitting back in the large chair behind the desk in Christian's study.

God, Ashlyn really was her, wasn't she? She was writing about her own issues, her own struggles. Ashlyn was asking all of the questions she should be asking herself. Instead she was trying to work things out on paper to avoid having to deal with it all.

She wasn't surprised that she'd left Ashlyn hanging, full of doubt and fear. That's exactly where she was herself. But Gabriel was not Christian. No, in real life, she was the one who held back. Gabriel was just the excuse in her mind for why she couldn't allow herself to hope for something more with Christian. Not because he wasn't able to do that, but because she feared she wasn't up to the task.

She wanted to keep writing, to get Ashlyn through her moment of crisis, but she couldn't concentrate. It was strange writing in Christian's study, being alone in his house. He'd had a meeting today at a gallery, and she'd been left on her own.

She'd gone immediately to her computer, which he'd set up in his office for her. The room was large, full of heavy European antiques. Tall bookcases lined two walls and held books of every description. Art books, of course, but also an astonishing collection of classic literature, some volumes so old they looked as though they'd turn to dust if she drew them from the shelves. Framed paintings were stacked against an empty wall, reminding her that Christian hadn't been in L.A. very long.

God, she had to stop thinking about him, had to clear her mind. But alone in his house, what else was there to think about?

The telephone on the desk caught her eye and she

quickly dialed April's cell phone number. Her friend picked up on the first ring.

"April, it's me, Rowan. Did I catch you at a good time?"

"I'm on my way to work. I'm glad you called. I've been wanting to talk to you. So much has happened."

"Are you alright?"

"Yes, I'm fine, I'm just ... confused."

"Lord, me too."

"You do sound a little breathless."

"Yes, that's exactly how I feel. I'm at Christian's house. I'm going to stay here for a while."

A moment of silence, and then, "I didn't expect you to go into this so quickly."

"Neither did I. It's a bit of a shock, really, if I let myself think about it. We went to my house last night, got a few of my things together."

"What about work?"

"I had no contracts this week, and I canceled one I had coming up. I feel like ... like I have to give this the time it deserves. To fully explore it. Do you know what I mean?"

"Yes, absolutely."

"I should probably go up to San Francisco to check on a client in a few days, but other than that I've left my schedule open, and truthfully, I could skip that trip, too. Maybe I will. Things are just too complicated right now." Rowan ran a hand through her hair, let out a deep sigh.

"But is it good?"

She had to think about how to answer for a moment. "Yes, it's good. Most of it, anyway. But no matter what he does with me, I always immediately need more; it's as though I can never be sated. And that really scares me, for the first time in a long time. And I feel like I have to confront that."

"Some people think BDSM is all about the physical side, but there's so much more to it than that. The physicality of it, the rituals, the symbols, always brings up our issues in the end, doesn't it?" She could hear a touch of strain in April's voice.

"How are things going for you?"

"Like I said, I'm a little confused." She sighed. "No, not confused. I guess I know perfectly well what's going on. I'm falling in love with him, Rowan."

"Oh, honey..."

"I know, I'm an idiot. You don't have to tell me that. But I really can't help myself. And I've decided that I can either go into this with my eyes wide open, or I can never see him again. Except that's really not an option at this point. Not until Decker tells me it's over. I can't stop it. I really can't."

"I understand. Now more than ever. Just...be careful with yourself, if you can."

"I'm trying. I'm going back to him tomorrow night."

"Keep in touch."

"I will. And what about you? Can you keep in touch? I mean, being at his house, how is that going to go? What have you agreed on?"

"I'm no slave. He doesn't have control over my every waking moment; I'm free to do as I wish when he's not here. It's all about what happens when we're in role together. He understands that. He's giving me some free rein to explore this in my own way, but only to a point. When we are in role he doesn't let me get away with much." She ran her fingers along the edge of the desk. The old wood was so smooth. Like his hands on her flesh. "He takes over when he needs to. It's as though...he can read me, read what I need."

"Well, that's good, then, isn't it?"

"I think so. Truly, April, I don't know where any of this is going. I don't know what's at the end of this journey. All I know is that I need to find out."

"And if it's love that's at the end?"

"I'm only here to find myself, April."

"Yes, but sometimes when we're finding ourselves, we find things we never expected, things we weren't necessarily looking for, don't we?"

"Yes, of course."

But love? No. She wasn't looking for love; she never had been.

Then why was it that her heart gave a small, dull twist in her chest at the idea of it, the idea of loving Christian Thorne?

No, Rowan.

She refused to believe that love was part of this particular journey. She was intent on finding the truth about *herself*.

But what if the truth was, she was falling in love with Christian?

EIGHT

⚜

"THIS IS YOUR USUAL EXCELLENT WORK, CHRISTIAN. Beautiful, lyrical, as always. But I'd love to see something new from you."

Sterling was dressed in his usual idea of business casual: the tailor-made slacks from his favorite design house in London, where his main gallery was; a cashmere sweater over a custom-made shirt; Italian loafers. Sterling was a man of exquisite taste. Years earlier, that taste had run to Christian himself, when Sterling had discovered his young, raw talent. Sterling never held Christian's heterosexuality against him, and had launched his career despite Christian's politely declining the older man's advances. It hadn't been an issue since then, and they'd had a long and successful working relationship, as well as a close friendship.

He looked at the older man now as he sat behind the large, ornate Louis XIV desk in his office at his Beverly Hills gallery. His full head of silver hair was flawlessly smoothed, his clear gray eyes intense, striking. He was perfectly serious. This was the first time in years he'd made any such solid remark on the direction of Christian's career, and it took him by surprise.

"Are you saying you think I've gotten stale?"

Too much truth there...

"Your work is still superb, but it's been a long time since I've seen something truly different." Sterling paused to make an elegant hand gesture in the air. "Something fresh, new."

Christian shifted in the delicate antique chair that seemed too small and fragile to hold him. He wasn't insulted. On the contrary, he respected Sterling's opinion about his work above anyone else's. And he knew his friend was right. He'd been searching for inspiration the last couple of years, but his search had been fruitless. That's one reason why he'd come home from Europe; he never did find what he was looking for there. Life had come to be nothing more than a meaningless pursuit of physical pleasures. He'd known for a while that he needed to find something that had a deeper meaning before he'd find his muse again.

He thought about his conversation with Rowan, telling her he wanted to paint her. Where had that come from? He'd been working almost exclusively in stone for over five years. Why this sudden urge to paint? But did it matter? He felt the urge to create again; that was the only important thing.

"I have an idea, Sterling. But it's not sculpture. Do you think my patrons would accept something that different from me? But no, I don't really care. I'm going to do it anyway." He let out a short, sharp laugh. It was true. He didn't care. And he felt compelled. So there was no question about it, really.

"Tell me what you have in mind."

"A series of paintings," he answered, realizing that it was all coming together in his mind as he was speaking. "I don't know exactly. But they'll be erotic." He thought for a moment about Rowan, about the texture of her skin, her beautiful face, her expression as she came into his hands. "Yes, definitely erotic."

"Your work is always, at the least, subtly erotic."

"Yes, but what I have in mind will be distinctly erotic. Edgier than the work I've been doing."

Sterling raised an eyebrow.

Christian grinned at him. "I have a new muse."

"Apparently. But for you to go back to painting now... that's quite a change for you. You've had muses before, by the dozens—"

Christian tapped his fingers on the arm of the chair and gave his friend a wry grin. "I'm aware of my sordid history, Sterling."

"But none of them has ever done more than inspire a single piece. This one must be special. I assume it's the woman you told me about on the phone?"

"It is. And she is special." He thought about her lovely face, her eyes, the emotion contained in every movement of her body, in the tension held in her muscles. "Something about her... she's made me remember there is a spiritual side to my work, just as there is in BDSM. I think I'd forgotten that. In both arenas."

How delicious that she was waiting at home for him.

His to do with as he wished. A plan was forming in his mind. He could hardly wait. If it were anyone but Sterling he would cut the meeting short and go home to her right now. Tie her up, paint her.

Yes. He would paint her.

"She's incredibly beautiful," he told Sterling almost unconsciously, simply speaking his thoughts aloud.

"Of course. They all are."

"No, you don't understand," he said, leaning forward in his chair and focusing now on his friend. "She is stunning, this woman. You would have to see her. She has the most incredible bone structure. Delicate, like a bird. And skin like polished ivory. I'll need to put her in stone eventually, but first, I have to paint her. I don't even know why. Hell, I don't care. I just need to do it." He was really getting worked up now, but it didn't matter. This was Sterling he was talking to.

Sterling's mouth quirked. "You really are taken with her, aren't you?"

"I . . ." But what could he say? Obviously he was physically obsessed with her, with her physical beauty, with the fact that he couldn't quite have her. But anything more?

There was a lot more to Rowan than the way she looked. But he couldn't explain it now. He shook his head. "You have to see her, Sterling. Even you could appreciate her."

"Even I? You know perfectly well that I am capable of appreciating beauty in any form. Even when I have no desire to sleep with it." He paused, his eyebrow raised once more. "Have you slept with her yet?"

"What? No. I don't intend to."

"Why don't I believe you?"

For some reason, Sterling's remark made him edgy, a little angry, even. He rose and began to pace the length of the office, his shoes scudding on the priceless Aubusson rug beneath his feet. "Look, just because I've been with a number of women doesn't mean I have to sleep with every woman I come into contact with."

"Of course not. But why not this particular woman?"

"It's part of our agreement."

Was that what he was really angry about?

"Christian, you do what you must. You don't have to justify yourself to me; that's not what I was asking for. But surely you must understand why I'm curious."

"I'm sorry. This woman, Rowan…she's got me in a state, I'm telling you, Sterling."

"I can see that."

"God, I'm pathetic." Christian smoothed a hand back over his ponytailed hair.

Sterling leaned back into his chair. "Not any more so than any other artist experiencing angst. You all go through this. You're all so excruciatingly tortured. Remember Rodin and his Camille Claudel? 'My very dearest down on both knees before your beautiful body which I embrace.' He wrote that to her, you know."

"Lord, I hope it's not that bad. It's torturous enough as it is. I don't want either one of us to end up in a mental institution like poor Camille. It's too tragic. No, it's all a little frustrating right now, that's all. I'll feel better when I can start to paint her."

"When do you intend to begin?"

"Now."

૭๏

Christian slammed the door shut behind him and went immediately upstairs to find her. She was in his second-floor office, sitting in front of her laptop. She looked so small behind his big desk, surrounded by all of his things, dwarfed by the size of the furnishings and the ceiling-high bookshelves. Tiny and vulnerable. Definitely out of her element. He loved her just like this, her dark blue eyes a little confused, her whole posture speaking of the fact that she was a bit off balance.

He really was a sadist.

"You're back."

"Yes, and I need you right away. Come upstairs with me."

He felt too pressed to begin to explain first. He watched a frown cross her lovely face, then she stood without saying anything. But she bit her lower lip, betraying the calm façade she presented. He noted she was fresh from the shower, dressed in a long midnight blue silk robe; the tips of her hair were still damp. She wore no makeup, but still, her skin was flawless. She looked beautiful. Perfect for what he had in mind. He wanted that look of clean innocence, a contrast to her lithe body, which was pure sex to him.

He held a hand out to her. "Come with me and I'll tell you everything."

He stepped closer to reach for her and was hit with the fresh, damp scent of her as his hand found hers. She smelled like the sun and the rain at the same time. It almost brought him to his knees. And when he realized she was probably naked beneath her silk robe, he wanted to strip it off her and take her there on his desk.

Control, Thorne.

But he was holding her small hand in his and she was waiting for him. He moved out of the room, up the stairs. She trailed along quietly until they reached the studio. She stopped just inside the doorway.

"Christian, what's going on?"

"I've just come from the gallery and I had a talk with my friend there, Sterling Price. No, that really doesn't matter right now. What matters is that I need to paint you."

"Paint me?"

Her brows rose in surprise. He needed to get her consent, of course, as with any other model. He wouldn't be able to stand it if she refused. But he had a feeling she wouldn't. She was becoming more and more pliant each day. The submissive side he'd seen deep within her was beginning to rise to the surface. And one of the best things about his driving need to paint her was that it would do her good, too, in this sense.

"Yes, I want to paint you. Maybe sculpt you later, but now, I need to paint, or at least to do a series of preliminary sketches. Will you do it, Rowan?"

He slid his hands onto her shoulders, looked into her eyes. Her body beneath his hands was warm, electric. Maybe painting her would be the only way to keep from fucking her. Maybe it would only make it worse.

Doesn't matter.

The only thing that mattered right now was doing it, finding a way to manifest her form on canvas. To render her flesh in that way, to make her presence eternal. He was long out of practice. He hoped he could do it.

Just do it.

"Rowan, I'm just beginning to understand what this means, that you inspire me on several levels. Levels that have been missing for too long. And I know I'll discover even more in the process of putting your image on canvas. All I need is your answer."

"Yes...I just...yes, of course you can paint me, if you really want to. Is this part of it? I mean, I'm trying to figure out what this will mean."

He laughed. "It means I'm an artist. There isn't always an explanation for what I do." He slid his hands down to her wrists, lifted them both to his lips, laid gentle kisses there. "I'm going to bind these delicate wrists of yours, bind them in chains."

When he raised his eyes he could see that hers were already glazing over. Oh, yes, there was a submissive in there, and she loved to be told what to do. She was going down already. He could see it in her eyes, feel it in her pulse fluttering beneath his thumbs, in the way her shoulders slacked as he spoke.

Perfect.

He let her wrists go and her hands settled slowly at her sides. When he pulled at the bow knotted at her waist, her robe fell open. He was right. Nothing under there. Just her small, lovely body, all that porcelain skin. The edges of the robe caught on the curve of her breasts. Her nipples were dark and hard already, making him want to touch them, to pinch them between his fingers.

Later. Later he would do a number of things to her beautiful body, to her head, and Lord knows when he'd be able to stop. But right now he wanted to lay her over the old chaise longue, bind her, pose her.

He led her across the room, slipped the robe from her shoulders and guided her to sit on the chaise. He took the quilt that was draped there and tossed it away.

"Go ahead and lean back into the pillows while I get everything prepared.

She immediately complied while he went to a large wooden chest against one wall and pulled out several lengths of heavy metal chain. He loved the look of this stuff, the medieval feel to it. The chains symbolized something to him, something dark and primal. He couldn't wait to see them on her.

She was leaning back against the pile of tattered old silk pillows, her body all long, smooth lines. He had to admit he was surprised at how easily she was submitting already. Important, but he couldn't think about it now. He went to her, knelt down, and wrapped the chains around her wrists. The contrast against her pale skin was incredible. The chain was thick, heavy. He twined it around several times, making it look even more harsh against her fragile flesh.

"Come on now, lie back."

He helped her to stretch out on the old chaise on her back, then pulled her arms over her head, so that her body was elongated as it was when he suspended her from the ceiling. She was trembling, just a series of delicate tremors running through her. Perhaps a part of her was still fighting this? But he could tell she was as excited by what they were about to do as he was.

"Yes, close your eyes if you want to. Doesn't matter right now. I'll get to your face later. I want to get the lines of your body first."

He picked up the first sketchpad he could find and began to draw.

He wanted to be exact: that flowing line of arm, breast, waist, hips, then the longer line of her legs. She was so damned gorgeous lying there. He got up, went to her, ran his fingers over her graceful, swanlike throat. She was still trembling, but it was more like a humming just beneath the surface of her skin. Her eyes stayed closed, her dark lashes resting against her flushed cheeks. Her breathing was even, despite the telltale flush of her arousal.

He tore his hands away from her, penciled in a few details on his sketchpad for a moment, looked back at her prone figure. She really was too beautiful to be believed. Every nerve in his body was on alert, his hands aching to touch her again.

He leaned in, brushed his fingertips over her nipples, one at a time, and she let out a soft sigh, her nipples going hard immediately. They were dark, full, ripe. His groin tightened in answer.

He went back to his pencil and paper, but he didn't dare to shade in the dark triangle of curls between her thighs. It would break his concentration utterly. She lay there, lambent in the haze of subspace, almost shockingly vulnerable. All the more so because he knew how strong she was on the inside. But how to capture that part of her?

Later, when he did this in paint, when he had more control over light and texture, he could show who she was in her eyes, in her lovely, soft mouth. This was preliminary.

But he knew already this would be brilliant. Beautiful. Erotic. Rowan.

Everything he wanted it to be.

He reached out and drew his finger over the high curve of her breasts. She shivered, her lips parting, and pulled in a gasping breath. And he knew if he slipped a hand between her thighs she'd be soaking wet. Again he paused, worked on the sketch for a few moments; then he had to touch her again, translating the feel of flesh and bone into his drawing of her, bringing it alive.

Or maybe he just needed to touch her.

He reached out and stroked her skin, which had gone from warm to hot. The flush had spread lower, over her breasts. Her breathing quickened as he touched her. Even though her eyes were still closed and she was deeply into that slumberous, trancelike space, he could read her desire. He placed his palm flat on her chest, between the swell of her breasts. Her heartbeat was absolutely thundering. He left his hand there, just watching her. Listening to her breath, which was coming in shorter, sharper pants.

He swept his hand lower, couldn't help himself, watching her face as his fingers slid over her stomach. She gasped when he reached the soft curls he had sworn to ignore. Her eyes opened, locked on his. Somehow, she was totally present in her body, connected.

That look hit him like a hammer blow. Fire surged through his veins, his mind.

He moved his hand back to the soft flesh of her belly. He was vaguely aware of his own panting breath. Beneath his hand her skin was absolutely molten with heat. And her liquid sapphire gaze remained fixed on his.

Her breath shifted, matched his own. He dropped his sketchpad on the floor.

"Rowan..."

"Yes, Christian," she whispered.

"Christ."

He wanted to read what was behind her steady gaze, but he was too mesmerized by it. By her. There was so much there, raw need, raw emotion. He could hardly stand it. His heart twisted in his chest. And the need to be inside her body was so strong he could barely fight it, didn't want to, really.

She watched him as he slid his hand lower once more, as he dipped between her luscious thighs. God, she was all soaking wet heat. She was quivering all over. He was so hard it hurt. He knew if he went any further he would lose all control. And she would let him.

Don't do it, Thorne. Just draw her. Do what you're supposed to do.

It took everything he had to pull his hand back.

He forced himself to step away, to just leave her there in her chains while he turned to stare out through the greenhouse glass. The light was waning outside the windows, the fog rolling in, thick and gray, swallowing the last of the day's light.

After several minutes, when he thought he had himself calmed down a little, he went to her, knelt on the floor beside the chaise. Her lashes lay dark against her pale cheeks, but he could see the faint glow of blue from beneath her translucent lids. Her lips were dark pink, slightly parted. She was still breathing in short, shallow gasps. When he touched her shoulder she stirred a little. He could tell she was still deep down in subspace, under that floating layer of cloud in her head that allowed her to lie still like this, despite what had just happened between them.

"Rowan. I'm going to remove the chains now."

"Yes," she murmured.

He reached up and drew her hands down, rolling her onto her side, then unwound the chain. Dangerous to even touch her now, but he had to do it. Her eyes were open. They were damp and shining, as though she were about to cry.

Damn it, that's not what he wanted. But he also understood some of what she must be feeling. He was feeling it himself.

He made himself concentrate on rubbing at the cool skin on her wrists, warming her flesh. She lay still, letting him do it.

He realized all at once and on some very deep level that this lovely, ethereal creature had put herself in his hands. Trusted him. Allowed him to use her body in the way he saw fit. She really had turned herself over to him, despite her inner struggle. How much strength had it taken for her to do that? Did she even realize it? Her strength made her all the more precious to him.

Yes, she was precious to him.

Another blow to the chest, this realization.

She had quieted now, her breath a gentle whisper. His throat tight, he leaned in and laid a kiss on her mouth. Softly; he didn't want to pull her out of her haze just yet. She was too gorgeous like this, all sleepy and pliant and dazed.

God, her lips were soft, so soft he had to do it again.

And this time, she kissed him back, her mouth pressing into his. So damn sweet he wanted to groan aloud.

It went through him all at once: shock, lust, the pure truth of her yielding. She wasn't just submitting. She was right there with him at that moment. It made his pulse jump, his chest pound. He pulled back.

He'd lose his goddamned mind if he didn't get to have her soon.

But no. It was part of what they'd negotiated, and he would never, ever break a contract. Taking advantage of a bottom who had been brought down into subspace, when she couldn't clearly think and speak for herself, was unforgivable.

Then get her consent before you play again.

God, where had that evil thought come from? But he was too worked up to think clearly himself. And if he got so damned turned on playing with her, just looking at her, for God's sake, could he still be a responsible Dom? Could he really say that he was in control?

Grabbing the discarded quilt from the floor, he laid it over Rowan's nude and still quiet body, then got up to pace the length of the studio.

He moved across the floor in long strides, stopping in front of the window to turn back and look at her. She seemed so small wrapped in the blanket. Her hair was a mass of raven waves. He smoothed a hand over his jaw and commanded himself again to calm down. If he couldn't keep it together, then maybe he wasn't the one for her to do this experiment with.

But it had gone far beyond any experiment, hadn't it? She'd gone into it far too easily, too fast. And there was a real connection between them. He knew it was more than chemistry, although that was as intense as any he'd ever experienced. More, so much more.

How ironic that having her, truly having her, was the one thing that was entirely impossible.

೦ಾ

April was tired after a long day at Precious, the trendy boutique where she worked. The high price of the merchandise meant a demanding clientele, and today had been particularly difficult. Still, she loved it, loved the clothes, loved dressing people. She'd thought for a long time of becoming a stylist, and L.A. was certainly the best location for it. She was working toward her degree in fashion merchandising and had only a year to go. School and work took up a lot of hours, but not enough lately to distract her mind from the ever-present thoughts of Decker.

She tossed her keys into a glass bowl on the small antique sideboard in her living room and headed into the bedroom, stripping off her sweater and her bra as she went. God, she hated bras; it was the first thing she took off when she got home every day. With her large, full breasts she knew she needed to wear one, but she still hated the feel of the damn things.

Luckily, she'd spent a lot of braless evenings lately. Everything-less. Decker always stripped her down the moment she arrived at his house.

In her bedroom, she tossed her sweater and bra onto the small blue and white striped damask chair in one corner, took off her skirt and added it to the small pile there.

She kicked off her shoes gently and picked them up to put away on the shelf in the closet. She adored her shoes, really had a thing for them; they always received much better treatment than did her clothing.

She lay down on her bed, luxuriating in the feel of the white down quilt, soft and plush beneath her skin. She wanted to close her eyes, think of him, imagine she was with him tonight. She hated that she was so obsessed with him, that she could barely think of anything else since their first night together. But she got tired of fighting it.

His face materialized in her mind's eye. So strong, so intense. His eyes were so dark they were almost black, making him more enigmatic than he already was by the sheer force of his personality.

His intrinsic air of command was what had first attracted her to him. Then she had come to know his talent, his creativity, his sharp instincts when it came to BDSM play, when it came to sex. And after her last night with him, when she'd finally been given some glimpse into who he was inside, into what his life was aside from what they did together, he'd become more attractive to her than ever. No wonder everyone was so drawn to him; he was that perfect combination of utter confidence and charm. And those moments of tenderness toward her, and when he was talking about his family, were devastating. Even more devastating than his dark good looks, his powerful body.

She shivered, recalling the texture of him. Hard and smooth all at the same time. He had those six-pack abs; she could feel every ridge when she ran her fingers over his stomach. God, she loved that. Loved touching him at those moments when they were just having sex and there were no dominant and submissive roles, when that all fell away and it was just the two of them touching each other all over.

Her body heated and she slid her hands over her breasts, cupping them, as he so often did. Of course, his big hands covered so much more of her flesh. Brushing her fingertips over her already hardening nipples, she teased herself. Decker might tease her, too, getting her as hot as he could before giving her any release, drawing it out for his own amusement.

He liked to make her beg to come, and she did it willingly. No problem. If he wanted her groveling at his feet she was happy to do so. More than happy; rapturous. She'd already known she was a submissive at heart when she'd met Decker, but with him the desire to please took on an altogether keener edge. Begging at his feet was her idea of heaven.

Closing her eyes, she pictured herself kneeling naked before him. A shiver of pleasure rippled through her and she smoothed one of her hands down over her stomach, moved it between her thighs.

In her mind, he stood over her, ordered her to touch herself. Told her exactly what he wanted her to do.

For him.

She slid her hand beneath her panties and found her damp cleft. She used her fingers to spread her swollen lips, opening her body up to her probing touch. Listening to his imaginary voice in her head, she slid two fingers inside while she used her thumb to press onto the tight bud of her clit.

His deep voice reverberated through her mind while

her body shuddered in pleasure at her touch. If only it was his hand on her, his big cock inside her. God, the man could fuck like a demon. He could go on forever. She moved her hand, pressing deeper inside her, her thumb circling, rubbing. And all the while it was his voice instructing her, commanding her. His face in her mind, his big hands on her body.

How many times had he touched her like this? Yes, just...like...this...

Her hips bucked into her hand as the first wave of her climax rolled over her.

Yes, fuck me...

The walls of her sex clenched, spasmed; pleasure shot through her system, lighting her on fire, her core exploding around her fingers.

When it was over she lay panting on the bed, her legs still trembling with the force of her climax. She rolled over and laid her head on one of the blue and white throw pillows, wishing it were his shoulder, wishing she could feel his body next to hers, smell his scent that was so completely male, purely *him*.

If only...

She sighed.

The telephone rang.

She bolted upright, made a grab for the phone on her nightstand. "Yes? Hello?"

"April."

Decker's voice flowed over her body like honey, thick, heavy, sweet, weighing her down. Her sex gave one last clench.

"Decker. Hi."

"You sound out of breath. Tell me what you've been doing."

Oh, God, could the man see through the phone, read her mind? But this was Decker; he could read her every breath, every nuance of expression. Could she really tell him what she'd been doing? Hell, he'd probably like it. And she always went right under just from the sound of his deep, sexy voice. She would have done anything he asked.

"I was . . . thinking of you."

"Were you? Tell me, little one."

God, she loved when he called her that. Made her want to come all over again.

"I was thinking of you, picturing you. And touching myself." Her body began to heat up once more.

A small chuckle from his end of the phone. "And did you come?"

"Yes!" Even she could hear her own panting breath.

"I like that. Do it again for me."

"What? Now?"

"Yes." ·

She laughed.

"I'm perfectly serious, April."

His somber, commanding tone sobered her. But it also caused a lancing shaft of heat to stab into her body, her sex coming alive instantly. She knew this tone. It was not to be argued with. Not that she really wanted to. She wanted only to please him.

"Are you naked?"

"I am now, Sir," she answered, slipping her panties off and throwing them onto the floor.

Another small chuckle. "Good girl. Tell me, where are you?"

"I'm lying on my bed, Sir."

"Perfect. Lie back, spread your legs. Spread them as though I were right there in front of you and you were presenting yourself to me."

Propping her head on the small pile of pillows, she did as he asked, spreading her thighs wide apart while her head began to empty out, focusing only on his voice in her ear.

"Now pinch your nipples for me. Do it hard. Do it the way I would. I want it to hurt. For me. Do you understand?"

"Yes, Sir." She did as he asked, twisting her nipples hard in her fingers, feeling the pain shoot through her body in a lovely stab of sensation.

"Does it hurt, April?"

"It feels good. Yes."

"Do it harder."

She pinched, hard, the pain biting into her flesh, making her gasp aloud.

"Very good. Are you wet? Are you ready for me?"

"Yes, Sir."

"Let's find out, shall we? Move your hand between your legs."

She slipped her hand between her thighs and brushed her sex. A tingle ran through her body. She could come in moments, she knew.

"Are you wet, April? Are you all hot and slick like you always are? Always ready for me to fuck you, aren't you, my girl?"

"Yes . . . yes, Sir."

Her sex was aching, begging for release.

"Move your hand for me. Slide your fingers over your pussy lips. I know you like that, like to start off with that soft, stroking motion."

She groaned, as much at the slow, husky tone of his voice as at her own fingers doing exactly as he asked. And yes, that, too, following his orders. She shivered.

He kept silent for a minute or two while she stroked herself, just her lips, not touching the swollen and aching nub yet, or slipping inside, as badly as she wanted to. She hadn't been told yet that she could.

"I can hear you breathe, April. I can hear you beginning to pant. I can hear your excitement. And it's making me hard. It's making me need you."

She moaned aloud.

"I want you to take those lovely little fingers of yours and brush them over your clit. Softly. Do it."

She did as instructed, teasing herself gently as he so often did. Pleasure rolled over her, making her thighs tense.

"Do you need to come yet, April?"

"Yes!"

"Ah, too bad I won't let you, then, isn't it?" A brief little laugh.

Wicked man.

But wasn't that one of the things she loved about him?

"Tell me, girl, do you own a vibrator? A dildo?"

"Uh, yes, Sir. A vibrator."

"Get it."

She rolled over and opened the drawer in her nightstand, pulled out a large, phallic vibrator.

"I have it, Sir."

"Describe it to me."

"It's big. And it's silver, shiny chrome, with ridges all along the shaft."

"You have excellent taste in toys, April."

She smiled, but she was distracted by the vibrator in her hand, by her needy sex begging for the toy to be used.

"Lie back again and turn it on."

Once again she did as asked. On her back on the bed, her legs spread wide, she touched the switch and the vibe buzzed to life.

"I want you to use it on yourself. Just the tip of your clit. But don't come yet; not until I tell you."

"Yes, Sir."

She touched the vibrator to her clit and shuddered all over with the need to come. She drew in a sharp, gasping breath.

"It's good, isn't it? But now I want it inside you. And I want you to imagine it's my hard cock inside of you. Push it in slowly, my girl. I know you can take all of it. You get so damned wet, and you can take all of me. Do it."

She pushed the pulsing instrument into her body, her sex, slippery with her excitement, swallowing it easily.

"Oh, God." She gasped.

"Is it good? Tell me."

"Yes. Oh … it's … I'm going to come!"

"No, April. Steel yourself. You can do it. Hold back."

She gritted her teeth.

"Just ride that edge. Hold on to that edge of sensation."

His voice was deep and gravelly with lust, and just the

sound of it was purely erotic to her. She tried to relax her muscles; her thighs, the walls of her sex. Sensation poured through her in an almost unbearable wave.

"Just let it be good. Feel every moment of it." A long pause, then, "I can hear you. You're panting now. I love to hear you like this. I wish I were there with you now, watching you push that chrome toy into your hot little pussy. I love it so damned much I've got my cock in my hand and I'm so hard I want to explode."

The picture that came into her head, of Decker holding his cock, stroking it, made her sex clench hard.

"Please, Sir..."

"Please what?" he growled.

"Please let me come!"

She heard only his harsh, panting breath for a moment. "Yes, come, little one. Come for me."

She twisted the vibrator, moved it in another fraction of an inch, the buzzing sending her hurtling over the edge. Her climax hit her hard and fast. She shut her eyes against the onslaught of sensation, and behind her lids a pure white light exploded, dazing her. Pleasure crashed through her in shattering waves, and on the other end of the phone she heard Decker's groan of pleasure. She imagined him coming, spurting into his hand.

Oh, God.

When it was over she slipped the chrome vibrator from her body and lay, stunned, on the bed.

"Are you there, April?"

"Yes, Sir." She was still trying to catch her breath.

"Tomorrow night. Bring your little toy for me. I have

some ideas. And, April . . . don't come again until I see you. Understood?"

"Yes, Sir."

"Good girl. Tomorrow, then."

She heard a click. He was gone.

But her body would remember his voice for the rest of the evening.

Hell, she'd remember everything about Decker for the rest of her life.

#

Rowan woke to the gray dawn sky. Streaks of pink were just beginning to peek through the veil of fog. Beside her, Christian's breath came in an even rhythm. Why did the peaceful cadence of his breathing make her want to cry?

She was beginning to get used to these early morning moments alone, with only the rising sun and her own thoughts for company, and Christian's sleeping form beside her.

She tried to remember the previous evening, but there was such a dreamlike quality to it, she wasn't quite sure it had really happened. Except for that seemingly endless moment of absolute clarity when their gazes had locked. At that moment, she'd felt as though he could see right into her, and for once she could see back. Was it ridiculous of her to feel that she knew something more about him now? Was it equally ridiculous for her to feel she had given him something of herself, something important?

She remembered quite clearly the cold metal chains

going around her wrists, that sensation of sinking into their cool touch, of giving herself over to it. And after that, the sensation of his hands on her body when he touched her as he sketched. And she really had sunk down deep, into the experience, into his touch, his gaze on her. But as deep down as she was in subspace, in the moment, she was hyperaware of every sensation, of every breath, his as much as her own. And exquisitely aware of the connection between them that shut out the rest of the world completely.

She'd seen this happen to others, people who went right under and into the hazy lair of subspace just by being bound, by being touched or spoken to in a certain way, but she'd never expected it to happen to her. And maybe it wouldn't happen with anyone other than him. But in turning herself over to Christian, giving herself into his care, his hands, she felt safe.

Had she ever in her life felt safe before?

Certainly not safe enough to do the things she was doing with Christian. When this was all over, how was she ever going to manage without that safety?

Her heart gave a hard squeeze and the tears wanted to come again.

She turned her head to look at him, and was surprised to find his blue-green eyes staring back at her.

"Oh..."

"Hey." His voice was rough with sleep. He reached out and stroked her cheek with one finger. "What's this?"

"Nothing, I'm fine." She turned her face away, wishing the damned tears away. She couldn't look at him now.

He propped himself up on one elbow. "You're not. Talk to me, Rowan."

She could only shake her head.

"Rowan." He took her chin and forced her to look back at him.

God, he was beautiful. She'd never seen a man with such beautiful features. Why did that only make her chest tighten more?

"Is it what we're doing together? Is this hurting you, Rowan? Because if it is, we'll stop. That was never my intention."

She shook her head again. "No. It's not that."

"Then what?"

She had to force the words out. "It scares me, all of this. It scares me that I love what we're doing together. That I'm so willing. What that says about me."

"Rowan, I'm here with you. I'll help you through this."

She looked into his eyes then. "Why are you so intent on helping me? I mean, why . . . all of this? This is no longer a game to you, unless I'm reading you wrong. So why do this with me?"

He gave a long sigh. "Because now I have to."

"Because . . . ?"

"Because I am someone who is driven to finish what I start. But I don't mean that in the impersonal way it sounds. I feel a sense of responsibility toward you that goes beyond being a dominant, being responsible for you in that way. It's part of who I am. It's about my life, the things that have made me who I am. Things I don't necessarily want to go into right now. Things that don't even have any direct relevance, except that you're a part of it." He paused, then said again, "I feel I *have* to do this."

She nodded, trying to understand. "And I have to keep some things to myself for now."

He tucked a strand of hair behind her ear, a brief, natural motion that was so tender it made her heart ache.

"Rowan, did something happen to you?"

A stab of panic went through her. "What do you mean?"

"Something bad, in your past."

How could he know that?

She shook her head, her hair swinging softly against her bare shoulders. "I've put it behind me."

"So something did happen."

"Alright, yes." She pulled in a long breath. "I had... there was a man in college. God, I don't know what to tell you. I had a pretty rotten experience with him. And I... I didn't come away entirely intact. But it was a long time ago. I'm a different person now. Stronger."

But the last word came out on a sob.

"Ah, Rowan."

Before she had time to think about it he pulled her into his arms, tight against his chest, and the damn tears were coming fast, sliding down her cheeks in hot, traitorous streaks.

She was still shaking her head, still trying to deny it. Foolish, but she was used to fighting it, these old memories, the old hurt. And with Christian's arms around her, his heart thudding beneath her cheek, it was too hard. She wanted to just let go, to let it all out. But she was afraid if she did, she'd never get it under control again.

He stroked her hair and whispered, "Someday we'll talk more about this."

"Just not now."

"Yes, not now."

She breathed out her relief on a long exhalation, paused and inhaled the warm honey scent of his sleepy body. Nothing had ever smelled better to her. Sexy and comforting at the same time. She just wanted to be here, to bask in his presence, to let her body buzz with desire, to let her mind empty.

"Why don't you get in the shower, then we'll go have some breakfast."

"You don't want me to cook for you naked on my knees?"

He laughed, a low sound that rumbled against her ear. "Feeling better, are we?"

She smiled to herself. "Maybe."

"In that case, naked breakfast might not be a bad idea. But there's something I want to show you today, and as much as I love to see you naked, you'll have to be dressed for this."

"Where are we going?"

"Ah, too many questions. You'll have to wait to find out. I have my secrets, too." He swept her into his arms and stood up with her, carried her down the short flight of stairs to the second floor, where he set her down outside the bathroom door. "Be ready in half an hour."

❧

Christian's Cadillac moved through the Los Angeles streets, gliding over the pavement soundlessly and with little sense of motion. He navigated traffic smoothly, driving as he did everything else, with the greatest confidence and ease. Rowan loved seeing him like this, out in the world. Loved seeing his assurance and innate physical grace against the backdrop of the busy city.

From behind her sunglasses, she studied his profile. In the winter sunlight, the tips of his lashes glowed auburn. She'd never noticed before how long they were. His hair was pulled away from his face, as it always was, revealing the strong lines of his features. She wished she could see his hair down, just once. It was so pale it was almost silver, and the straight strands looked thick and silky. What would it be like to feel all that hair draped against her naked skin as he held himself over her, made love to her?

But no, that wasn't going to happen. It was in their contract: no sex. And when had she begun to think of it as making love, anyway? She shook her head, trying to clear her mind of the image that made her body burn with desire and her heart ache.

"You alright?" His voice startled her out of her musings.

"What? Yes. I'm fine."

He turned a quick smile on her before focusing once more on the road. "Are you?"

She didn't say anything.

"I've learned to read you. I can see those wheels turning in your head. What else is going on?"

"What else? What isn't?" She turned to watch the scenery rolling past the windows of the car. Shops and restaurants slipped by, the big, sleek body of the Cadillac reflected in the windows. She caught a glimpse of her own reflection. Did she really look so small and pale behind her big sunglasses?

"I know you're struggling, Rowan," he said quietly.

"We've already talked about that."

"Yes. But that doesn't mean we don't ever need to discuss it again." He paused. "You know, we all go through this transition period going into the lifestyle, whether from the top or the bottom."

She lifted her hand and touched her fingertips to the window. The glass was cool against her skin. "I'm not sure I ever really did."

"Didn't you?"

"I felt as soon as I became a top that it was the right thing for me. It worked for me from the start."

"Working for you is not necessarily the same thing as being right for you."

"You only say that because I'm bottoming for you now." She was angry again. Defensive.

"Not only because you're bottoming for me, Rowan. But because you slipped into it so easily, so beautifully. Do you know how responsive you are? How easily you go down into subspace? Last night—"

"Don't hold last night over my head!"

He glanced at her again, then back to the road in front of him. "Last night was incredible."

"Last night was . . . Last night doesn't mean that I'm not still a top."

"I don't agree. I think it means exactly that." His voice was quiet, but firm.

"I'm not a weak person, Christian. Just because I can play at being the bottom . . . it means nothing!"

"You're not playing at anything and we both know it. And it's me you're talking to, Rowan. It's me you're doing this with. You know damn well I won't hold it over your head. I'm not him."

She couldn't deny it. She was being foolish. But she couldn't let it go. She dragged her hair away from her face, her fingers tangling in the waves. She gave a frustrated tug.

"Okay. You're right. All I'm saying is that this one experience with you does not define who or what I am."

"Of course not."

Why was he being so damned agreeable?

He went on. "But it does indicate a specific ability, a need. There is no way last night would have happened if this were entirely unnatural for you. Christ, Rowan, last night was . . . powerful! How can you deny that? It was a breakthrough of sorts, even with you lying there, perfectly still. I have some understanding of what had to be going on in your head. I've seen it before. So have you. And you know exactly what I'm talking about."

She hated that he was right. She wasn't ready to agree with him, to throw her strength away so easily.

No matter how good it felt to hand herself over to him. To submit.

"Alright, yes, there is something to it, of course there is." Her hands fell into her lap and she had to fight not to twist them together.

"Do you miss being a top? Do you miss your submissive boys?"

She shook her head, then said quietly, "No."

"Don't you think that means something?"

"Maybe it means I'm distracted right now."

"Do you honestly think that's the whole truth?"

"I don't know. This is all happening so fast. I can't wrap my head around it. I'm okay while it's happening, but then later..." She stopped and gave another helpless shake of her head.

"But then when you stop to think about it, you're always ready to run again. Is that it?"

"Yes!"

"I won't let you."

That should have made her angry, his quiet declaration. But it didn't. It made her feel safe. As though she had no choice in the matter. How did that even make sense?

She turned to gaze out the window again. They were deep in the center of Beverly Hills. The classic architecture, the gold accents and elegant striped awnings of Rodeo Drive were familiar to her. Yet she felt totally out of her element on the inside. She had to find a way to calm down.

Christian's voice was low, certain. "Someday you will open up to me, Rowan. And on that day, you will be free of these fears, these thoughts that hold you back. I promise you."

He reached over and gave her hand a squeeze. Her whole body gave a small shudder of pleasure. Her heart surged once more in her chest, but whether it was a surge of fear or of hope, she couldn't tell. She remained silent.

"Here we are."

He pulled the car over and a valet opened her door. She stepped onto the street.

"The Price Gallery?"

He smiled, a flash of strong, white teeth that warmed her insides and made her wish she were back at his house, naked in his bed. "I want to show you my work."

"I've been curious about your work. You always keep your larger pieces covered."

"One of those artistic eccentricities. I don't show anyone anything until it's done. Come."

He held the heavy door open for her and ushered her into the building. They passed through a marble-lined foyer, past enormous urns overflowing with European-style floral arrangements, and into the main gallery. Immediately a chic young woman in a designer suit, her blond hair pulled back into a classic chignon, stepped from behind a desk and came to greet them.

"Mr. Thorne, how nice to see you. May I bring you and your guest a drink? A cappuccino, perhaps? Or champagne?"

He turned to Rowan. "Anything?"

"No, thank you."

"Nothing for us, thank you, Jeanette. Is Sterling in?"

"Mr. Price is in his office. I'll notify him right away that you're here."

She left and they moved into the gallery. The space was enormous, with vaulted ceilings and white marble floors. In the first display room were statues done in marble and stone; large pieces with lovely, sinuous lines that immediately brought to mind the classic masters: Canova, Rodin. Rowan moved in to take a closer look.

"Are these yours?"

"Yes."

"They're gorgeous."

She stood before one life-size piece depicting two nude women twined in an embrace. Their lips were a breath apart, as though at any moment they would seal in a kiss. Their bodies were pressed close together, their breasts crushed against one another.

"This is beautiful. Erotic. But I'm sure you've heard that before. And I'm certainly no expert."

"Your opinion is important to me."

She turned to him. He was perfectly serious.

"Why?"

He paused, his brows, so much darker than his hair, drawing together. He looked as though he was trying to find a way to word his answer.

"Ah, Christian, there you are."

Rowan turned to see the tall, elegant man to whom the English-accented voice belonged. His gray hair was combed away from a sharp-featured face that was handsome even though the lines on his skin showed his years.

Christian laid a warm hand on the small of her back. "Rowan, this is Sterling Price, my oldest and closest friend. Sterling, Rowan Cassidy."

The older gentleman reached out to take her hand. "Lovely, yes."

"It's nice to meet you, Mr. Price."

He hadn't let go of her hand. "But you must call me Sterling, my dear."

She nodded her head.

"What do you think of his work?" Sterling gave a small wave of his hand.

"I think it's beautiful. Sensual." Her gaze wandered back to the statue of the two women. "The lines are so smooth, fluid. It makes me want to touch it."

Christian was beside her. He said quietly into her hair, "Do it. Touch it, if you like."

She reached out and slid her fingertips along the cheekbone of one of the female figures. The stone was cool beneath her skin, but warmed quickly. She had a sudden urge to touch their almost-joined lips. She pulled her hand away as heat built in her body. Even this statue held an aura of sex for her. Everything did lately.

She turned to Christian. "Who are they?"

"Just models."

Would she soon be nothing more than just a model? Her stomach gave a quick, tight squeeze. And she knew with sudden, aching clarity that she couldn't stand for that to happen. Knew that Christian was making a huge impact on her life. On her very soul. And she had to be important to him. If not, then what did all of this mean?

She was afraid to find out. But what was it she was really afraid of? That she would mean nothing to Christian? Or that he would mean far too much to her?

ထရ

Christian watched Rowan move around the gallery, watched the way she examined each piece of sculpture as though she was truly drawn to it. He was inordinately pleased with himself, with her response to his work. And he'd seen the way Sterling had looked at her. His friend must have some understanding now of what he'd been saying about her, about his need to immortalize her on canvas, in stone.

Christ, when she'd touched that first piece, the two women, his cock had sprung to life, filling and aching so he could barely breathe. Something about the way she used her hands...

Sterling was still eyeing her as she stepped from one piece to another. Her black hair was gorgeous under the gallery lights, a shining curtain of jet waves cascading down her delicate back. Made Christian want to wrap his fist around it and pull her head back so he could take her mouth and...

Jesus, man, get it under control!

"Oh, I love this one..." Her voice was a breathy exhalation of awe.

She stood before a tiny piece, a nude figure in miniature of a woman laid out on her back, arms draped over her head, very much in the same position Rowan had been in the night before. Even though the stone was no more than sixteen inches in length, he'd worked for months on the detail. It was one of his favorite pieces.

He left Sterling's side to cross the room to where Rowan stood, her blue eyes aglow.

"She's called *Nyad*. One of the few pieces I did without a model."

"She's gorgeous. No, that's not even the right word. There's a dreamlike quality to her." She ran one slow finger down the statue, from the form's clasped hands to the delicate ankles.

"You should have her." He knew instantly it was the right thing to do.

"What?" She gave a small laugh. "No, I couldn't."

"You must. I insist." He turned to find Sterling smiling benevolently at him, one brow raised. Oh, yes, they would have to talk later. "Sterling, can you please have someone take care of this for me? Have it sent to my place."

"Of course."

"Thank you."

Sterling disappeared toward the back of the gallery. Christian turned back to Rowan.

"You can't mean this." She was shaking her head, her dark fall of hair brushing her shoulders.

"I never do or say anything I don't mean."

She gazed into his eyes, hers full of emotion she was trying very hard to hide. "I think I'm beginning to understand that. Thank you."

"You're welcome."

Why did it please him so much to make her happy? The solid warmth of satisfaction filled him, buoyed him, just seeing her smile.

He wanted to bring her pleasure. He'd known that from the start. But that was beginning to change, wasn't it? To expand beyond what either of them had expected.

Don't get carried away.

Still, it was hard not to, with Rowan right here in front of him. Her skin was almost translucent, like fragile, pale silk, and that mouth of hers, so damn sexy, especially when she smiled, as she did now.

He wanted to kiss her. Wanted it almost more than he'd wanted anything in his life. He didn't really give a damn anymore about any agreement.

He stepped forward. She tilted her chin and raised her

gaze to his. He touched her cheek with one fingertip, drew it down the line of her jaw. Her long, dark lashes fluttered against the high curves of her cheekbones, bringing his attention back to her pink mouth. Her lips parted, she looked back up at him. She blinked once more, her eyes dilating, her cheeks flushed with color.

His heart was pounding. It would be so easy. Just move in, take her mouth, crush it beneath his.

"Christian, I'll have the piece to your house this evening."

Damn it.

He turned to Sterling. "Thank you."

It took him a few moments to force his breathing back into a normal, steady rhythm. Behind him, he heard Rowan draw in a deep breath.

He didn't know whether to curse his friend, or to be grateful to have been saved from making a mistake.

But would it be a mistake? He didn't know anymore. Yes, they had an agreement, more than that, a contract, which in their world was sacred.

But there was such a thing as renegotiation.

No, he didn't feel that would be fair to Rowan. It would seem too much as though he were taking advantage of her when she was confused.

He knew all this, but it wasn't helping right now. He was damn tired of being noble.

Maybe he wasn't the Dom he'd thought himself to be. Hell, nothing was what he'd thought it to be lately. Not since Rowan. And she was standing there, she and Sterling both, waiting for him to say something.

He cleared his throat.

"Well, why don't we go have some lunch? Sterling, can you join us?"

"Thank you, not today. But we'll catch up later."

He didn't miss Sterling's pointed tone. Yes, they'd talk later. But he didn't feel like explaining his thoughts, his actions, right now. Not even to himself.

လ၁

The terrace at the Ivy was crowded with the usual Hollywood elite, but they were seated quickly at an umbrella-shaded table in a corner against the quaint white picket fence. The dim February sunshine was coming through the scattered clouds, making it warm enough to eat outside.

He loved the way the sun glinted in her hair, in glowing touches of fire blue. What was his obsession with her hair today? But he had to admit he was beginning to become obsessed with everything about her. He wished he could see the color of her eyes behind her dark glasses.

They ordered; salads for them both. He was too amped up today to eat anything heavier. But he ordered a nice bottle of wine, a good vintage pinot noir. Rowan seemed relaxed, happy, comfortable in this environment.

"Have you eaten here before?" he asked her.

"Of course. It's the best place to stop after a day of shopping."

"Ah, you're one of those women who shop."

"It's a favorite pastime. But I have other, more noble pursuits."

He laughed. "Like what?"

"I love to read. I'll read almost anything. I love the classics; I'll read Dickens, Shakespeare."

"That fits you."

Their wine arrived. He approved the first pour with a nod and the waiter filled their glasses. He picked his up and sipped.

Rowan's fingers rested on the stem of her glass. "I also love to read romance novels."

"Really?" Why did that amuse him?

Her gorgeous mouth quirked in a small grin. "Yes. Really. And biographies, history, suspense novels."

"What else?" He leaned toward her. He was suddenly voracious; he wanted to know everything about her.

"Well, you've seen my collection of photographic art. I love art of any kind, love to go to museums. I particularly love the small collections at the Getty."

"Then you must have seen the Robert Adams exhibition there."

"Yes, just a few weeks ago. I love his work. It's so... stark, raw."

"Exactly. He's one of my favorite photographic artists."

"I was thinking... when we were at the gallery just now I glimpsed a piece of surrealist sculpture in another room. And I made this sort of connection. Do you know the painting *The Garden of Earthly Delights* by Hieronymus Bosch?"

"Of course. It portrays the various sins of the flesh, in all its lurid glory. Some people think it's erotic." He took a sip of his wine, wondering where she was going with this.

"I sometimes think of those of us in the BDSM lifestyle like that, in terms of that painting. But sensual and sinuous, rather than vulgar and sad, the way Bosch thought of it from his Puritan perspective. I mean, he called it a garden of delights, but what he meant was a garden of immorality, of sins, as you said."

Christian grinned. "I'm perfectly happy to be a sinner."

She shook her head. "What I'm saying is, the way we live is delight and sin all at the same time."

"That only makes for a more beautiful and intriguing garden."

He felt a surge of excitement that she knew art, that she had such an interest in it. That she thought about these things. He leaned forward in his chair. "What do you think of sculpture?"

She smiled. "I love yours. But you know that."

There was that wash of pure pleasure again.

"What about you, Christian? What do you like to do besides sculpt and paint and hurt pretty little girls?"

He laughed. He loved those moments when her wicked side emerged.

"I like to travel. But I've done enough of that for a while."

"How long did you live in Europe?"

"Five years. It was enough. I need to be here for a while. I got to a point in my life where I felt the urge to set down roots. This is home for me. So, here I am."

She leaned forward, rested her chin in her hand. Her lush little mouth was so pink and alluring, he had to make an effort to pay attention to what she was saying.

"Why now? I mean, why do you think you suddenly felt this need to settle down?"

"I don't know that it was sudden. It was a sort of evolution. I traveled the world, lived in foreign cities. It was all exciting enough at first, but then it just became the norm to live in Paris, London, Berlin. Whatever. It all became the same. The people all became the same."

"And people aren't all the same in Los Angeles?"

"Maybe." He paused, sipped his wine. "You're different."

That seemed to take her by surprise. She sat back, turned her head away for a moment, then back to face him.

"Am I?"

"Yes."

She pulled her sunglasses off, revealing her gaze to him. She searched his face, as though looking for something. The truth, maybe? There was something in her eyes that hit him right in the gut. Then she took a deep, sighing breath and put her dark glasses back on.

What had that been about?

Their salads arrived and they ate in relative silence, chatting here and there about inconsequential things. But once back in his car, he could feel the sense of being alone with her, isolated from the rest of the world. Which, he realized, was exactly what he wanted.

He took the surface streets back to the beach. She was quiet on the ride, giving him time to think about their conversations; today's, and the other talks they'd had during their time together.

She was coming to trust him, and more importantly, to trust herself. She was no longer constantly questioning, fighting. And she was really beginning to open up to him, to let him in.

She was a most amazing woman.

When he glanced over at her, her head instantly turned toward him, as though she'd felt him looking at her. Tension hummed between them. His groin tightened as he watched her breasts rise and fall beneath her thin sweater. She was feeling it, too.

They reached Venice and he pulled into the driveway, helped her out of the car. He fumbled with his keys at the back door, his nerves strung tight suddenly. Why did he feel like this? Like some kid on his first date.

He opened the door and led her inside, tossed his keys on the counter.

Rowan was standing there, waiting for him. He moved toward her and reaching out, took off her sunglasses and laid them on the counter behind him. She had that look in her sapphire eyes again, that searching look. Her dark brows were drawn together. He moved closer, so that she had to tilt her delicate chin to look up at him.

Her eyes were shadowed, emotion flashing through them. He thought he knew just how she felt. A lot had happened just in the last twenty-four hours, and it had changed the dynamic between them. They both sensed it. Impossible not to.

God, he needed to touch her. Knew he was about to. Knew she would let him.

"Christian?" Her voice was a breathy whisper.

Damn it.

He couldn't stop himself. Didn't want to.

He took her chin in his hand and bent over her, brushed her lips with his. She was so damned sweet. Her whole body seemed to melt into him instantly.

He pressed his lips to hers again, harder this time, really feeling the texture of her mouth. His whole body hardened at the contact.

More.

He pulled back a fraction of an inch, tasted her satin lips with his tongue. She let out a moan that made his cock strain beneath his slacks. Then he moved in and really kissed her. Her mouth opened immediately, her lips parting to let him in. His tongue first swept her teeth, then met her tongue. She was open and eager, yielding to him completely.

He wrapped his hands around her small waist, dragged her body closer, so that she was pressed right up against him. The soft crush of her breasts against his chest was almost too much. And her tongue was in his mouth now.

Jesus.

He broke the kiss. She was panting as hard as he was.

He took her chin in his hand once more, looked into her eyes. They were glazed with lust. Her lips were swollen, slightly parted, flushed with color.

"I won't do anything without your consent, Rowan. You know that."

"Yes."

"You have to tell me you want this."

A stab of panic lanced through him. What the hell would he do if she said no? "Do you?"

"Yes!"

His body surged with an almost unbearable pleasure at her answer. Then he swept her into his arms and carried her up the two flights of stairs to his bed.

T E N

Rowan didn't want to stop to question what was happening. All she knew was that for once she was exactly where she needed to be at that moment, in Christian's arms.

They entered the studio and he quickly moved across the room and sat her on his big bed. She was breathless with anticipation, ignoring the warnings going off in the back of her mind.

Christian pulled his shirt off, revealing his broad, beautiful chest, then bent over her and slid her sweater over her head. The censorious voices in her brain faded away. She couldn't wait for him to put his hands on her. Couldn't wait to touch him, finally. She didn't care that they'd agreed not to do this. She only knew that she needed him.

He knelt at the end of the bed and gently pulled her boots from her feet, then helped her off with her wool slacks before removing his own, leaving him in a pair of black boxer-briefs. His erection was huge, straining against the cotton fabric. She wanted it in her hands. In her mouth. Inside her body.

Then he reached back and pulled the black band from his hair, letting it fall loose around his shoulders. Long, thick strands of the palest blond. She couldn't wait to touch it. He looked different with his hair down, more frankly sexual, with that corn silk around his strong face, such a contrast to his angular features. God, if she'd seen him like this sooner, she'd never have been able to keep her hands off him.

He snaked one hand behind her neck and laid her back on the bed, covering her body with his. His hair fell forward, cool satin brushing her cheeks, her shoulders, making her shiver. She could feel every ridge and plane of him; he felt so good pressed against her. Her nipples swelled, peaked to two hard points, craving his touch. She wanted her bra off *now*.

He settled in, his body pressing into hers. She loved the weight of him, the touch of his skin against her needy flesh. She wrapped her arms around his broad back, pulling him closer. His silky hair was all around her now. She breathed in the clean scent of it. Reaching up, she let her fingers tangle in his thick locks. Yes, exactly like silk, and so heavy in her hands. She turned her head to brush her lips against it.

Lovely.

When his engorged cock came to rest in the vee between her thighs she thought she'd lose her mind. Groaning, she moved her hips, trying to let him know what she so desperately needed.

He bent his head and started kissing her again, and she was momentarily distracted by his lips, his hot, wet tongue in her mouth. God, the man knew how to kiss. Knew how to light every nerve in her body with his clever mouth. He pushed his tongue in, out, pausing to bite and nip at her lips, to lick them, to suck.

Then he moved his head away and swept his lips over her throat, hitting that sweet spot where her neck met her collarbone, and pausing to lick and suck there. Her breasts ached, her sex filled and pulsed with need as his long hair feathered over her skin with every motion, adding to the sensations he was causing with his mouth.

When he moved his head lower and bit her nipple through the sheer fabric of her bra she thought she would come right then and there.

"Please, Christian," she begged.

He raised his big body from hers long enough to unclasp her bra and take her breasts into his hands.

Oh, yes, this was what she craved. He kneaded her bare flesh in his palms, drew back to tease her hard nipples with his fingertips. Her body surged, arching into his touch. He lowered his head and took one nipple into his mouth. The damp heat stunned her; her sex, her body, filled with an almost crushing desire.

"Yes," she breathed.

His mouth on her almost sent her over the edge. Then he was moving his hands down her body, leaving tiny sparks of nearly orgasmic sensation as they went. He tore her thong down over her legs, and she spread her thighs for him. Then his hands were everywhere at once, sliding over her thighs, down her calves, back up. She strained beneath him, needing him to touch her *there*, wild with need and his hot, sucking mouth at her breast.

Finally, he slipped a hand between her thighs and teased her cleft with his fingertips. She was going to come any moment.

"Please, Christian."

"What do you need?" His voice was deep and rough.

"I need you to touch me. I need to come. I need you to fuck me. Please."

She reached down and wrapped her fingers around his cock. It was thick and hot in her hand, a shaft of steel-hard velvet. She gave a squeeze. He moaned.

"Then come for me, Rowan."

He took her nipple into his mouth once more, then moved his hand over her mound so that his palm pressed onto her clit, rubbing hard, while he slipped two of his fingers inside her. A shock of sensation jolted her, and her orgasm came crashing down on her like a thunderbolt.

She cried out, bucked her hips into his hand. Pleasure stabbed at her body; her nipples, her sex. Wave after wave of crushing intensity. And before it was over he had pulled a condom from the nightstand, sheathed himself, and was lowering himself over her, between her thighs, and pushing into her.

He was so big, she wasn't certain she could take him. But her body quickly opened to him, and he slid inside.

"Christ, you feel like heaven, Rowan," he ground out. Then he started to move.

His hips thrust, and she gasped in pleasure. He filled her completely. She could swear she felt every ridge on his cock, the round, pulsing head. He drew out, then slowly pushed back into her. Her sex clenched, held him tight.

"Faster, Christian." She slid her hands down over the firm flesh of his ass and pulled him closer. His skin was smooth and hot beneath her palms.

"I don't want to hurt you."

"You won't. I need this."

He groaned, bent his head to suck on that tender spot at her neck, his hair falling all over her bare flesh once more, and pushed deeper inside her. Pleasure shafted through her. He drew back, thrust again, harder this time.

"Yes, that's what I need," she murmured, lost in sensation.

He moved faster, thrusting harder, deeper, and she felt another climax begin to build. His hands were everywhere, gliding over her skin; her sides, her thighs; then they slid under her and he grabbed her ass, tilting her hips so that he could move even deeper inside. She burrowed into his neck, inhaled his masculine scent. *Wonderful.* She opened her mouth and sucked at his flesh, his skin like honey beneath her tongue; he tasted exactly as he smelled.

He started a strong, even rhythm, pumping into her. Each powerful thrust brought her climax closer to the surface, until it was a keen edge her body rode, waiting for release. She wanted to hold back, to enjoy the sheer pleasure of it for as long as she could, the exquisite knowledge that this was *him* inside her. But he pounded into her, his cock moving in and out of her body, and it was too much for her.

The first waves of her climax shot through her like lightning, burning her, branding her. Sensation spread until she was shaking all over with it. Her sex clenched around his swollen cock while he plunged wildly into her. He groaned aloud, every muscle in his body tensing, and together they came in a wanton frenzy, their moans driving each other on.

Finally, he collapsed on top of her, his breath coming in ragged gasps. They were both damp with sweat. The musky scent of sex was everywhere. She was weak and limp, her limbs still buzzing with the tremendous power of her orgasm. She didn't want to move, wasn't sure she could if she had to.

And she loved the weight of him on her, didn't want him to leave her.

Yes, stay with me.

Her heart squeezed. She knew there was no promise of permanence here. She'd never asked for there to be, never wanted it before. Why now?

Don't think about it.

That was getting to be a mantra for her, wasn't it? But now was not the time. Now she simply wanted to enjoy the last trembling vibrations of climax moving through her body. Wanted to luxuriate in the satisfied weakness of her limbs, and the sensation of Christian's body so close to hers.

She focused on the rough cadence of his breathing. Their bodies were fused together with sweat. She moved her face into his neck and inhaled, wanting to remember the scent of him, the scent of them together.

Minutes passed. Finally, he raised his head and kissed her gently on the mouth. It was a sweet kiss, a grateful kiss. She knew just how he felt. She was grateful, too, to finally give their bodies to each other in this way. Even if it never happened again.

Would it?

But she didn't want to think about the consequences or the future now. She wanted him to kiss her again.

He did, pressing his lips onto hers, opening them with his tongue, moving into her mouth in slow, sweet strokes. Her body began to buzz with lust once more.

He pulled away, rolled onto his back, taking her with him so that her head rested on his chest. His fingers tangled in her hair. Beneath her ear, his heart beat in a slow, steady rhythm. She knew that rhythm, knew it in every cell of her being. Why did that make her want to cry?

She had to get her ranging emotions under control. She knew too damned well what could happen if she really let herself feel something for this man. She couldn't allow it. She bit her lip, bit back the threatening tears.

No, she would get her feelings under control. When this thirty days was over, she would be back in command of herself, which was how it had to be. Control was the key. How had she ever thought it was a good idea to give that up? Look where it had gotten her, every time.

She had made a mistake, a huge error in judgment. She'd been too cocky, thinking she could keep it all together under these circumstances. But it wasn't too late to fix it. Was it?

⨯⨯

She knew she hadn't slept more than a few fitful hours when she felt Christian stir. She glanced at the clock: seven A.M. She'd been up thinking and just listening to him breathe until at least three. He rolled over, kissed her forehead. Such a tender move, she thought sleepily.

"Rowan," he whispered, his voice rough with sleep.

"Hmm?"

"I just remembered I have a meeting. I have to get up. Promise me you'll stay here today."

"Why wouldn't I?"

But even as she said it she knew she'd been planning since last night to take off, to get away so she could get her head on straight.

"I know we need to talk about what happened last night. About the fact that I broke our contract. And we will, I swear to you. I'll only be gone a few hours. Promise me."

He knew her, didn't he? Knew her first reaction was to run away. And what did that say about her? It was different seeing herself through someone else's eyes. She wasn't entirely happy with what she saw there.

"Alright, yes. I'll stay."

Blinking away the tightness in her chest, she looked up at him. His eyes were shadowed in the morning light, but it was emotion more than the half-light of day coming in through the windows that caused the shifting in his gaze.

She wished he would kiss her again. She wished she were brave enough to wrap her arms around his neck and pull him to her body. But she couldn't make herself do it.

His hair was still loose from last night, a long sheet of pale blond, the color of moonlight. Even tangled a bit from sleep, it was unbelievably gorgeous. She remembered the silky feel of it on her skin. The scent of it.

God.

It was better he was going for a while today. She really had to pull herself together.

He lifted her hand to his lips and laid a soft kiss across her knuckles.

"I'll be back as soon as I can."

Then he was up and out of the bed. She watched him as he stalked, naked, across the room, and she really saw for the first time the way he was made; the long, muscular legs, the tight buttocks. His back rippled with muscle. She loved the way his hair hung down over his shoulders. She could fall in love with hair like that.

She could fall in love with him.

But that was exactly the point, wasn't it? She could not allow that to happen.

Panic set in as she realized there was still too much time left in their agreement. Too much time alone with him; almost another two weeks. She had to get away, for a little while at least, or she was really going to come apart.

Once she was sure he'd had enough time to get in the shower, she threw on a heavy robe he had hanging from a hook on the wall and crept downstairs to the kitchen. She pulled her cell phone from her purse and dialed northern California.

ॐ

Rowan leaned back into her seat and waited for the plane to level out. She hated takeoff and landing; it always made her nervous.

Finally, the bell dinged and the flight attendant announced that they could get up and move around the cabin. Rowan pulled a file out of her briefcase and quickly checked her itinerary and hotel reservations for San Francisco.

She'd been meaning to make a follow-up visit to this client, anyway. Now was as good a time as any. They'd been pleased when she'd called that morning to tell them she was coming.

Christian had not been pleased at all. But he'd had to accept it when she told him it was business. He didn't have to know she'd volunteered for this trip, that it wasn't entirely necessary. By the time he'd returned to the house, she'd had twenty minutes before the taxi would come to take her to the airport. No time to talk.

She didn't want to talk yet. She wasn't ready for some big conversation. She had to figure things out in her own head first. And leaving L.A. was the only way she could do that. If she'd stayed, she would have just ended up back in his bed, mindless, senseless, breathless.

She was already half mindless. She couldn't believe she'd forgotten her laptop. She was thinking that she might ask Christian to overnight it to her. But she could get by with the company's computer system for the next two days. She was thankful she always kept her briefcase and a garment bag with a business suit in the trunk of her car so she hadn't had to go back to her apartment first. It was enough to carry her through two days.

What would she do when she got back? It depended, she supposed, on the conclusions she came to while she was away. And the conclusions Christian came to as well.

All she could think about, even now, was his body stretched out over hers, the scent of his hair, the way he fit her perfectly, custom made for her. And the way he made her feel when he looked at her, when he touched her. As though she were everything. But she knew she wasn't.

He needed a woman who could give her heart to him. A woman without secrets. A woman who was whole.

She knew deep down she would have to give him up sooner or later. And that was the question, wasn't it? Would it be sooner? Or later?

ॐ

Ashlyn watched Gabriel stretch, his long arms reaching high over his head, the muscles lengthening, flexing. She loved waking to him in the morning, watching him as he slept. She loved his heavy, dark lashes, his long, lean body, the hard-cut muscle everywhere.

She was afraid to think of what else she might love about him.

He was warm in the bed next to her, and her body was already responding, molten heat flickering like a tongue at her sex. When he turned his head and smiled at her sleepily, her chest constricted.

He rolled over, right on top of her, and began to kiss in a long line down her neck, between her breasts, lower still. His tongue danced at her navel, traced a path down her abdomen, making her sex clench in anticipation.

He moved her thighs apart with his hands, ordered her to hold still before bending his head to his task. She moaned when his tongue lanced out, hot and wet against her clit. God, he knew just how to do it, too, knew her body after all these nights together. Knew just what she needed, how she liked it. He tortured her with pleasure.

His tongue was driving harder now, licking and sucking. Her body warmed, tingled, rose in a dizzying spiral to that crest. She balanced there for one lovely, excruciating moment. Then he pushed his fingers inside her and sucked on her clit hard. She came, exploded, light rippling behind her tightly closed eyelids. Tremors of pleasure washed over her, leaving her shaking and hot all over.

Yes, he knew exactly what her body desired. But she could never let him know what she craved most.

This was more than just sex, more than the BDSM play. And it hurt. It hurt that it could never really be more. That she could never really have him in the way her heart was beginning to yearn for.

She knew what she had to do. She had given him her body, but her heart she would hold safe. No matter how much it hurt to do it. At least she would come away intact.

Christian closed Rowan's laptop and sat, stunned, at his desk. Not just by the writing, which he thought was really good. No, more than that, he thought it was excellent. But he could so clearly see what she was doing here. Did she even know?

He could see her own struggle within the character she wrote about; it was right there, in between every word she'd typed. Did she see it? Was this her way of working her own issues out, or was this a subconscious act?

Why had she never told him she was a writer? Why would this be a secret, especially from him? He was an artist; this was something he could understand, this connection between emotion and creation.

But she held a lot of secrets close, didn't she?

He got up and stalked the length of his office. He shouldn't have looked at her work. It had been inexcusably invasive of him. But she'd left her laptop right here, wide open, and when he'd gone to move it aside the screensaver had faded away, leaving the open document there for him to see. He was surprised she hadn't been more careful.

Maybe some part of her had wanted him to see it? Maybe deep down she wanted to share this with him.

That was probably wishful thinking. She was still as closed to him as she'd ever been, beyond a certain point. He felt compelled to get through to her, to help her. To heal her.

But who the hell was he to do this if she didn't want him to?

The telephone on the desk rang and he jumped on it, anticipating Rowan's voice.

"Hello?"

"Christian, Sterling here."

"Ah, yes, hi."

Sterling let out a low chuckle. "Don't sound so glad to hear from me."

"Sorry. It's not you."

Another chuckle. "Never thought I'd see the day when the infamous international playboy was lovesick."

"Come on, Sterling. I've slept with my share of women, but I could hardly be called a playboy. And that term is out-dated, anyway."

"Is lovesick outdated, too?"

"Yes, maybe. I don't know. But I'm just...anxious to hear from her. She left on a trip today. I want to know that she got into San Francisco safely."

"When was the last time you worried about anyone, Christian?"

That caught him up short. Sterling had a damned good point. Since his mother had died he hadn't had anyone to worry about, except his sister. But she was safely married; she wasn't his worry any longer. And anyone outside of his family? He didn't care about anyone else that much, except perhaps Sterling.

Until now.

"What were you calling about, Sterling?"

"I wanted to let you know that statue should be at your place by tomorrow. Unless you need it sooner. Then I can send a messenger rather than our usual trucking company."

"No, tomorrow will be fine." He absentmindedly ran his fingers along the edge of the desk. "Sterling, let me ask you something."

"Anything, my boy. You know that."

"What made you say that? That you believe I'm love-sick?"

He expected another laugh, but his friend's voice was somber. "I've never seen you look at a woman the way you did at Rowan here in the gallery. And you've never given a piece of your art to a woman, that I know of. Hell, you've only given me two pieces and I've known you your entire adult life, been deeply involved in your career. It's in everything; the way you speak to her, the way you touch her, as though she is something very precious to you."

"She is," Christian said quietly, running a hand back over his ponytail.

"What are you going to do about her?" Sterling asked.

"I don't know. And it's not entirely up to me."

"She has a lot of strength. I could see it in her. She's a most interesting woman."

"Yes, she is." Christian glanced at her gray laptop sitting on his desk, the words still glowing on the screen. "A very interesting, enigmatic woman. She confuses the hell out of me."

"May I offer a word of advice?"

"Of course."

"Don't let her get away, Christian. I think you need her, whether you're ready to admit it or not."

He was quiet for a moment. Sterling knew him like nobody else on earth.

"Sterling."

"Yes?"

"I am in love with this woman. Whether she loves me back or not. And I don't know what the hell I'm going to do about it."

ঙ৶

Rowan sat at the small writing desk in her room at the San Francisco Hyatt, her briefcase open on the floor beside her, files open and scattered across the desktop. Outside, the sun was setting and the fog of the city was rolling in, as it always seemed to do, no matter what time of year. She was tired. Her head ached. And she missed Christian.

It had been alright during the day while she'd kept busy with work, surrounded by people. But now, alone in her room with night closing in, she had time to think.

That had been her real mission in leaving town, though, hadn't it? To think, finally. Now that she was here, the prospect of the process itself seemed almost too much for her. But she would do it. She had to.

She stood up and went to the phone beside the bed and dialed room service, ordered a bottle of red wine, a decent Cabernet from the Napa Valley. The wine would help her to unwind, which she desperately needed to do. A glass of wine and a hot shower, yes.

A few minutes later a knock at the door and a white-jacketed waiter wheeled in a small cart with the bottle of wine, two glasses, a corkscrew. He silently opened the bottle, poured, held a small glass out for her inspection. She tasted, nodded her approval, tucked some bills into his hand and he was gone. She knocked back the rest of the glass in one gulp. A shame to ruin a perfectly good glass of wine, but she needed it. She would savor the next one.

She poured herself another glass and picked up the phone again, thinking to dial Christian's house, to tell him she'd arrived safely. The dial tone droned in her ear. But she couldn't bring herself to make the call. Instead she dialed April's number. She picked up immediately.

"Hello."

"April, it's me. Rowan."

"Hi. Are you in San Francisco?"

"Yes. I know I came here to think and it's ridiculous that I'm calling you when I could have stayed in L.A. and talked to you, but I'm driving myself crazy."

"Tell me what's going on."

Rowan paced the floor, thinking as she spoke.

"It's Christian. And it's me. We had sex."

April was quiet for a moment. "Okay. It's not the end of the world. I mean, I know you broke your agreement, but obviously you both wanted to."

"It's not the contract. It's . . . the sex. It's what happened between us. God, I sound like I just lost my virginity to him. I don't know why the sex is so damn important."

"Sometimes it just is," April said quietly.

"I feel like I'm losing all control here. It's more than what's going on between us physically. He's really getting under my skin. Into my heart, if you want to know the truth. And I feel like my mind and my body belong to someone else. To him."

"Is it just too different for you? That you feel the need to dominate?"

"No. I really don't. My need for extreme sex is more than being met by Christian. And I'm discovering that the need is pretty basic. It almost doesn't matter what direction I approach it from, on that level. But to yield to another person, to give myself over completely . . . no, I can't do it. Not long-term."

"Can't you? You're doing it now."

"I don't know. But it's more than that. This is bringing up old issues, old wounds. And I don't always like what it makes me see about myself."

"That just makes this a learning experience."

"I can't learn at his expense." She paused in her pacing, rubbed her aching temple with her fingers. "I'm in love with him, April. And it scares me to death. I've known it for a while, but I haven't wanted to face it. God, I fell half in love with him the first night I was alone with him. He bound me in flowers, for God's sake. What kind of man does that?"

April was quiet, letting her talk it out.

"He has shaken my whole world, made me question

everything I thought I knew about myself. He is the only man in the world for whom I will go down on my knees. But I'm not a submissive."

"You keep saying that, but you've been submitting to him the last few weeks, enjoying it. You just told me it fulfills a need in you. Why are you hanging on so tenaciously to this need for control?"

"I don't know. I just need to, I need the control to make me feel safe." She paused, ran a hand through her hair. "Lord, I'm turning into my mother."

That idea hit her like a blow to the chest. Her mother: brilliant, manic control freak. Cold, unreachable.

Was that really who she wanted to be?

And when had that happened? She sipped from her glass, thinking, remembering. It was after that terrible year with Danny. In the process of pulling herself back together, building her strength, she had built a wall around herself. She hadn't truly let anyone in since then.

Her eyes stung with tears. Too awful, that she'd lived like this the whole time. She'd felt so secure in the knowledge that Danny no longer had any control over her life, but that was a lie. Because what he'd done to her still affected her every interaction with other people. That's what he had turned her into.

She was beyond being angry about it. And she wouldn't wallow in the sense of defeat this epiphany had brought. But she could certainly try to begin to change it.

"I don't know what to do, April."

"It sounds to me like you want to be with him, if you can stop fighting it."

"But how can I risk opening to him? What if I end up broken again? I just don't know."

"How can you not? How can you turn away from him, from your feelings for him?"

"I have two more days here to figure that out." And to miss him so much it made her skin ache.

She knew already she was going back to him. Consequences be damned. She had to. Because she couldn't stay away.

ELEVEN

April watched Decker pace back and forth before her. He'd had her strip down the moment she'd arrived at his house, as usual. Then he'd picked her up, carried her upstairs, and laid her down on his big bed. She'd brought her chrome toy, just as he had asked. He held it now in one hand; in the other was a small flogger, the tails made of square-cut lengths of black rubber. It was a toy they both loved. She adored the sharp sting of the rubber; he admired the red welts it left on her skin. She shivered in anticipation, looking at the devices he had armed himself with. When he moved closer, standing right over her, her sex quivered as well.

He started right in with the evil little whip, stroking it over her breasts, her stomach. The rubber brushed her skin, so lightly she barely felt it, but she knew this wouldn't last long. He was building her up, bringing the blood to the surface, warming her. He bent down, leaned in closer, until she could feel the faint pant of his breath on her cheek as he worked. He moved the flogger, focusing now on her nipples, which were rock-hard and wanting. He struck a little harder, the rubber tails stinging, exciting her, making her blood pound in her veins.

Yes.

Her sex was wet already, and she couldn't stop thinking of the chrome vibrator he still held. He moved down, the flogger slapping against her stomach, her abdomen.

"Open for me, April."

She obeyed immediately, spreading her thighs, allowing the flogger to caress her mound in quick, steady strokes, the rubber biting tantalizingly into her flesh.

"Tell me what you need, April."

"I need..." She paused, trying to catch enough breath to speak. He knew what she wanted, of course; he simply loved to hear her ask for it. "I want the vibe, Sir. Please."

"Then you shall have it."

She watched as he lowered the sleek tool between her legs, closed her eyes at the first cool contact. He swept it lightly over her cleft, back and forth, teasing her. The rubber flogger was still moving across her nipples in hot, stinging arcs. She moaned and arched her hips.

"No, April. Hold still."

She bit her lip and tried, but her sex was aching with need, desire pulsing through her body in a steady beat.

"That's better, my girl."

To her surprise, he moved in and pressed the buzzing vibrator right against her clit, held it there. She started to come almost instantly, and he didn't order her to hold back. She let the climax wash over her, sharp currents of pleasure rolling through her system.

"Again," he said, his voice hoarse.

He held the vibrator to her, and the buzzing instrument did its work; that and the flogger still torturing her tender nipples. They were absolutely on fire, fueling the sensations in her sex. The second climax came quickly, hard and fast and intense. She shook all over as pleasure stabbed through her.

When the last tremors had passed, she was panting. She looked up at him, and his dark gaze was fixed on her face. She didn't know what to think of it. But before she had time to wonder, he was turning her over onto her stomach.

"On your knees now. Put your head down, arch your back. Yes."

She did as he asked, there was no question about it. She held herself up, her arms and legs shaky with the after-effects of her orgasms.

"Spread your legs wider. Good."

He immediately went to work with the flogger again, even strokes that were tiny, sharp bites of pure pleasure. Then he moved down, flogging the inside of her thighs, forcing them farther apart. He knew she loved it like this, being wide open to him. He teased her lips with the vibrator. Her sex clenched, wanting it inside her. But he kept teasing, until she couldn't help but surge back against it.

He gave a small chuckle. "Eager, are you, my girl?"

But rather than continue to tease her, as he would usually do, he plunged the vibrator right into her, making her gasp. The pain and the humming of the vibe inside hit her hard, her sex clenching, going into another climax already. She panted, moaned, and came again, harder this time, with the vibrator pressed against her g-spot.

"Oh, my God..." She collapsed onto the bed. She

knew she shouldn't do it, knew she was expected to hold herself up until ordered to do otherwise. She didn't care.

But rather than reprimanding her, Decker stroked her back with his hand. His touch was gentle, and she thought dazedly that he meant to whip her with the rubber flogger again, but he kept smoothing his hand over her flesh, his palm warming her.

She loved when he touched her like this. Loved it too much, perhaps. It made her want to cry, that tenderness, coming from him. But in a moment he was on her yet again, pushing the chrome vibrator between her legs and right into her. She couldn't believe he was doing this. But she opened to him, let him do whatever he wanted, if it would make him happy.

He used the flogger on her back again while he probed her, the rubber tails hitting her in a hard, quick tempo. She knew the welts would come up fast, just the way he liked it. And a surge of pleasure warmed her at the thought that she was pleasing him.

The biting pain of the flogger and the vibe moving inside her, then pulling out to press against her clit, then back in again, made it hard for her to find a rhythm, to catch her breath. The stimulation was overwhelming; she had to simply give in to it. She came once more, hard spasms making her sex clench, making her body shake. Her mind was going blank; she couldn't think anymore.

Before the last tremors had left her body, he turned her over onto her back again and immediately began to flog her. He moved the little whip over her body, her stomach, down the front of her thighs, before moving down to the bottoms of her feet.

Oh, she loved this, loved even the elegant term for it: *bastinado*. That was her last conscious thought before he pressed the vibe against her mound once more.

"Come on, girl. Come for me again. Do it."

She was helpless against him, against the onslaught of sensation, his voice, his command. Once more her body shuddered with the pulsing beat of orgasm. Her sex clenched, she cried out, trembling all over.

Finally, he seemed satisfied with the number of orgasms, and stopped the flogging, moved the vibrator away.

She had no idea how much time had passed before her body calmed, and she opened her eyes, barely able to focus.

How many times had he made her come? She'd lost track. Her body was so sore by now she figured she'd be useless for a week. But she still wanted him. Even in the wake of climax after climax, she still felt a fierce need to feel him inside her body. It wasn't about not being sated. It was about being left unfulfilled. She didn't know how to explain that, even to herself.

He'd had a raging hard-on all night—she'd seen it right from the first moment, the ridge outlined against the fabric of his jeans—but he hadn't fucked her. He usually liked to end their sessions by fucking her senseless. Why was he holding back?

She watched him now, as he stood over her. His breath was coming in hard gasps, and she could see his swollen cock straining against his tight black jeans. If he wanted her, why didn't he take her?

"Decker? Sir?"

"What?" Was that anger she heard in his voice? Frustration?

He was quiet for a minute. Then he loosened his hold on her and used one hand to smooth over his short, dark crop of hair. He inhaled, blew out a long breath.

"I don't know."

She was sure she was going to cry. But somehow she held it together long enough to tell him, "Then I'd better go now."

She started to get up, but he held on to her.

"You don't have to go now, April."

"Yes, I do."

He loosened his grip and she stood, moved around the room finding her clothes. He was silent while she got dressed. She didn't look at him until she had her clothes and shoes on, had found her purse. He was sitting still on the edge of the bed, his hands resting on his knees.

"You don't have to go like this." His voice was low, husky, and laced with that accent that always turned her knees to liquid.

It took every bit of strength she had to turn away from him. But she had to do it.

"Good-bye, Decker."

❧

April sat at the small mosaic-tiled café table in her kitchen, sipping tea and allowing herself to wallow.

It had been two miserable days since she'd left Decker's house, and not a word from him. But what had she really expected? She'd been the one to say good-bye.

She couldn't place any blame on him, couldn't claim that he'd behaved inappropriately or unkindly. He'd just been honest with her about what he was capable of. Or incapable of. She was the one who couldn't handle it.

Damn him! Why couldn't he do this? Why couldn't he love her?

Tears stung behind her eyelids but she would not let herself cry over him. She had to find a position of strength in this somehow, or her brave show of leaving was for nothing. There had to be some purpose in her walking away, turning her back on Decker before he turned away from her. Right now, it was awfully hard to remember what the point was exactly.

She sniffed, took a sip of her fragrant tea, tried to calm herself.

God, she missed him. And she knew it was only going to get worse. She'd spent the last two days staring at the phone, wishing he'd call, dying to call him. But to what end?

She wished Rowan were in town. She could really use a talk with her. She was just going round and round in her head, having the same conversation with herself over and over. And it didn't help. The pain never went away.

How could she ever get over having to leave the man she loved?

And now, here she was, as miserable as she'd ever been, and what had she accomplished, really? Oh, yes, she had beat him to the punch, retained her pride, but it had still knocked the wind out of her. Was that something to be proud of?

Anger fused with the misery permeating her system. She was angry with herself. Because the truth was that she had accepted defeat.

Wasn't he worth fighting for? Was she just going to lie down and take it? Just because she was a submissive didn't mean she had to bend to his will without question. In the bedroom, certainly, but out here in the real world, when her heart and her happiness were on the line, didn't she have a right—no, a responsibility—to fight for what she wanted?

She stood up and took her teacup to the sink, setting it down so forcefully it clattered and cracked, the remains of her tea spilling over the counter.

Damn it.

She lifted the broken pieces and threw them across the room. They bounced against the opposite wall with a satisfying clink.

The tears threatened again, but she swallowed them hard and they faded away.

She stared at the bits of china on the kitchen floor. She would be stronger than that. And she would show *him* her strength.

She would not be so easily broken.

◊

He'd tried to insist on picking her up at the airport, but Rowan had managed to out-stubborn him, and took a door-to-door shuttle back to Venice. Now she stood on Christian's doorstep, as she had so many times before, the scent of the sea all around her, her heart fluttering, her pulse hot and thready. All because she was going to see him again. How was it she could feel this way about a man she'd known for not quite three weeks?

She hadn't felt this way about a man in a very long time.

Maybe never. She'd only been gone two days, but it felt like a month.

And now, here she was, her pulse and her heart hammering away. Needing to knock on the door, to see him, be with him. And afraid at the same time.

She shook her head, set her bags down on the wood decking, lifted her hand, and knocked. She waited, her blood rocketing through her veins. The house was quiet, the door remained closed. Where was he?

She knocked again, her heart thudding harder. Finally, the door opened, and there he stood, as beautiful as ever. The first thing she noticed was that he'd left his hair down. It was the first time she'd seen it like this, other than their last night in bed. Her sex, her entire body, clenched in memory.

She focused in on his face and saw his smile. Gorgeous. Made her weak in the knees. A silly, old-fashioned expression, but that's exactly what happened to her.

"Rowan. I've been waiting for you."

She stepped through the door and into his arms. They slid around her waist; she couldn't help it, couldn't have stopped it. And they felt so good. He felt good. And smelled good. She wanted to fall right into him. She wanted to be naked. Without thinking about it, her arms went around his neck, his hair silky and warm against the back of her hands.

They stood silently, holding each other, for a long time. And bit by bit, her muscles relaxed, melted into him. It was as though he knew that if he held on tight enough, long enough, he could help her let all the tension and doubt go.

It worked. That and more. Emotion lodged like a stone

in her chest, tightened her throat. But it was okay. As long as his strong arms were around her, she was okay. Just being with him made the rest fade into the background, as though his solid embrace absorbed it all: the doubt, the fear, the confusion.

Finally he let her go, stood back with his hands on her shoulders and looked her over.

"How are you? Are you hungry?"

"No, I'm fine. I ate before I left San Francisco."

"Come on, why don't you take a shower? You'll feel better. I always feel grimy and tense after I fly."

He reached through the still-open doorway to retrieve her bags, set them down in the kitchen, then took her hand and led her upstairs. There was something homey and welcoming about following him up there, her hand in his, about being instantly welcomed into his home in this way.

He took her right into the bathroom on the second floor, with its clean white tile and towels in soothing neutral sandstone shades. She loved this bathroom; it had one of those enormous shower stalls with three shower heads: one overhead rainfall, and two handheld sprayers. It even had a built-in bench seat. Pure decadence.

Christian reached into the shower to let the water heat, leaving Rowan in the middle of the room. She still had her black trench coat on, but he didn't seem to notice anything unusual. He came over to her, cupped her face in his hands, and kissed her.

His lips were soft, feathering across hers. She melted inside immediately, as much from his hands on her cheeks as the touch of his mouth; so tender, so lovely. But then he really began to kiss her and she forgot all about anything but his lips, his hot, searching tongue, his teeth that paused to nip her lower lip. She shivered with the absolute pleasure of it.

Her hands went to his broad shoulders and she hung on while he pressed his lips to hers, over and over, opening her mouth with his tongue, moving inside. His mouth was hot and sweet, unbearably tantalizing. She wanted more.

As if hearing her silent wish, he moved back enough to pull her coat off, then her slacks, her blouse. She didn't have time to think about how he managed the buttons without his lips ever leaving hers; she was simply grateful.

Her bra and panties came right off, then his own clothes disappeared somehow. Naked finally, he pulled her body in close, until they were skin against skin. She'd never felt anything more erotic in her life.

Until he pulled her into the shower.

They moved through a thick veil of steam until they were under the water; it fell over them like warm rain. The water caressed her skin, and Christian caressed her body, his hands everywhere: her shoulders, her breasts, her sides, her hips. She loved his big, warm hands on her flesh, leaving a trail of pure desire all over her skin, heating her to the core. Finally his hands curved around her bottom, holding her, pulling her up hard against him while his erection pressed into her stomach.

She snaked a hand down between them to wrap her fingers around his swollen cock. He groaned and her sex went wet at once. A familiar sense of power shifted through her, yet it was completely new at the same time. This was different from the way it had ever been with any of her "boys."

She loved that she could make him moan at her touch. The power was in that alone, in giving him pleasure.

Ignoring her own body's needs, she slid to her knees on the warm tiles and gazed at his cock. She stared in awe for a moment, at the sheer beauty of the way it was made, at every silky ridge, the rounded head. And then she took him into her mouth.

His hands went into her hair at once, while another groan, louder this time, escaped him. And she took his shaft deeper into her mouth, swallowed him until she felt the head nudge the back of her throat, relaxed and took him deeper still.

She slid her hands over his strong thighs and moved back, his cock sliding out between her lips, then back in as she took him again, slowly. His cock filled her mouth, her throat.

Lovely.

He tasted so good, sweet and clean and all male. And she could feel the muscles in his thighs tense as she moved her mouth on him, down, then up again, pausing to lick at the sensitive head. She loved the sounds he was making, sounds of pure pleasure. When she pulled back to look up at him, his head had fallen back, his eyes closed. He looked like a statue to her, that beautiful, that still, except for the trembling in his thighs beneath her hands. She loved it.

She went to take him in her mouth again, but he murmured, "Not now," and pulled her up to face him.

He kissed her while the warm water fell, slid down over her skin like heated satin. He reached behind her, found a bar of soap and ran it over her back, then down the front of her body, over the front of his, making them both slick with suds. He wrapped an arm around her and crushed her to him, their bodies meeting as if they were mermaids in the ocean.

That's what it felt like to her, with the water and the slipperiness of their soapy skin.

His hands danced over her, cupping her breasts, covering the bottom curve of them, then sliding up to tease her nipples. Ripple after ripple of sensation cruised over her skin, down her spine, between her legs, as he played her nipples with his fingertips. When he began to squeeze them, pleasure shot down to her sex, drenching her. She ground her hips, pressing her mound onto his muscular thigh, seeking relief.

"Christ, you feel good, Rowan." His voice dropped an octave as he moved his mouth right next to her ear. "Are you wet for me? Ready? Let's find out."

He turned her in his arms so that he was behind her. He spent a moment smoothing the soap over her back, her buttocks. Then with a firm hand on the back of her neck, he pressed her forward, bending her body. She went right down, bracing her hands on the wall of the shower, yielding to him, to whatever he wanted her to do.

His hands slid over her ass, massaging, slipping on the soap.

"Move your legs apart. Yes, beautiful."

With one hand he held her hip; with the other he guided his cock to her opening. Her sex clenched in anticipation as the head of his cock nudged at her sex. She tried to move back, to impale herself, but he wouldn't let her.

"Not yet, Rowan."

God, she was shaking with need. His hand on the back of her neck again, keeping her bent over. She couldn't say why that excited her even more.

He eased his cock in, perhaps an inch. Pleasure radiated through her body in swift, stinging currents.

"Please, Christian." She panted.

He gave her a little more, pressing a little deeper inside her. And then he reached around with one hand and smoothed his fingers over her cleft until he found the tender spot that ached for his touch. She surged into his hand, then back onto his cock, everything feeling too damn good. She didn't know what to do.

He didn't lose her clit for one moment. Massaging it with his fingers, he thrust his hips, burying his cock inside her. He filled her, stretched her, and it was pain and pleasure all at the same time. He kept massaging, pinching, sensation building on sensation until she was shivering all over with it.

She was moving her hips in time with his, tilting back as he pumped into her, his body slippery and wet, slapping against her ass cheeks with every thrust.

She was beginning to pant in long sobbing breaths, so close to the edge. And when he curled his fist in her hair, bringing her head up, and rubbed her whole mound with the heel of his hand, her orgasm came crashing over her in a powerful tide. She sobbed out his name. Her sex convulsed around his thick cock, still pumping into her, driving her on.

And before it was over, he'd turned her around, locked her against his body. His mouth came down hard on hers as he backed her into the tiled wall of the shower, pulling her up, and she wrapped her legs around his waist. He pressed his cock into her once more. And suddenly she was coming again, harder this time, as he drove into her with pummeling force. Her sex clenched, lightning flashes went off in her head, spinning, out of control, her body nothing but exquisite sensation.

Christian threw his head back, let out a harsh groan, and went rigid all over as he came, his cock still pushing into her, over and over, the hard tiles against her back the only thing holding her up.

When it was over they were both shaking, silent as the warm water flowed over their still-joined bodies. For some time there was no sound but the cascading water and their own panting breath.

Still impaled, her legs firmly around his waist, she breathed in the steam, laced with the clean smell of soap. And beneath it, the musky scent of sex was everywhere.

She didn't want to move, didn't care about anything but keeping their bodies this close.

Finally, he wrapped his hands around her waist and lifted her a bit, set her on her feet. She felt immediately bereft, but he pulled her into his arms and held her tight against his chest.

She didn't want to speak, to do anything to ruin the moment, to alter the way she felt. Her skin was so warm, her body lambent and spent. A lovely sensation. And Christian was right there, the comforting rise and fall of his wide chest beneath her cheek.

They stood under the fall of water as they had earlier, but this time they were quiet, content just to hold each other. Rowan closed her eyes, and let the moment just *be*.

Christian stroked her wet hair, then her cheek, her shoulder.

"Rowan."

"Shh. Don't say anything."

He paused. "I need to tell you—"

"No, no. You don't need to tell me anything." She buried her face into his chest.

"I read your story. The book you're writing."

"What?" Her chest tightened, her stomach clenched.

"You left your laptop here, left it open. I didn't mean to. I know that's a lousy excuse, but it was right there in front of me. And I know it's strange that I'm telling you this now, but I really did mean to tell you as soon as you'd returned."

She held her breath. Her secret, her secret writing! She'd never shared that with anyone; it was too personal.

"Don't you want to know what I thought of it?"

"I'm not sure."

"Well I'll tell you, anyway. I thought it was amazing."

She lifted her head, her heart hammering. "You did?"

"And I think it was very revealing, but we don't have to talk about that right now."

She pressed her cheek into his chest once more. "Thank God for small favors," she mumbled.

She still couldn't believe he'd read her work. That he'd intruded on something so private. He was right; it was revealing. She'd realized a little at a time as she worked on the book how much of her own story was in Ashlyn. But for some reason, it felt okay, because it was *him*. It felt important that he'd seen it, that he understood.

Her heart opened a little more to him. She knew right away that this made her even more vulnerable.

She pulled away to look at him. Water clung to his high cheekbones, his long lashes, his full mouth, the strong, straight line of his jaw. He blinked those ocean eyes at her and she felt it deep inside her. Not in her sex, but deeper, in her chest, in the center of her being, where it really counted.

She was overcome with love. And gripped by fear. And she still had no idea which would win out.

Christian held her against his body. Even beneath the warm water, in the swirling steam of the shower, she trembled in his arms.

He would have thought it was the orgasm—his had left him shaky—if he hadn't felt that tensing in her body a moment ago.

Why now? Why, after the most mind-blowing sex of his life? It had been even better than the first time. Something about the water, the hot steam . . . Christ, something about Rowan, that's what it was.

He wanted to ask her what she was thinking, but she didn't want to talk. Again.

She would damn well have to talk sometime. Or at least listen. Because he was in love with her. And he wasn't going to keep quiet about it for long.

He snaked a hand up the back of her neck, curled his fingers into her wet hair, pulled her even closer. With his other hand he grabbed one of the handheld shower heads and began to rinse the soap from her body. He sensed her muscles relaxing a bit beneath the hot spray. He lifted her hair and washed the back of her neck, letting the water do its job on her shoulders. She let out a small moan.

"Feel good?" he asked her.

"Oh, yes..."

He moved the sprayer down her back, then pulled away from her to rinse the front of her body. When the stream of water hit her breasts her nipples went hard.

His cock filled again at the sight of her dark pink nipples, erect, needy.

He moved the sprayer back and forth across her breasts, teasing, letting the water stroke her flesh. When he glanced at her face, her eyes were closed. Her face was so damn beautiful. Those high, curving cheekbones, her long dark lashes. That luscious hooker's mouth. Pure sex.

But he had to look back to her breasts. They were perfect: high, round, the skin there milky white. Her nipples always darkened when she got excited, and they were a deep red now, stiff and swollen.

He moved the sprayer lower, watching her breathing change as he shifted it to spray at the vee between her smooth thighs. Her legs parted a little, then, with the urging of his hand on her thigh, a bit more.

Holding her with one arm around her slim waist, he moved the sprayer back and forth, letting the warm water caress her mound, then changing the angle so that it would tease her clit.

Rowan let out a small sigh.

"Good?"

"Yes. Oh, yes."

Her hands were digging into his shoulders as she hung on to him, leaning her weight into him.

"Here, come sit down."

He rinsed the tiled bench seat for a moment to warm it, then had her perch on the edge. With a hand on the center of her chest, he made her lean back.

He knelt on the tiles before her. Using his hand, he parted her thighs until she was wide open to him. She let him do it, didn't even struggle. He could see her pink nether lips beneath the narrow strip of dark hair there, the luscious, swollen nub peeking out from between the folds.

Beautiful!

His cock throbbed at the sight.

He moved the sprayer over the front of her body, letting it heat her skin. Her eyes remained closed, but he could see from the rapid rise and fall of her gorgeous breasts how excited she was. He moved her legs wider, spread her wide open, and took another long look at her pussy, so pink and tight he could barely stand it. Then he shot the spray of water right between her legs.

She let out a groan, arched her back.

"More, Rowan?"

"Yes. More. Please."

He played the water over her sex, used his fingers to spread her swollen lips apart so he could get to her clit. She went a little wild when he did that, gasping and writhing.

And suddenly, he couldn't stand it anymore. He dove right in, kissing those hot, swollen lips, sucking and licking at her, thrusting his tongue inside her.

Christ, she tasted like heaven.

And suddenly he remembered the scene she'd written, about her characters, Ashlyn and Gabriel, doing just this. Knowing that she'd written about it, thought about it, made doing it to her even better.

He kept at it, sucking, licking, scraping with his teeth, and he held the sprayer so that the heat of the water cascaded over her at the same time.

When he pushed two fingers inside her tight, waiting little hole, she came immediately, her body arching up off the bench seat, into his face. He sucked harder, moved his fingers inside her. The walls of her sex clenched around them, squeezing hard, and he shoved them deeper.

"Christian!"

Still he worked her with his fingers, with his mouth. Her pussy was on fire, hot and clenching. His cock was rock-hard, but he wasn't going to stop until she finished coming.

Finally, the spasms tapered off and she calmed. Her lashes fluttered open and she looked at him, gave him a small, lazy smile. Her eyes were glowing with blue fire.

Yes, he had to have her, right now. Pulling her forward on the bench, wrapping her legs around him, he drove his cock into her, hard. She was so damn wet it was easy, sliding right in, up to the hilt.

Her arms twined around his neck and she latched her wicked little mouth onto his neck, sucking and biting. He loved it.

He drove deeper, faster. She was so damn tight. So hot. He'd never felt anything like it. Never felt anything like Rowan Cassidy.

"Yes, Christian," she whispered into his ear, urging him on. "Yes, yes, yes . . ."

His hips slamming into her now, he thrust hard, harder. He was panting. She was panting. And then she was coming again, her tight, wet sheath clamping so hard around his cock, he lost it. He pounded into her as he came, her own orgasm, her moans, making him come so hard he felt like he was shattering. Just coming apart all over.

The shower heads were still going, water falling warm all around them. He wanted to stay in there with her forever. But after a while the water began to cool.

Rowan was still half lying on the bench seat, her limbs limp. He shut off the water, scooped her into his arms and stepped out of the shower. Setting her on her feet, he grabbed a towel and dried her very carefully. She stood perfectly still, perfectly silent, just letting him do what he wanted.

He couldn't resist slipping a hand between her thighs to feel the slick heat of her sex. Made him want to be hard again already.

He took another towel and ran it over her hair. It lay in a dark tangle around her shoulders. Her eyes looked bluer than ever.

When she was dry, he quickly toweled himself off, wrapped them both in the thick white terry robes he kept on the back of the door, then picked her up to carry her to bed, just because he felt like it. She was nearly weightless in his arms. He didn't often realize how small she was, how delicately built. The sheer strength of her personality made her seem larger than she was.

It was cooler upstairs, raining outside. With all of the windows, the glass greenhouse roof, the rain was like soft music coming down, casting odd splatters of shadows everywhere when he turned a low lamp on at the studio end of the big room.

He set Rowan down on the bed. She lay back against

the pillows. He knelt on the bed beside her, leaned over her, kissed her lovely pink mouth. She kissed him back, lazily, her lips parting easily for him.

He never wanted to stop kissing her. But he also wanted to make her come again. He didn't even know why. He just had to do it, to bring her pleasure, to hear her moans, to feel her body arch beneath his hands.

He parted her thick robe, moved his mouth down and took one nipple into his mouth. Her skin was still hot from the shower, her nipple coming to attention immediately.

"Ah, Christian!"

He laughed. He couldn't help it. And he was definitely going to make her come again. "Just one more time."

"You're insatiable."

"Let's see if you are."

He moved his head inevitably downward, kissing her rib cage, over her belly, lower. She moved her legs open for him, and he went to work with his hands and his mouth, just the way she liked it, licking and sucking, pushing his fingers inside her, filling himself with her sweetness, until she came once more, thrashing on the bed, crying out his name.

And all around them the dark sky hid the stars and the rain fell, washing the earth clean.

TWELVE

APRIL WOVE UP THE TWISTING CANYON ROAD IN HER small blue Saturn. The way to Decker's house had become familiar enough that she could find it even in the dark. But a rare L.A. rain had begun to fall, and the streets were slippery, the lights of oncoming cars reflecting off the wet pavement. Her pounding heart wasn't helping, either. It was hard to concentrate on the road when she was so full of emotion, so nervous.

She'd felt brave enough when she'd left her house, her temper flaring. But now, having had a little time to make the drive, slowed by the wet roads, the damp, gray night closing in around her, she wasn't as sure of herself.

Yes, she knew she loved him, suspected he loved her. Hell, he *did* love her. He'd practically admitted it to her. He just couldn't face it. But she wasn't as certain anymore that she could convince him to face his feelings for her. Who the hell did she think she was, anyway, that she could have that kind of power over him? And Decker, of all people. The playboy of the Los Angeles BDSM scene.

She still wanted him in the most heart-wrenching, soul-shattering way.

Her eyes stung with tears she refused to shed as she carefully rounded turn after turn in the road. Well, she had nothing more to lose by trying. If she didn't, she'd already lost him for sure. She didn't think she could live with that, without at least making the effort.

Some of her resolve back in place, she pulled to the curb in front of Decker's hillside home. Lights burned through the shuttered windows. Good, he was home, at least. Too bad she hadn't brought an umbrella.

She got out of her car, ran through the downpour across the street, and began the ascent up the steep stairs. Her hair was drenched in seconds, water trickling into the collar of her coat. She reached the top finally, stood for a moment to catch her breath at the front door, then rang the bell.

Seconds ticked by while her stomach tied itself into a neat little knot and the tears burned behind her eyelids.

I will not cry.

The door opened.

A woman stood in the doorway, a girl she recognized from Club Privé but didn't really know. Dark, spiky hair, tall and lithe, her athletic body clad in only a very short black latex dress and a narrow leather collar. She was barefoot.

"Who is it?" Decker's voice coming from somewhere inside the house.

"Can I help you?" the woman asked, obviously not recognizing her.

Well, she could hardly blame her. She was soaked to the skin, her hair plastered to her head, her makeup likely washed off. She must look like hell. And this woman, so nice and neat. So pretty.

Decker came to stand behind the woman in the doorway.

"April? What are you doing here?"

Her heart dropped from her chest to her stomach with a sickening thud and she truly thought for a moment that she might be sick.

No, not here, not in front of them.

She shook her head as the tears came back, fierce and hot, burning her eyes, spilling over her lids. She didn't care suddenly.

She said quietly, "I really don't know."

She caught his gaze, forcing him to look at her over the woman's shoulder, to make an excuse if he dared. His dark eyes stared into hers, a series of emotions flashing through them, but he didn't say a word. He gave a small, helpless shake of his head, ran a hand over his short thatch of dark hair.

She waited. Nothing.

Again she shook her head, and muttered, "I really don't know what I'm doing here," before turning to flee.

She heard him call her name as she ran down the stairs, but what could he possibly say to her that would make this any better?

She let herself back into her car and sat behind the steering wheel, shaking, as her heart turned to stone, grew brittle, broke apart.

What a fool she was!

Two days. Two days and he'd already replaced her with another girl. She stuck her key in the ignition and started the car, blasting the heat. She was shivering, trembling all over.

God, she was angry! Angry with herself, angry with him. And hurt so deeply she couldn't even comprehend it right now.

Beneath the hurt and anger was another layer, a layer of shame. How could she have fooled herself into thinking this disaster of a relationship could ever be anything else? It had been doomed from the start, and she was a complete idiot to have let herself think, even for one moment, that there could be more between them.

Damn him!

But no, she had only herself to blame. Decker had never led her on, had he? She just hadn't wanted to see the truth.

Rain pounded on the roof of her car as she made her way down the hill. The streets were quiet. She managed to make it home, even with her heart crumbling into tiny shattered pieces in her chest. Managed to make it all the way into her bedroom, to strip her wet clothes off and climb into bed before the tears came. And when they did, they were hot and furious, taking over her body with long, wrenching sobs.

She curled into the blankets, a pillow held tight against her chest, as though it would help ease the pain there. But it didn't help. Nothing did. She felt as though nothing ever would.

෴

She was sure she'd never be able to move again.

Eyes closed, Rowan took in air in long gulps, trying to

fill her lungs, to calm her madly racing pulse. Her entire body still vibrated with the force of orgasm after orgasm. She'd never come so much, or so hard, in her life.

And there hadn't been one single moment of BDSM play. Not one moment when she or Christian were in the roles of dominant and submissive.

What did it mean?

But she was frankly too exhausted to figure it out now.

She felt Christian's weight on the bed and opened her eyes. His were absolutely glowing, as though he'd been the one to come just now. But there was something more in that blue-green gaze than lust. He smiled down at her, lifted one of her limp hands and kissed it, over and over, softly, as though her hand itself was something to be treasured, adored.

Christian trailed his mouth up the inside of her arm, over that most tender skin, until he reached her shoulder. He stopped there, paused to lift her hair away, bent and kissed her shoulder, her throat.

Another shiver of desire flooded her system. And at the same time, his movements were so achingly tender she could hardly stand it. When he gently brushed her hair from her cheek her eyes burned with tears.

Not now.

He whispered, "I have something to show you."

"What is it?" she managed despite the tightness in her throat.

"Come and see."

He pulled her robe around her, helped her to sit up. She'd barely caught her breath. But he stood and she followed, swaying a bit. Christian steadied her, one arm around her waist, and walked her across the room to sit her down on the old velvet chaise.

He left her for a moment to turn lights on around the studio, just a few floor lamps. She heard the rain falling on the roof, a gentle background to the golden light bathing this end of the room. It was then she noticed a large canvas on an easel set up in a corner, covered in a white drop cloth. Behind it was the deep velvet sky, black, seemingly infinite through the walls of greenhouse glass.

Christian came to stand beside the easel. God, he was so beautiful to her. His still-damp blond hair fell around his shoulders, framing his face in softness, making her think of the way he touched her. He reached up, held the edge of the drop cloth in his hand. His eyes were focused on her, intense. Rowan swallowed hard. Her pulse fluttered.

"This is what I did while you were away." A small smile as he slid the cloth aside, revealing a painting done all in sepia tones, like one of those antique prints of angels or statuary.

A painting of her.

The work was exquisite, she could see that right away. Her figure, laid out on this very antique chaise longue, her arms bound and stretched over her head in one long, fluid line. It was her, yet not her. More dreamlike, more beautiful than she could ever really be. Was this how he saw her?

Her throat constricted as she held back tears. When she looked at him he was watching her carefully, his jaw held tight. He looked like some ancient royalty, with his long white robe, his broad shoulders, his noble features. Strong, intimidating, except that there was so much emotion in his face. Was it for her? Or his painting?

Did she want to know?

"It's lovely." She shook her head at the inadequacy of the words. "It's so . . . so beautiful. I don't know how to say it. It almost doesn't look like me."

"It looks exactly like you, Rowan," he said, his voice quiet.

She started to shake her head but he quickly dropped the cloth and came to her, kneeling on the floor in front of her.

"No, don't even try to deny it. It's you, and it's beautiful. You're beautiful." He took her face in his hands, gazed into her eyes. His were so blue and green, shifting with the shadows of emotion, deep, endless.

She blinked, cast her eyes downward, but there were his lips, ripe and lush, red from kissing her still. His lips alone made her want to cry. Her heart was hammering away in her chest. She didn't know what to do with her hands. With herself. With everything she was feeling for this man that she had sworn not to—not for anyone. Ever again.

But here she was and she loved him, damn it. What the hell was she supposed to do now?

The tears escaped, fell onto her hot cheeks. He silently rubbed them away with his thumbs, asking nothing, no explanation. What kind of man did that?

She cried helplessly, quietly, soft tears drifting down her cheeks. There was no sobbing, no heavy torrent of tears, and she wasn't even entirely sure why she cried, what it was about exactly; the painting, the way he looked at her, the things they'd done together.

And Christian just let her cry, wiping her tears away as they fell. Finally he asked, "So, does this mean you like it?"

That made her laugh. "Of course!"

She looked at his face again. He was the picture of patience, simply waiting for her crying jag to end. Suddenly she felt ridiculous. She shook her head.

"I'm sorry."

"Don't be. Art should be an emotional experience."

"Yes, but it's not all because of that. Not all about the painting, your beautiful painting." She took a deep breath. How to explain?

"Go on," he urged gently.

She locked her eyes on his. "Christian, what are we doing here? You know this can't go on."

His dark brows shot up. "Why not?"

"There are twelve days left in our agreement. When our time is over, I will go back to being a dominant, and you will go back to ... training some other girl."

"How can you be so certain of that?"

"Because that's how life works. People don't change, really."

"I don't agree with that." He was quiet a moment, waiting for her response.

"I'm not—" She started to protest, to deny his accusation, but he was right. She wasn't going to lie to him. "Sometimes things happen to people, things that damage you. Damaged me." Her fingers flexed on the edge of the chaise, the old velvet rough beneath her hands.

"Why does that have to be a permanent condition?"

He was being so patient. She didn't want to get into this subject. "Do we have to discuss this?"

"Yes, damn it! When you're talking about walking away from me because of what that son of a bitch did to you, yes, we do. Because you know as well as I do that this has turned into something. Something real."

She looked away, pulled one of the small pillows into her lap, hugged it close to her body. She said quietly, because the words hurt coming out, "It may be real, but we still have to face reality. And the reality is, I am not a true submissive, Christian. Yes, I can do certain things with you, but I can't change who I am."

"Bottoming has been too easy for you for that to be the whole truth. I don't understand why you're being so stubborn about this, when everything that's happened between us tells me something different."

Suddenly anger burned through her system. "You men! God, you think that just because I've done these things with you, they define me, make me some sort of slave girl!"

"That's not what I'm saying at all, and you know it." He was trying to keep his temper now, too, she could tell. She could see it in the clenching muscle in his jaw, the tight line of his lips.

She shook her head again, empty inside. Drained suddenly. "I don't think I can do this anymore."

His brows drew together. "What do you mean?"

"Be with you, like this. I can't do the thirty days."

He clearly wasn't expecting that. Her words silenced him. She couldn't bear to look at him, at his ocean eyes, his fall of soft, pale hair, the shock on his face. Instead she looked over his shoulder, past the painting he'd done of her, out into the dark night. It was cold and empty out there, exactly how she felt on the inside at the prospect of never seeing him again.

But she would, wouldn't she? She'd run into him at the

club, have to watch him play with the submissive girls there, his hands on their flesh.

Too awful.

But what choice did she have? Was she supposed to abandon her life because of him? Wasn't that the whole point?

Finally he said, "I can't make you stay."

"No."

He got up, walked to the windows, looked out into the night. The set of his shoulders was filled with tension. He stood there for a long while, ran both hands back over his hair. When he turned around she could see the grief etched in the tender skin around his eyes. She hadn't wanted to do that to him. But she had no choice. Better now than later.

"Do you want to go now?"

She nodded, just a small dip of her head. "I think it's best, don't you?"

"No. I don't think any of this is what's best. But I won't stop you. You aren't a slave, after all. You do what you need to do. But I want it clear that I think you're acting rashly. I think you're throwing something away, something valuable. I think you're acting on fear."

"Yes, you're probably right." She wasn't about to deny it. But the profound ache in her chest was a clear sign that she'd already gotten in too deep. How had she allowed this to happen?

"I'm sorry, Christian. I don't know what else to say."

His voice was almost a whisper. "Say you'll stay. Say you'll stay with me, try to work through your feelings. I can help you."

"Why? Why do you feel this need to help me, to fix me?" Her voice was harsher than she'd intended.

He shook his head. "Because if I don't, it feels like a failure on my part. Because as a good dominant, you are my responsibility. Your well-being is in my hands. And if I've done something to bring up feelings in you, old hurts, then I am responsible for handling the fallout."

"Fallout? Look, my past is behind me. I put it there. And I'm fine."

"Are you? You can't even talk about what happened to you."

She ran a hand through her tangled hair, focused on the slats of the wood floor. "It's . . . not easy to talk about."

"The things that most shape our lives never are."

She did not want to tell him the ugly details. But she felt on some level that he deserved to know. And more than that, she felt a need to explain herself to him, to justify her actions.

"It was my sophomore year in college. I felt truly independent for the first time, away from home, away from my mother. My mother is the kind of woman who has utter control over everything around her, and of course that included me. And she didn't like me having any ideas that weren't hers. When I left home I was finally able to think for myself. It made me feel powerful, for the first time in my life. So when I met Danny, I was in a good place. I felt strong. And I was . . . I'd had these feelings for a long time. He was my first really serious relationship." She paused, bit her lip. The hard part was coming.

"I let him know what I wanted. And he didn't call me a freak or anything. He wanted to try it, too. I was so proud of myself for asking for what I wanted. Hell, for even knowing what I wanted."

"You bottomed for him, didn't you?"

"Yes." Cold suddenly, she wrapped the robe tighter around her body. Just talking about it made her feel small and frail. "It was fun at first. A little spanking, and I had him tie me up with his belts. It was thrilling, frankly. But then... things got out of hand. Ugly."

She glanced at Christian. He nodded, encouraging her to go on.

"Looking back now, I know that he never really got it, what a BDSM relationship is all about. He was just into the thrill. It was all about sex for him. And I didn't know any better. I was... I was into the submission; at least, I thought I was."

She pushed her hair behind her ear, took a moment to think, to calm down.

"It got worse as the year wore on. He was really abusing the power I'd so stupidly handed over to him. And I was letting it happen. He took more and more of me. Until there was very little left."

She paused, took in a deep breath, pushed her hair away from her face.

"Then he... got drunk one night. Well, he got drunk a lot, if you want to know the truth. But so did a lot of guys in college. But sometimes when Danny got drunk he got mean. So, he came over to my apartment one night and... and he was trying to be charming at first, but he was so... so drunk. Disgusting. I'd been ready to break things off with him for a while at that point. I don't know why I waited. I wish to God I hadn't."

She had to pause, had to breathe, in, out, cleansing her lungs. Her stomach was a hard knot.

"So ... he came over, wanted to fool around, wanted to tie me up again. But I didn't want him to. And he ... he called me a whore, that usual abusive macho bullshit. Told me I was the one who wanted it. And he did it anyway."

"Christ, Rowan."

Her eyes burned. But she refused to cry one more tear for Danny. She said quietly, "I think you can guess the rest."

He was silent for a good full minute, absorbing what she'd just told him. Shocked, maybe?

"Do you feel any sense of relief at having talked about this just now?"

"Honestly? No, I don't. I don't need to talk about it anymore. I swore after that night nothing like that would ever happen to me again. That I would be in charge. Of my life, my sexuality. I swore I would never allow a man that kind of power over me again. And I've done that. I've gathered my strength, built on it. It's all I have to hang on to. Because he damaged me. And that damage will always be there, no matter how deeply I bury it."

"That doesn't make sense. Rowan, you're the one who said that what we've been doing together doesn't define you. Neither does what you've done before me. Why does it have to be about extremes?"

"Because it is about extremes. Isn't that what this lifestyle is about? We are extreme people, Christian. How can you deny that?"

"Alright. Okay. But, Rowan, now that this is out in the open, I can help you deal with it."

"You're not my savior, Christian. Why do you think you have to do this for me? Do you think I'm weak?"

"No! Of course not."

"Then why?"

"I've already told you why."

"But there's more, isn't there?"

He paused, looked away for a moment, then back at her. "What else?"

God, what had made her ask that? She didn't want to know, didn't want to do anything that would draw them closer. She couldn't stand it.

He took a few long steps toward her, until he was standing right before her again. And again he went down on one knee, placing his hands on either side of her body on the old chaise. He searched her face, his eyes so intent, so full, she could barely look at him. Her heart gave a sharp squeeze of pain.

"What else, Rowan? I think you know. Do you really want me to say it? Because I will. I will give you that piece of myself. I will tear myself up like that for you. For *you*. Do you understand what I'm saying?"

Tears choked her, her throat closing up, her eyes flooding. She turned her head away. "No, Christian, don't."

But he took her chin firmly in his hand, forced her to look at him. His face was beautiful to her behind the blurry sheen of her tears.

"I love you, Rowan. I am in love with you."

"No..."

"Denying it won't make it go away. You don't have to accept it, you don't have to say it back. But there it is, out on the table."

She was crying in earnest now, the pain of it filling her entire body. She leaned her face into her hands. She could not look at him, at the truth shining through his eyes.

"Please don't," she begged.

"Are you still leaving?" His voice was harsh.

She dropped her hands, took a deep lungful of air. Nodded through her tears. She choked the words out. "Yes. I have to."

He nodded once, stood, went again to the tall windows, his arms crossed over his chest. He didn't say another word as she rose and went downstairs to gather her clothes. He was still standing there even after she'd gotten dressed and come back into the studio. She came up behind him.

"I'm . . . I'm going to go now."

He didn't say a word.

"Please say something, Christian."

"What more do you want from me? I've said everything I had to say."

He was right. There was nothing left to say. She turned and left the room.

THIRTEEN

ROWAN HAD TO STOP CRYING. TEARS HAD NEVER DONE her much good. And these were no easy tears; they held no release. They were tight, scalding tears that did nothing to cleanse, to heal. She had been victim to these same tears for three days. She was exhausted, weakened to the core, taken over by grief.

She glanced over at the small, lovely statue on her dresser. *Nyad.* It had arrived that morning by messenger. There had been no note. It was the only form of communication she'd had with Christian since she'd left his house, said good-bye to his back. He hadn't looked at her. She couldn't blame him. She could hardly stand to look at his statue now, this object he had made with his own hands. But she couldn't bear to remove it from her bedroom, either, to put it away somewhere out of her sight.

She moved to the window and stared out at the city. The sky was gray and gloomy, the late afternoon fog beginning to roll in even this far from the coast. She could only imagine how thick and impenetrable it would be out at the beach, at Venice. At Christian's house.

No.

A new wave of sorrow coursed through her, tightening her stomach, her shoulders, as though it were a physical, palpable thing. Agonizing.

She couldn't bear to think of him, and yet her mind refused to allow her to think of anything else. She'd been trying to write, to distract herself, but she couldn't do it. The words refused to come.

There was far too much of her in that story. Christian had been so right about its being revealing. She had been using it to explore her submissive side, even before she'd met him. And once she'd been with him for a while, had begun to explore these things in real life, she no longer needed to write about it.

Would Ashlyn's story end on a happier note than her own? She didn't know. And it didn't matter anymore. She only needed to know what was going to happen to her, how she would survive this grief.

She sniffed, wiped her face with a tissue. She picked up the teacup that sat next to her laptop on her small writing desk, but found the tea was cold. She had no idea how long she'd let it sit there.

Picking up the cup, she rose and headed to the kitchen, padding down the narrow hallway in her fuzzy slippers. The apartment was cold; she'd forgotten to turn on the heat. She flicked the thermostat on as she passed it. The living room she moved past quickly. It seemed too big, too cold and stark, and she didn't want to linger there. She needed the safety of her bedroom, with her big bed and the piles of pillows. The living room, with its enormous windows, seemed too reminiscent of the greenhouse windows of Christian's studio, of his bedroom.

God, God, God.

Like a knife to the heart, thinking about Christian, about being in his bed, in his arms.

In the kitchen she filled the kettle, turned the flame up high on the stove, and waited for the water to boil, trying not to think, to ignore the sharp ache lancing through her body. Silent moments ticked by before the water heated and the kettle whistled. She poured the water over a new tea bag, Earl Grey, her favorite, and the doorbell rang.

She froze.

Her pulse fluttered and her hand went automatically to her chest, as though to protect her aching heart.

She thought she'd hyperventilate by the time she reached the door. She drew in one deep breath, which did nothing to calm her, before she opened it.

April stood on the other side, dressed in jeans and a baby blue sweater that would have matched her eyes, except that now they were rimmed in red. The dark smudges beneath them told Rowan that April had slept as little recently as she had herself. Her sleek, strawberry hair was done in two long braids, making her look young, fragile.

Rowan took the girl's hand and brought her inside, shutting the door behind her. "Are you okay? What's going on?"

April took a deep, hiccupping breath. "You don't look so good yourself."

Rowan just shook her head, bit her lip. April hadn't let go of her hand.

"Rowan? Can we sit down? I'm so tired…"

"Of course." She started to lead her into the living room, but paused. "Here, let's go into my bedroom. It's too . . . empty in here."

They settled into the pair of sleek, modern chairs upholstered in a deep shade of eggplant velvet that flanked one of the windows. Rowan pulled a small silk pillow into her lap.

They both remained silent for a while, just sitting together, taking what small comfort they could from each other.

Finally April spoke. "Decker and I are over."

"I'm sorry." Rowan's heart surged with sympathy, making her own loss even more glaring, more present.

"You can say 'I told you so.' "

"I wouldn't do that."

"No. That's why I came. I wasn't looking for more self-flagellation, masochist that I am." She tried to smile, but it was a pale effort. "And you? What's happened? I've been trying to reach you on your cell phone for days."

"I've . . . left him."

Again they sat in silence for a while. Finally April said, a small smile on her lips, "I guess misery really does love company."

"We're too pathetic, aren't we?" Rowan pushed her heavy hair away from her face. "How did we let this happen?"

April shrugged. "Well, for me the answer is easy. I've never made good choices when it came to men. Decker is another in a long line of mistakes. I knew from the beginning he'd break my heart. I was right."

Rowan reached out to take her hand. "Oh, April. I'm so sorry."

"No, I'm okay. Or I will be. What about you? What happened?"

"I got in too deep. I don't...I don't usually do that."

"Why not?"

She dropped April's hand, sat back in her chair. "It's complicated."

"Isn't it always?"

"Yes. I suppose you're right. But this time..." She had to stop. Her throat was closing up on her again.

"This time what?"

Rowan just shook her head.

"Whatever happened with you and Christian, it must have been important."

"Yes."

"Are you still in love with him?" April asked quietly.

"Yes." It came out in a whisper.

"Then why aren't you with him?"

"Because he deserves more."

"I don't understand. Is it this stuff we talked about before? About you not being able to truly submit to him?"

Rowan shook her head. "I can't let all of my power go like that, on a daily basis. It makes me too helpless. Too powerless. But it's more than that. It's my past, everything that happened with Danny."

"Don't let what that jerk did to you stand in your way, Rowan. If you do, then he's won. Can't you see that?"

"It's not just Danny, either. Not exactly. It's what I became after him. I closed off a part of myself, April. I shut down. I know it. And I also know that means something is missing in me. How can I give Christian all he deserves in a relationship if I'm so screwed up?"

"Have you told him this?"

"Yes." She pulled at a thread on the pillow, twisted it between her fingers.

"And he still wants you?"

"He thinks he does."

"Come on. He's a grown man. I'm sure he knows what he wants, and he wants you. I think you should go to him, talk to him."

Rowan shook her head. "I can't."

"Why not?"

"I left him. He told me he loved me and I turned away from him. I hurt him, April. I don't think he'd want me back now."

"Are you joking? Of course he wants you back. You have to go to him. Rowan, you have to go!" April leaned forward in her chair now, her face intent. "You have a chance. You have to take it, even though you're scared. If I had that same chance, I'd be with Decker in a minute. But I don't." She looked down at her lap, tugged on the end of one long braid. "Shit."

"What happened with Decker?"

"Oh, he sent me away. Or, he would have if I hadn't left. I knew from the start he would eventually. But I fell for him anyway. And then I decided I wasn't going to let him do it, and I went to his house and...I found some subbie girl there. It was fairly awful."

"God, I'm so sorry, April."

"The thing is, he pretty much admitted to me that he

couldn't see me anymore because he was starting to have feelings for me. That makes it worse somehow, you know?"

"Yes, I know exactly," Rowan said quietly. "What are you going to do about it?"

April gave a short, sharp laugh. "What can I do? I'm going to get over him."

Rowan only wished her own answer were so easy. She didn't think she was capable of getting over Christian.

"Are you going to call him, Rowan? See him? I think you two should talk. He didn't reject you, the way Decker did me. You have a chance."

"God, I don't know right now."

"I guess I'm having a hard time understanding why you would turn your back on the possibility of love. It's hard for me to get that when it's everything I've ever wanted."

Rowan watched the expression on April's face. Her brows were drawn together, her blue eyes blazing with emotion. And she knew she was right. She knew it. But damn it, she was still too scared.

Could she find the strength to face her fears? And could she do it before it was too late to turn back?

∞

Early dawn. The sky glowed with shades of pink and gold as the sun made its way over the horizon, fighting through the thin layer of mist to light the sky in a spectacular blaze of color.

Christian watched through the windows of his studio. He was cold, exhausted. Too tired and distracted to appreciate the beauty of the sky. His hands and his shoulders were sore from working the stone all night. He'd been at it for four days now, ever since Rowan had left.

It was her taking form in the stone, that mysterious piece of stone that had called out to him when he'd first come back to L.A. He hadn't been able to read it, to figure out what it needed to be, until the other night.

The stone was Rowan, or it would be. The pale marble had that same cool, silky texture as her skin; it warmed beneath his hands almost as quickly as she did.

As she *had*. That was over and done with, wasn't it?
Christ.

There had been moments when he'd wanted to knock the half-formed sculpture to the ground, smash it, smash any reminder of her.

Then why hadn't he washed the pillowcase she'd last slept on? Why had he so carefully hung the robe she'd worn on the hook by the bed? Why hadn't he been able to sleep in the bed they'd shared together since she'd left, spending those scant hours in which he slept on the old velvet chaise, leaving the bed as some kind of shrine?

He ran a hand over the stubble on his jaw. He hadn't shaved since then, either. Hadn't left the house. Hadn't left the studio other than to eat and shower once each day. Hadn't answered his phone. Sterling had called twice, leaving messages. He should call him back. But he wasn't ready to talk to him, to have to explain anything. He just wanted to work, finally.

How ironic that Rowan had been the muse he'd needed to kick-start his work for him again, only to leave as soon as he'd found her. And now she was the only subject he could draw, paint, sculpt. There were sketches of her lying everywhere: on the floor, the small tables scattered around the studio, the old gold chaise. He'd started a few paintings, just studies, really, on small canvases, done in ocher, burnt umber, and white. He liked to sketch like that sometimes, as much as he did in pencil or charcoal. Every last one was her.

He smoothed his hand over the white marble, seeking the textures unconsciously; face, shoulder, breast. There was no other woman for him. There never would be again.

She hadn't called him, not even after he'd had "Nyad" delivered to her apartment.

Damn it. He couldn't waste his life pining away over a woman. He'd never done this before. Why now?

Because he'd never loved a woman the way he loved Rowan.

She loved him. He knew she did. It wasn't just misguided ego speaking. He knew it down to his bones. She talked about all this strength she'd built over the years, but how strong was she, really, if she couldn't face her feelings?

No, that wasn't fair. She wasn't weak; he didn't really believe that. She had a right to be scared. Hell, it scared him. But he wasn't willing to walk away from it.

Then why had he allowed her to?

He'd told himself he was respecting her decision. That he was being noble. But who the fuck did he think he was? No, maybe the truth of it was that he was a coward.

So, what the hell was he going to do about it?

He could not stand the idea of living without her forever.

His lost muse. Too awful.

This was crazy, living like this, like some mad European

artist from another century, crazed, tortured. If he wasn't careful he'd be cutting his ear off to send to her.

Christ, he was really falling apart, wasn't he?

He glanced again at the drawings and paintings of her littering every surface. He'd find more downstairs, he knew, on the kitchen table, on the counters. He'd sketched her on notepads, on napkins while he ate. Maybe he really was crazy, spending his days and nights like this.

And maybe it was crazy to think they had a chance, but he wasn't going to just lie down and die like this. He wasn't going to let Rowan make this decision all by herself, damn it.

Fuck it. No more. He was going after her.

ඏ

April stretched and yawned, momentarily confused. She looked around the room: soft gray walls, black lacquer furniture, touches of red and orange. Very clean, very Zen. Rowan's guest room. The little touches, like the tall hematite vase with one long-stemmed bird-of-paradise, the gorgeous two-foot-tall bronze Singapore Buddha, the tight red bolster pillows, were so Rowan. Beautiful, every detail perfectly composed.

It was a moment before she remembered what she was doing here, their little sob-fest the night before. Well, nobody had sobbed, but they may as well have. They'd stayed up late, drinking tea, talking, sometimes just sitting quietly together. At one A.M. Rowan had suggested April stay with her rather than drive home so late.

She glanced at the clock. It was not quite seven in the morning. She was still tired, but there was no way she could sleep anymore, even in the calm luxury of Rowan's guest room. Her mind was already going.

She got up, went into the guest bath Rowan had showed her the night before, and took a quick, scalding hot shower, then went to the kitchen to make coffee.

Rowan was already there, dressed in a long kimono robe in bright red, a stark contrast to her dark hair and pale, tired face.

"Hi."

"Good morning. Coffee is already on. Did you sleep okay?"

"Yes, just not long enough. But I've been thinking..."

"What about?" Rowan poured coffee into a big mug and set it down on the center island, next to a small pitcher of milk and a sugar bowl. April added two spoonfuls of sugar to her cup and stirred.

"I was thinking about some of the things we talked about last night. And I think... God, I know you'll think I'm nuts, but I'm going back to talk to Decker."

Rowan raised an eyebrow, but only said, "When?"

"This morning. Now. Before he has a chance to leave for work. It shouldn't take me more than twenty minutes to get to his place from here."

"Do you know what you want to say to him when you get there?"

April bit her lip. "I'm not sure. All I know is that I have to do it. Remember what I said to you about taking risks? Well, I'm going to take my own advice. I know he loves me.

He knows it, too. I'm going to make him face it. I don't want to lose him, Rowan." She paused, sipped her coffee. "Do you think I'm insane, doing this?"

"I think you're brave. Braver than I am."

"Why can't you do it, too? Talk to him. Do it, Rowan." She took one more quick sip before setting her cup on the counter. "I'm going now."

Rowan came around the counter and hugged her. "Good for you."

April pulled back. "You can do it, too, Rowan. You can."

"Maybe you're right..."

"Just...make that decision. Be strong. You *are* strong, you know, whether you recognize it or not. I can see you want to. Go to him."

"Maybe."

"I'll call you later, okay?"

"Okay. Good luck."

"Thanks. I'll need all the luck I can get!"

❧

The door closed behind April, and Rowan turned, leaning her back against the door. Her heart was pounding. Because she knew April was right, about everything. She had to go to him, to give this a chance. Even if he was angry, turned her away. She had to try or she'd regret it all her life.

Fear bubbled up in her, threatened to close her throat again, to choke her, but she fought it down.

Nobody said love was easy. You had to fight for it, even if sometimes you had to fight yourself.

She'd already showered; she'd woken at six o'clock.

Now she slid into a pair of white jeans and a white sweater. The color of surrender. Well, that's what she was doing, wasn't it?

She had one last moment of cold, stabbing doubt as she locked her front door behind her. She stood frozen in the hall outside her apartment, her heart beating so wildly she actually felt faint. But she pictured Christian's face in her mind, letting that image warm her, calm her. She would go to him. *Now*.

ഝ

Christian pulled up in front of Rowan's building. As he slid the Cadillac into an open spot at the curb, a silver BMW came squealing out of the underground parking lot and shot off down the street. Rowan's car? No, it couldn't be. Half the people in L.A. drove BMWs. He was imagining things now, thinking he saw her everywhere.

So this was what obsession was like . . .

He got out, took the elevator up to her floor, knocked at her door. No answer. He rang the bell and waited. Nothing. He put his ear to the solid wood, feeling a bit foolish. No sound came from inside the apartment. Maybe that *had* been her car? Where would she be going so early in the morning?

His pulse surged in his veins. Suddenly, he knew somehow with a deep certainty that she was on her way to Venice, to his house. He didn't understand why he felt so sure about it, but he knew it all the way down in his bones.

Wishful thinking? Perhaps. But he was going there now anyway.

He nearly ran down the hall, punched the button for the elevator twice, three times. It seemed to take forever to get there, for the doors to open. Then he was in, going down, and finally, he pushed through the heavy glass door of her building and climbed back into the Cadillac.

He sped through the streets, annoyed when he ran into traffic on Olympic Boulevard. Turning, he wove through the back streets, heading west, toward home. Toward Rowan.

He'd feel like an idiot if she wasn't there when he arrived.

Her little car was faster than his, even though his Cadillac had a more powerful engine. He drove as fast as he could manage on the narrow avenues. He didn't care if he got a ticket, but he didn't want to leave Rowan waiting too long; she might turn around and leave.

He made the last right turn into the narrow street behind his house. His heart gave a heavy thud when he saw her car there. A surge of relief welled up in him, as well as a hard, hammering anticipation and the fear that she hadn't come here to say the things he wanted to hear.

He took one last deep breath, filling his lungs with the cool salt air, and got out of his car. This was it.

∾

Rowan stood at Christian's door, shivering in the damp morning air. She always forgot how much colder it was this close to the beach. She'd knocked, rung the bell, but he wasn't there. She hadn't seen his car in the driveway, but she'd hoped, anyway.

She turned and leaned her back against the closed door. Where could he be? It was far too early for any of his usual appointments at the gallery. Maybe he'd gone out of town? Maybe he'd gone back to Europe. She had no way of knowing; she hadn't spoken to him for days. He could be anywhere.

He could be distracting himself with some other woman. And he'd have every right to. She'd turned him away.

Despair hit her like a cold fist, making her feel as though she'd been knocked flat. She hung her head, wrapped her arms around her body. What now?

Her eyes filled with tears. She shouldn't have come here like this. She shouldn't do this to him. To herself. What had she been thinking? This was a mistake.

Her whole life felt like a mistake.

She put her face in her hands and cried. It started with one long sob that drew itself out and became a low, keening cry. Her chest was so tight she had to fight to breathe. It didn't matter. All that mattered was how horribly she'd screwed things up. And now they both had to pay the price.

Another sob, deep and wrenching, took her body over, swept through her on a wave of excruciating pain and emptiness. She sank back against the door, her legs suddenly unable to hold her up, and crumpled into her grief.

"I've got you."

Christian's arms went around her; she knew it was him just by his scent and the feel of his strong arms encasing her body, pulling her against him. Blind with tears, it was all she needed to know.

"Shh, I've got you, Rowan. I'm here." He tipped her

face up to his. She fought him at first; she didn't want him
to see her like this.

"Rowan." That familiar, commanding tone, yet now it
was a comfort to her, reassuring. She looked up at him.
"I'm here," he said again. "And you're here. I knew you
would be."

She had no idea what that meant, but it didn't matter.
He was here, as he'd said, and his arms were around her
and she loved him.

He moved one arm away to unlock the door, nudged it
open with his foot. The inviting warmth of his home
flowed out to her. "Rowan, come inside."

FOURTEEN

APRIL TOOK THE LAST STEPS TO DECKER'S FRONT door slowly. It struck her suddenly that he might not be alone. How awful would that be, to face that again? But she didn't give a damn. He would have to listen to her anyway. She had a few things to say to him and he was going to have to hear her out.

She didn't hesitate as she lifted her hand and knocked on the door. When there was no answer she knocked again, louder this time. She kept knocking until she heard his muffled voice, laced with irritation and that Irish accent of his.

"Who the hell is it? Do y'know what time it is?"

The door swung open and there he stood, in nothing but a pair of rumpled gray pajama bottoms. Sexy as hell with his broad, bare chest, a sprinkle of dark hair in a line down his abdomen leading into the waistband of his pajamas. He seemed taller and more imposing than ever, towering over her. But she refused to allow herself to be intimidated.

"We need to talk, Decker."

"April?"

His face was covered in dark stubble. He blinked a few times. He looked dazed, as though she'd woken him up.

"Are you going to invite me in?"

"What?"

She shook her head and pushed her way past him. He closed the door and turned around to face her.

"What's going on?"

"I know you love me," she accused. "And I'm not going to let you hide from it anymore."

He scraped a hand over his short thatch of hair. A vein pulsed in his neck. His eyes were dark as night. Unreadable.

Oh, God. Had she been wrong? Her pulse fluttered with doubt.

He blinked again. "Maybe we'd better sit down."

He walked into the living room without pausing to see if she followed him. He gestured helplessly to the sofa. She sat, and he settled down on the edge of the coffee table, facing her.

"I don't know what to say to you, April."

Fear sizzled in her veins, making her go hot all over, making her chest ache. She'd been so sure!

"Maybe it was a mistake, coming here," she muttered, trying to stand. But his hand on her shoulder stopped her. She looked into his eyes, trying to figure out what was going on behind them. "Are you telling me this wasn't a mistake, showing up here like this? Are you telling me I'm right?"

He nodded his head, slowly.

"God, Decker, talk to me! You're confusing the hell out of me."

"Maybe because I'm confused. I'm not used to being confused. I don't much like it."

Her head was spinning now. What was he talking about?

"So you...do you love me, Decker?"

Had she actually asked him that? She waited for him to answer, feeling as though she were dangling off the edge of a cliff, waiting for him to either grab her back to safety, or push her over the edge.

His hands came up to cup her face. She wanted to cry at the pure tenderness of it. He looked into her eyes, and finally she saw his open a bit, saw the shadows fade away until the dark brown depths were lit from within. She'd never seen him look like this. It left her breathless.

"I didn't think you'd ever come back. I wouldn't have, if I were you," he told her. She didn't know what to say. "But I'm damn glad you did."

And then he leaned in and kissed her.

Decker had kissed her before, but never like this. This time it was all sweet and pliant. Tender. Romantic. It made her go soft inside. It made her come apart. Her eyes burned with tears.

He kept on kissing her, holding her face carefully in his hands, as though she might break. Kiss after gentle kiss, until she couldn't think anymore, until she couldn't hold back the tears that wanted to fall from her eyes. There was nothing she could do about it. She was helpless in his hands.

Her tears fell, hot over her cheeks, over his hands. And

he whispered between kisses, "I'm sorry. Lord, I'm sorry, so sorry."

He kissed her tears from her face, moving his lips over her cheeks, her closed eyelids. And he told her again, "I'm sorry, April."

She was warm all over, warm and melting and hopeful and still scared to death that he would ask her to leave.

"Tell me, Decker. Tell me I don't have to go again."

"God, no!"

His hands were in her hair, pulling her braids apart so he could bury his fingers in it. He pulled her head back, trailed kisses along her throat, making it impossible for her to think, to be afraid any longer. Her arms went around his neck. His skin was burning hot beneath her hands. All she could think about was being with him, completely. She didn't protest when he laid her back on the couch, moving his big body over hers.

Her whole system was molten with desire, a desire made all the more urgent by her swelling heart. She loved him, needed him, needed him to be a part of her.

Somehow their clothes came off, leaving them naked and panting. He was still kissing her, all over now, his mouth leaving a burning trail of pleasure from her lips to her shoulder, her collarbone to the curves of her breasts. Hot, soft kisses that left her skin on fire, a fire that blazed, spread, heating her to the core.

She spread her thighs and took him into her body, her legs wrapping around his wide back. He held himself up on his arms, looked into her eyes as he moved inside her. Wordlessly, he let her know with each tender thrust that this was different. They were different.

When her climax came, it rolled over her in waves as soft as water, shaking her to the center of her being. And he came, too, never taking his eyes from hers, until she sank into the midnight brown of his gaze, down deep, deeper. Until she knew his heart was in her hands.

The tears came again. But this time they didn't hurt at all.

ඏ

It took some time, but Rowan's shoulders finally sagged, her whole body softened against his. She was full of misery, fear, exhaustion. Love.

"Rowan." He smoothed her hair from her face. "Talk to me. Tell me why you came here. You must have something to say to me."

"Yes." Her voice was quiet, almost a whisper.

"Come on. Look at me."

She raised her head, her eyes locking onto his. She could see hope there, and fear and love. She breathed a sigh of relief.

"I have to . . . to tell you what I need, Christian. If we're going to be together, I need you to know."

He nodded, urging her to continue.

"I want to be with you. But I can't be what you want. I don't know what to do."

"I want *you*, Rowan."

She shook her head. "But you'd have to take me as I am. And I'm not a bottom. I could not live like that every day. I don't even know that I could serve you at the dungeon like the other sub girls do. God, I don't even know if I could go there with you like that."

"I've never asked you to do any of those things."

"No. You wouldn't, knowing what you do about me. But it must be in the back of your mind."

"I admit I had plans at first. When this was nothing more than a challenge between us. Before I knew you."

"I have limits."

"Yes. But everyone has their limits."

"But can you live with mine? Can you live like that and be happy? Because I don't see myself ever changing, Christian, even for you."

He was quiet, thoughtful, his brows drawn together. Her heart throbbed like a steel hammer in her chest, sharp and painful.

Finally, he said quietly, "When have I ever asked you to change for me? All I wanted was for you to find your true self. I think you have. And I'm not saying that to be right. I'm saying it because I think it's the truth. You are a bottom, Rowan, in the sense that you derive pleasure from playing that role. Are you denying that?"

"No. I can't anymore. I've seen the truth of that since my first night with you."

"Then what?"

Another sob rose in her throat. "I can't stand the idea of being with you and not making you happy. Of depriving you of everything you need because you settled for me." The sob broke. "God, that sounds so damned submissive!"

She started to turn her face away, to hide from him, but he wouldn't let her. He took her chin in his hand, made her look at him. "Rowan, I would never, ever feel that I've settled. How can you think that? You are who I want to be

with. Not some slave girl from the club. Why can't you accept that? And why can't you accept that a part of you, at
least, is submissive? That's not a bad thing, Rowan. How
can you have spent these years in the lifestyle and still think
that being submissive equals being weak? Is that what
you've told April about it? The other people in your discussion group?"

"No, of course not."

"It's not any different for you." His eyes were blazing,
hot with emotion. "Remember when you talked to me
about Bosch's painting *The Garden of Earthly Delights*? I got
that, what you were saying about it. That the garden is
wicked and sinful, yet beautiful in its own way, too. Well,
it's all about perspective, Rowan. You need to see the
beauty in *all* of it. In what you do, too. You have to stop
hiding from yourself. You have to stop running from me. I
already told you I love you. But I can't be with you if you
keep running away, from me, from the truth about who you
are. And if it's still that hard for you, then I don't know if
you're ready to be with me, or anyone."

"What are you saying?" Her body filled with dread.

"I'm saying that as much as I want you with me, I can't
do this if you aren't able to let that old baggage go and just
be with me. Be the person you are, without fighting it all
the time. Because I've realized that I can't fight it out for
you, as much as I want to, as much as I've tried. That was
wrong of me, I understand that now. You have to get there
on your own."

He searched her face, his eyes boring into hers. The
colors were dark, swirling, brilliant with emotion. She

swallowed hard. She understood what he was saying. He was right. But could she do it? And if not, it wasn't fair of her to pretend.

"I love you, Christian."

"I know."

"I need to think..."

He let her go immediately. She was chilled without the safety of his arms around her. She stepped back, looked up into his face. It had hardened, gone cold.

"Go. Think. Just don't take too long. I'll wait. But not forever."

He turned and walked from the room. A moment later she heard his heavy tread on the stairs.

She looked around frantically, not sure what to do next. That's when she noticed there were sketches everywhere, drawings of her. She picked one up from the counter, a small piece of white paper. It was her face, drawn in pencil, her hair a halo of dark curls. The expression made her pause. Something about the eyes; she was clearly a woman in love. Was that how she looked to him? How long had he known?

She should leave. But she couldn't make herself do it. Instead, she went to sit at the kitchen table, looked out the window. The air was thick with fog. She closed her eyes against the pain coursing through her body. He was right. About everything. And so was April. How could she turn away from this man, from the way she felt about him? How could she have any respect for herself if she let her past decide this for her?

Her past had governed her for too long. She had

changed who she was because of what had happened to her, or she thought she had. She realized now with sudden, stark clarity that she'd been punishing herself. That on some very deep level, she had come to believe Danny's abuse of her was punishment for wanting him to do those things to her, for submitting to him.

Her stomach clenched into a hard knot of pain. God, all these years wasted in some twisted lie she'd told herself to justify what had happened. And now, she was about to throw away the most important thing in her life because of it.

It was time she chose to live with the truth. It was time she truly did put her past behind her. It was time she let love into her life, even if it hurt.

Grasping the paper in her hand she took to the stairs. She knew where she'd find him.

She paused at the door to his studio. He was in there, his back to her, his hand resting on a piece of white marble, the edges ragged here and there, a work in progress. Knowing he never showed anyone his unfinished work, she felt momentarily intrusive. But some things were more important than art.

"Christian?"

His shoulders went rigid, she could see that even beneath the sweater he wore. He was silent a moment. He kept his back to her. She could hardly blame him. But she felt suddenly desperate. What if it was too late? What if the things she'd said to him, her inability to accept his love, had hurt him too deeply? Rendered him unable to forgive her? He'd said he would wait, but she may have ruined things already with that one small, stupid sentence she had uttered out of fear.

Her heart beating faster than it ever had in her life, she sank to her knees on the hard wood floor, and waited.

Finally, he turned, and his expression was one of pure shock.

"Rowan? What the hell are you doing?"

Her throat was so tight with hope and fear it was a struggle to get the words out, but she had to do it. Her voice was a harsh whisper. "I want you to know that I am giving myself to you. In love. And with respect. And with total trust."

He shook his head. "You don't have to do this."

"Yes, I do. I need you to know that I love you, and that I can do this for you."

"Christ, Rowan." He came to her. "Not like this. It's not necessary."

"It is. We both know it. I needed to trust you, to trust myself with you, and I had to show you that I do. I need to know if you'll have me."

She searched his face, his blue-green eyes. He loved her, she knew it already, could see it in his face. But she was still afraid.

"Rowan..." His hands moved over her face like a blind man's. "I need you to tell me what happened. What you're thinking."

"I'm trying not to think so much anymore. You're right, about so many things. The moment you turned away, I realized how foolish I've been, constantly pushing you away when all I want is to be with you.

"Today I finally understood that you're right. That I have to fix myself, love myself, that I have to truly put my past behind me and allow you to love me." A sob welled in her throat, choking her, and she had to swallow it back.

"Once I came to realize that, it was like an opening-up inside me. But that openness is frightening. I want to get past the fear." She paused, looking for the right words. "It's as though I've unlocked the gate, and walked into this dark, secret garden inside myself. And it's more lush and beautiful and varied than I could ever have imagined. And it's you who gave me that."

"You've had it in you to do it yourself the whole time."

"Maybe. But until I found you I had no reason to."

"And now?"

"And now I can love you. And I can allow myself to believe that you love me, that if you tell me you don't need something I can't give you, it's the truth."

She needed him to kiss her, to let her know everything was alright, that she hadn't come too late.

"Thank God," he said before he bent his head and pressed his lips to hers.

His mouth was soft and urgent at the same time. His hands were holding her cheeks, and she held his as she kissed him back. On the floor, on her knees, it was the most romantic kiss of her life.

Christian slid his hands down, over her shoulders, down to her waist, and lifted her to her feet. She wrapped her arms around him, her eyes brimming with tears again. She buried her face in his neck, breathed in the honeyed scent of him.

"Rowan." She looked up at him, meeting those amazing ocean eyes. He smoothed her hair from her face with one hand. "What now? Where do we go from here?"

"Anywhere you want. I'm going with you."

He smiled, stroked her face again, and her heart surged, swelled.

"You are finally, truly mine."

"Yes."

His arms went around her and he lifted her off the ground, held her, carried her to the old velvet chaise. He laid her down tenderly, silently removed her clothes. She held still, luxuriating in the touch of his hands on her skin, the brush of his fingers as he unbuttoned her sweater, slid her clothes from her body.

He stood back and looked at her. She could feel herself slipping away a bit; not enough to get lost in, just enough so that she was aware of her yielding. Her body. Her mind. And for the very first time, her heart.

He shook his head and murmured, "I can see this is different. You're different. You're everything I could ever want."

Her body was turning to liquid heat beneath his steady gaze. She could feel him taking her in with his eyes, loving her. And she gloried in this moment; just this, just being *his*.

He pulled his shirt off, and then his jeans, his eyes never leaving hers, until he stood naked before her. She had never seen a more beautiful sight.

He lowered his body over hers, the sweet crush of him making her dizzy with need, every surface and plane of their bodies connected.

"I'm going to make love to you, my Rowan."

She smiled. "Yes . . ."

"And then I'm going to tie you up, work you over with my hands."

"Yes!"

"And then I'm going to make love to you again, for the next eighty years."

"Yes, Christian. I am yours."

He kissed her again; her lips, her chin, her cheeks, then whispered, "And I am yours."

Yes, she thought, *you are mine*. And then he deepened the kiss and all conscious thought was wiped away in the beauty of the moment.

They were together in the garden at last.

∞

Tuesday night, the monthly meeting at the club. Rowan watched as everyone settled into their chairs. April, sitting across from her, was leaning over, speaking quietly with a young woman Rowan had never seen before. Nice that April was talking with one of the new ones. That first transition into the lifestyle was always so hard.

So were some of the later transitions, as she knew all too well.

"Let's get started, everyone. I'm Rowan, and many of you already know me as a top, a dominant, here at the club. Last month we talked a bit about making that first discovery about yourself, when you first come into the lifestyle. Tonight I'm going to talk about transition again. My own, recent transition."

She looked across at April, who gave her a reassuring smile.

"I guess what I want to say is that getting to know yourself is a process. And it's a mistake to think we ever know it all. We change as we go through life. We must, because to never change is to stay static. Stagnant. Sometimes making that change is difficult... very difficult. Frightening, even."

She paused to look around at the faces of the people watching her, listening. She caught April's eye again. She looked happy. Glowing. Well, she was probably glowing herself.

"The point is, knowing who we are, accepting our own truth, is the most precious gift we can give ourselves, no matter what we have to overcome to do it."

Several people nodded in agreement.

April spoke up, a twinkle in her blue eyes. "What are you trying to tell us, Rowan?"

She took a deep breath, pulling air into her lungs. "I'm trying to tell you that I've made a transition. That I've discovered my true self. And that self is a bottom."

A hushed murmur went through the group, but saying it was easier than she'd thought it would be. The murmurs were followed by nods and smiles of encouragement, acceptance. But the most important part was that she accepted herself.

"I've discovered that I need to be what I am, finally. And that it wasn't healthy to deny myself the way I did for so long. But I've gotten to the core of who and what I am now. I'm not saying it was easy. But anything worth having is worth fighting for." She paused, shifted in her chair. "I'm done fighting."

She felt the truth of that, all the way down to the depths of her soul. She knew exactly who she was, what she wanted, and with Christian she had everything she'd ever wanted, and more.

Love had shown her the way. But it was her own strength that had taken her there.

ABOUT THE AUTHOR

EDEN BRADLEY has been writing since she could hold a pen in her hand. When she is not writing, you'll find her wandering museums, cooking, eating, shopping, and reading everything she can get her hands on.

Eden lives in southern California with a small menagerie and the love of her life.

If you enjoyed *The Dark Garden* look for

THE

DARKER SIDE

OF PLEASURE

by

EDEN BRADLEY

Coming soon
Read on for a preview

THE DARKER SIDE OF PLEASURE

THE BONDS OF LOVE

Chapter One

Bondage. The word reverberated through Jillian's head, through her body, making her muscles tense and quiver.

Her stomach clenched as she pulled her sporty BMW into the driveway after a long day at work. She peered up at the sleek, modern expanse of redwood and glass her husband had designed for them six years ago, right after they'd married and moved to Seattle.

She took a deep breath and forced her hands to stop gripping the steering wheel. Tonight was the night. The night she and Cameron were going to start trying to put their marriage back together.

She yanked a little too hard on the parking brake, then grabbed her purse and the pretty pink shopping bag that held the new lingerie she'd bought for the occasion. Cameron was right. It had been ages since she'd dressed up for him. Hell, she'd been sleeping in the guest room for months. Not that that was his fault. It was her. She knew that. She just couldn't stand to be so close to him, with so much distance between them. It hurt too much.

Her nerves jangled as much as her keys did when she opened the front door. "Cam? You home?"

No answer. She exhaled a sigh of relief. She needed some time to make herself ready. Not just physically, but emotionally, too. Even though they'd talked about this almost a week ago. Maybe she'd had too much time to think about it. She did have a tendency to overanalyze things. She let her purse fall to the hardwood floor, gripped the lingerie bag, and headed down the hall.

Stripping off her clothes in the half-dark bedroom felt like a ritual, somehow. The house was quiet. The soft glow of twilight filtered through the Japanese paper shades that covered the ceiling-high bedroom windows. There was the faint scent of him in the air, that sense of intimacy in the room where they'd slept until she'd moved into the guest room a few months ago. But they hadn't made love for too long before that. And on those rare occasions when they had, she felt as though she wasn't entirely present in her own body, like she was watching it from the outside. But tonight was supposed to help change that. The idea made her stomach clench up again.

She stepped into the slate-tiled bathroom and blasted the hot water, wanting the sheer force and heat of it to wash her nerves away. This was her own husband, after all. She closed her eyes as she moved beneath the spray and let the water sluice over her, trying to steer her mind down a more positive path.

Cameron. He'd been so young when they'd first met, only twenty-one. She was an old lady of twenty-five at the time. But he was so mature for his age, so somber and responsible. And there was always something of the darkness about him that made him seem older than he was. Perhaps it was the tattoo that circled his right bicep, a sinuous circle in a dark tribal design. Maori, he'd told her. She loved it. She'd loved his tall, lean, yet muscular body. God, he had the greatest abs she'd ever seen on a human being. And she loved the way his straight, coal-black hair fell into his eyes, even the dark-framed glasses he wore for reading.

That's how Jillian had first seen him, in her English Lit class in college. He was bent over a book, and he glanced up as she passed a printed handout to him. And those smoky gray eyes peered up at her. Eyes fringed in thick, sooty lashes any woman would envy. Those startling eyes and that serious expression on his angular features, yet his mouth was lush and sensual, a stark contrast.

He still wore those glasses. And even after all they'd been through, a small shiver of excitement would course through her whenever he put them on. If only he had come to bed early enough to read, while she was still awake, while she'd still been sleeping in their bed.

But no, she shouldn't think about that. Tonight was for new beginnings, not old pain.

She shut off the water, stepped out onto the cool tiles, and began to rub scented lotion into her skin. It was Cameron's favorite vanilla scent, the one he used to say made him want to run his tongue all over her body. Her sex gave a quick, involuntary squeeze, surprising her.

Drawing her pale green silk summer robe around her shoulders, she went to pull her purchase out of the bag. The bra was black and lacy, with demi-cups that barely covered her breasts. The matching thong was a whisper of lace. It made her feel sexy, she had to admit, admiring her reflection in the big full-length mirror in her walk-in closet. Despite her breasts and thighs, which weren't as firm at the age of thirty-three as they'd been when she and Cam had met eight years ago.

No, don't think about that now.

She pulled her long honey-blond hair up with her hands, considering, then decided to leave it down. Cam liked it better that way.

When she drew the first black lace stocking over one leg, she began to get a real sense of ritual, of formal preparation. For some reason she didn't understand, it sent a small thrill through her, raising gooseflesh on the back of her neck. And when she slid her feet into the impossibly high black pumps Cam had insisted she buy, the feeling was complete. She understood suddenly that she was doing this for him, but that it also fulfilled some need in her: to please in order to feel whole.

This was a new concept for her. She'd been inside her own head for so long, immersed in her grief, that she'd forgotten to look outside. To look at her husband.

When Cam had first suggested they try to find their way back to each other through sex, she'd balked. In fact, that was putting it lightly. She'd flat out refused, thought he was being selfish and ridiculous. But then he'd reminded her that sex was intimacy, and that bondage was the purest form of mutual trust. It took her a while to absorb that, but she eventually came to realize he had a valid point. And they needed to try something, anything, before the gap between them grew any wider. Tonight was to be a true test.

She drew the stockings up her legs, her hand brushing the honey-colored curls at the apex of her thighs. Blood rushed to the area so fast, she had to cup her mound with her hand and press there. Strange! Why was she so hyper-sensitive, when she'd been completely shut down for almost a year?

The loud rumbling of her husband's prized Harley pulling into the driveway brought her head and her hand up fast. Cam!

She took one last, desperate look in the mirror, added a little lip gloss with a shaking hand. She was ready for him.

She thought she was. She shivered in fear and anticipation as his steps drew nearer. The door opened with a graceful swing, and there he was. Her husband. He looked so damn good standing there, she had to smile.

He smiled back. "Almost like the old Jillian. I love it when you smile like that. Like you mean it."

"I do." She dropped her head, suddenly shy.

He crossed the room, slid his hands around her waist, ran them up her sides, traced the curve of her breasts. "God, you're beautiful."

His words warmed her, but it was still hard for her to look at him. He tipped her chin up with his fingers. She thought he'd want to talk more, but he just leaned in and kissed her. That lush, kissable mouth of his covered hers, and when he parted his lips she could taste mint, and underneath it the faint sweetness of scotch. So he'd been nervous, too. She suddenly wanted to cry. This was why she'd been avoiding him, why she hadn't been able to sleep in the bed next to his big, warm body.

He pulled away and said simply, "Are you ready?"

Her stomach grabbed again, but she nodded. "Yes. But what are you . . . I mean, how is this all going to happen?"

"We talked about it, remember? If this is going to work, you have to trust me enough to turn yourself over to me. That's what tonight is all about. We have to learn to trust each other again. Do you remember your safe words?"

"Yes. Yellow for slow down, red for stop."

"Good."

He stepped back and his eyes roamed over her. She knew she looked better than usual in this outfit, so she didn't mind. And she could see his eyes glittering as he looked at her, his pupils widening with lust. He placed his hands on his hips, licked his lips. He gestured toward the bed with his chin.

"Sit down."

She just looked at him for a moment. She wasn't used to this simple, commanding tone from him. He didn't sound mean, but it was clear she shouldn't try to argue with him. A chill of pleasure ran up her spine.

"Now."

Another command; this time his tone was low and demanding. Her sex exploded with heat. She sat.

Cam paced the room slowly, looking at her from all angles, before he said, "Get rid of the bra."

She unhooked it immediately, her full breasts springing from the lacy confines. They felt plump and tender and they wanted to be touched, something she hadn't felt in a long time. The fact that she could have this sort of reaction to nothing more than a certain tone of voice was almost shocking. She was trying hard not to analyze it.

Cam walked up to her and touched her breasts with his fingertips, just lazily brushed them over the curved underside, traced them around the edges of the areolas. Her nipples sprang up, hard and ready. But he didn't touch them.

When she looked up at his face he was smiling, just one corner of his mouth quirked up. Rakish, sexy.

He stepped back again and unbuttoned his shirt. She had always loved him without a shirt. He had one of those long, lean, cut torsos, with just the right amount of silky black hair in a line down the center of his well-defined abs. He was built like a pro basketball player: well over six feet tall, with broad shoulders and those lanky, beautifully defined muscles. His black work slacks hung low on his narrow hips and she could see that he was hard already, the outline of his large erection shadowed against the fine wool.

She squirmed on the edge of the bed, her lace thong growing damp.

"I'm going to ask you to do things for me tonight you've never done before. Are you ready to do that, Jillian?"

She swallowed, hard. Was she? Her natural mental response was to fight against the whole idea. She was normally someone who was strong, in control. But her body was rebelling already. Still, how could it be this simple? She knew that Cam's angle had been that bondage was all about trust, that there had to be complete trust in order to make it work. He saw it as a way to get back to each other. It made a sort of weird sense, but she still had her doubts.

Cam repeated, "Are you ready?"

His voice seemed so different tonight; his whole

persona was different. Confident. Commanding. But it was still Cam. She could do this. She would do it for him. For them. And judging from the unexpected way her body was responding already, for herself.

"Yes. I'm ready."

He turned then and moved to the tall dresser, pulled a CD from the top drawer and popped it into the CD player. She recognized the trancelike tones of Enigma immediately. She watched him as he lit a pair of tall pillar candles. The scent of amber wafted into the air, and the warm candlelight was soft and sultry, aided by the glow of sunset outside the windows.

He bent and opened a bottom drawer and took out a long coiled length of black rope. She hadn't known it was in there, didn't know where he'd found it. She didn't really care right now. All she could think of was that he was going to use it on her. Nerves and pleasure washed through her in an exciting, confusing tide.

Cam came to stand before her while the music played, and he rested his hands on her shoulders. After a moment, he swept his fingers up her neck in gentle strokes, then back down, over her arms to her wrists. Gently, he gathered them into one of his big hands and pulled her arms up over her head. She shivered again, feeling unsure, vulnerable.

"Cam?"

"It's okay."

His soft voice was reassuring, but he didn't release her wrists. With his free hand he began to stroke her breasts again, and despite her hammering pulse her body responded to his touch. Her breasts filled, her nipples aching as he teased her skin with the lightest touch. When he finally brushed one hard nipple with his fingertip her whole body arched toward him.

"Patience, Jillian." He sounded amused.

She moaned softly. He rewarded her by tweaking one nipple, rather hard, but she liked it. Somehow it was just what she needed. Her sex began to pound and she squeezed her legs together.

"Lie back on the bed," Cam said.

"Why? What are you going to—"

"Shh. No questions. You're mine tonight. Turn yourself over to me, Jillian."

Yes. She wanted this. And not just because she was following the plan. Now that they'd started she knew she was going to like it, even if it scared her a little. Or maybe the fear was part of what drew her?

She lay down on the bed.

When Cam came to stand over her with the ropes in his hands, her body gave a convulsive shudder. Of need. Of lust. She had never felt anything like it. Gazing up at his tall silhouette in the dim light, she suddenly knew she'd never wanted anything so much in her life. To give herself over. To let herself go. This was exactly what she needed. Yet at the same time, she struggled with the notion. How could this be what she needed? Wasn't it proof of her own weakness?

Cam bent over her and kissed her gently on the lips, then took her lower lip between his strong, white teeth and bit down. It hurt a little.

"You're mine, Jillian. Say it."

The chill that ran through her was part lust, part awe. And she knew that after tonight, she would never be the same again.

"Yes, Cam. I'm yours."

He smiled at her. "Very good. I want you to lie perfectly still now. I'm going to play with you a bit before I tie you up."

Tie you up. Oh my. He really was going to tie her up. A thrill ran through her, bringing goose-bumps to her skin once more, but this time they ran the entire length of her body.

But she didn't have long to think about it. Cam's hands were on her, stroking her stomach, running up her thighs. They seemed to be everywhere at once. She watched him, a look of intense concentration on his face. Finally his hands came back to her breasts, covering both of them, massaging, kneading. Her nipples were hard, hot nubs against his palms.

He looked up at her face, his gray eyes watching her as he took both nipples between his fingers and thumbs and began to roll them. Fire shot from her nipples straight to her already aching sex. She tried hard not to squirm. But when he pinched, hard, she shot up off the bed.

"No, Jillian." He pressed her back down onto the mattress. "Lie still."

She tried. She drew in a deep, shuddering breath, and then he began again, pulling at her nipples, twisting, pinching. They were so hard and engorged she thought they would burst. And her sex was full and throbbing. She wanted his hands there. But she knew she had to wait. To trust him.

Cam kept working her nipples, and she wondered for the first time in her life if it were possible to come just from that. She didn't know how long it went on, an impossibly long period of time in which she was finally able to shut her brain down, to stop thinking, analyzing. Her nipples were sore, but she didn't care. She bit down on her lip to keep from crying out, to keep from moving, but her thighs spread open of their own accord. God, she needed him to touch her there. To use his hands, his mouth. She didn't care. But she didn't want him to stop torturing her breasts.

Finally he bent his head and flicked his hot, wet tongue at one rigid tip. She groaned. He moved his head and flicked at the other one. Then, using both hands, he pushed the full mounds of her breasts together and moved his head back and forth, his tongue a damp spike of heat as it flickered over her stiffened nipples. His hands felt so good on her, so firm on her flesh, and his tongue was driving her crazy. She almost begged him to take her into his mouth. And then, as if reading her mind, he did.

He drew one nipple in and sucked. He was almost too gentle. She could hardly stand it. She gathered and bunched the bedspread in her hands, trying to hold still, to keep from crying out, from begging him to suck harder. Her sex was absolutely drenched by now. Her whole body quivered.

And suddenly he pulled back.

"Cam?" Her own voice sounded loud and breathless in her ears.

He straightened up, half-turned away from her and ran a hand through his dark hair.

"Cam, what is it?"

She heard his long, slow exhalation. Waited for him to turn back around, to talk to her. Her thighs clenched around the damp, swollen folds of flesh between them.

"Maybe we need to talk about this some more."

"What?" A startled laugh escaped her lips. "Now? When I'm just beginning to…" She couldn't finish the sentence, couldn't say out loud that her body was responding in a way it hadn't for months. Couldn't tell him how desperately she craved his touch. Why couldn't she say it?

When his eyes met hers she saw the confusion there, saw that his breath was coming in short, sharp pants.

"This is… already more intense than I expected."

Also available:

The Ninety Days of Genevieve
Lucinda Carrington

He is an arrogant, worldly entrepreneur who always gets what he wants.

And what he wants is for Genevieve to spend the next ninety days submitting to his every desire . . .

A dark, sensual tale of love and obsession, featuring a very steamy relationship between an inexperienced heroine and a masterful and rich older man.

Praise for The Ninety Days of Genevieve

'This month's essential reading . . . For fans of the renaissance of erotic fiction comes Lucinda Carrington's tale of love and obsession'
Stylist

'sizzling . . . It's full of expertly written sex scenes that will appeal to any woman who has ever fantasised about bondage, lust, exhibitionism and voyeurism! . . . an excellent plot, well written characters and heaps of charm'
Handbag.com

Also available:

In Too Deep
Portia Da Costa

Lust among the stacks . . .

Librarian Gwendolyne Price starts finding indecent proposals and sexy stories in her suggestion box. Shocked that they seem to be tailored specifically to her own deepest sexual fantasies, she begins a tantalising relationship with a man she's never met.

But pretty soon, erotic letters and toe-curlingly sensual emails just aren't enough. She has to meet her mysterious correspondent in the flesh . . .

Praise for Portia Da Costa

'Imaginative, playful and a lot of fun'
For Women